IMAGES OF MISS LINDFORS

An Ashtabula Love Story

Joseph Pasquarella

Saint Petersburg, Florida

ISBN: 978-1-64719-600-4

Published by BookLocker.com, Inc., St. Petersburg, Florida.

Printed on acid-free paper.

BookLocker.com, Inc.
2021

First Edition

"You've heered talk o'Johnstown?"

Harvey considered. "Yes, I have. But I don't know why.

It sticks in my head same as Ashtabula."

"Both was big accidents – thet's why, Harve."

—Rudyard Kipling, *Captains Courageous* (1897)

Dedication

This book is dedicated to all the great people who have lived and worked in the city of Ashtabula, Ohio, and who love and appreciate its rich history. Also, to the city itself, who at the time of this writing, has been for almost 145 years, eulogizing and in mourning for the many unrecognized dead of the horrific Ashtabula Bridge disaster of December 29, 1876.

Prologue

October 2012

It was a picture-perfect early autumn day in northeastern Ohio. Caroline and Joe, a married couple in their late forties, were motoring up the highway on their way to their one-night getaway in Ashtabula, in the heart of Lake Erie's beautiful and luxuriant wine region. The one-hour car ride would also provide the harried duo with some ample time to chat and catch up on each other's thoughts and feelings. They were destined for Di Matteo's Winery. The aromatic vineyard, which grew on six lush acres just about a mile from the shores of Lake Erie, also doubled as a quaint four-unit bed-and-breakfast-style inn, complete with a tastefully inviting restaurant and gift shop. The two were planning on a one-day respite of dining, wine tasting, and spending some peaceful time on the scenic lakefront. It was a break the two of them desperately were in want of.

It was not that they couldn't afford a longer, more extensively traveled vacation; it was the time away from their work that the two of them could not afford. Both had extremely onerous workloads. Caroline, a former nursing supervisor, now worked from home on her computer doing medical billing for some of the doctors she had previously been employed with at the hospital. Joe owned and operated a safety product distribution company. Both endeavors had the couple hopping, with no letup in sight. The one-day escape would have to suffice. Both would see to it that it would.

They arrived just before their 2:00 p.m. check-in time. The owner-operators of the establishment, Paul and Tracy, a married couple a few years Joe and Caroline's senior, invited them to stow their belongings in their room and then led them out back to show them around the picturesque estate. Paul explained that the business had been in the family for nearly forty years, when his father began it in 1973 by planting the vineyard. It took three years for the viticulture to be complete. "Then in 1976, we opened the winery. It has been my life ever since," Paul said as he pointed across the fertile vineyard. "In 1992, Tracy and I added the bed-and-breakfast."

"Well, it certainly is a beautiful place," Caroline observed.

"We've been harvesting a lot recently; this is a busy time of year for us," Paul added.

There were two more couples who had been booked at the inn for the night but were not scheduled to get in until after 5:00. Paul invited Joe and Caroline to come around the side of the inn and sit with him and Tracy under the vine-covered pergola and sample some of their delicious wines that were grown, vented, and bottled on the premises. Tracy graciously brought out a meat-and-cheese tray from the kitchen that was arrayed with a delectable selection of northeastern Ohio's finest varieties.

The four of them sat out there enjoying the atmosphere. The wafting full-bodied aroma of the lingering grape gleanings from the vineyard was pleasantly finding its way into everyone's olfactory bulb. Paul had brought out a new bottle of their favorite blush wine for the table to sample. He also brandished a sweet red, a Riesling, and both a white and a pink Catawba. The generous host, his pouring hand at the ready, didn't leave a single bottle without being uncorked, as the four newfound wine buddies shared a relaxing time of conversation and laughter.

Joe mentioned how nice the area was and how ideal the weather was for them. Paul asked Joe and Caroline if they had any plans to run up to the lake later that afternoon. They answered in the affirmative as Caroline complimented the city's alluring surroundings.

"A lot of famous people came from Ashtabula," Joe noted.

Paul agreed and rattled off a list of well-known celebrities from the city who had made it big nationally. He and Tracy boasted of the two women from there who went on to become famous actresses. Another famous television personality hailed from there, as well. They nodded as Joe pointed out that a championship college football coach had grown up in that town, as well. "He played high school ball over at Saint John's on the east side of town," Paul confirmed as he pointed in the general direction.

They discussed the city's once-burgeoning harbor activity of decades prior when, as Paul pointed out, it was one of the nation's—if not the world's—busiest ports. "In fact, at one point, years ago it was the second only to Singapore in terms of sheer volume of both massive amounts of imported and exported material!" he exclaimed.

The conversation paused for a few seconds as the four of them enjoyed a delicious taste of wine from their several glasses. After a moment, Paul piped back up with suggestions of some of Ashtabula's strange urban legend tales. The two of them sat up and listened intently, their senses already piqued by the imbibed fruit of the vine, as he and Tracy spun a few yarns from the city's haunted past and present. "The ghost of Walnut Beach was a legend I remember hearing about," Paul said, beaming. When Joe asked him what that was all about, Paul went on to relate the old account of a ghostly figure of an elderly man who could be seen walking on the waters of Lake Erie, just off the coast of Walnut Beach on the west side of the harbor area. Paul went on to account how years ago the old man's ship had wrecked, and he had lost his entire family when they drowned. "They say that he's wandering around out there, searching for his lost family," Paul added, as Caroline and Joe became amused.

At Tracy's prodding, Paul continued on by telling everyone about Ashtabula's legendary haunted library. "I guess when it was under construction many years ago, a fire broke out and a few of the workers perished. Now they supposedly haunt the library."

Tracy chimed in by saying that books have been known to mysteriously fall from the shelves, and people attest to always feeling like they are being watched. Caroline jumped into the mix by telling them that the hospital she had previously worked at was haunted. "We never saw the ghost," she told them, "but we always heard a woman's whisper, very eerie whisper, like she was trying to warn us from something. We always heard movement about the room, like footsteps."

When Paul and Tracy reacted in playfully shocked surprise, Caroline turned to Joe and asked him if he remembered her telling him about the ghost. "We called her Martha—remember I used to tell you about her, honey?" Everyone chuckled and took another sip of the tasty wine.

"How about the story about that one guy in Ashtabula?" Tracy excitedly asked Paul. "What was his name, Paul? He lived here in the early or mid-1980s. It was a remarkable story."

"Which one was that? The one about the guy who moved up here to the old Swedetown area off Columbus Avenue?"

"Yeah, remember?" Tracy queried.

"Oh, yeah," Paul mused." I remember. What was his name… David something… no, Daniel something. His last name began with a *D*."

"Yeah!" Tracy exclaimed. "We have time. Tell Caroline and Joe about him. I always get goose bumps when I hear the story. It's remarkable!"

Yes, it is," Paul concurred. "It is quite a remarkable story."

Paul leaned forward and grasped a freshly uncorked bottle of pink Catawba wine. "Everybody sit back, and I'll pour you a glass of wine," he playfully ordered." Everybody relax and enjoy a nice glass of our finest Catawba, and I'll regale you with this fascinating account of Daniel Du … whatever his last name was." Paul poured everyone at the table some wine into their fashionable glasses and then set the bottle back on the table. He sat back and drew a long breath of air. He slowly exhaled, took a sip from his glass, and then gently set it back down. "Whether this story is true or make-believe, whether it is fact or pure fantasy, whether it really happened or whether it's pure urban legend, I cannot say for certain. But it is quite a fascinating story. It all began in the autumn of 1984…"

1

October 1984

It was a tale that began on a beautifully sunny, early Saturday October morning in 1984, with thirty-four-year-old Danny Dubenion speeding up Ohio Route 11 in northeast Ohio's Ashtabula County in his old, albeit flawlessly restored, 1965 Astro-blue Buick Wildcat convertible. While heading up the scenic, brilliantly red and yellow splashed tree-lined highway, he was thoroughly enjoying the tunes emanating from his cassette tape filled with music from the 1950s and '60s. He was racing to meet the movers who were to join him at his newly rented century home on East Fifteenth Street, just off Columbus Avenue, in Ashtabula. It was an area of the old shipping town that, decades prior, was known as Swedetown because of its large influx of Swedish immigrants who arrived many years earlier to ply their trade in the shipping and railroad line of work.

Danny was moving to Ashtabula from Niles, Ohio, a city about fifty miles south the of the Lake Erie town. He was working in Niles as a quality control technician for a titanium-producing factory, a job that entailed performing various testing for the semiprecious metal that is used in jet aircraft engines and airframes, as well as weapons for the military and other high-tech functions. Danny was still working for the same company but had accepted a job transfer to its Ashtabula facility, where he would be making more money as the new assistant quality control laboratory manager and senior technician.

Danny was still single and, although his parents still lived in the area, he was relatively unattached and figured he would make the move and take advantage of the opportunity. After all, Niles was only fifty miles away, so he could visit often enough. Besides, Danny was heavily involved with the Niles Historical Society, as well as the McKinley Presidential Library and Museum. Fifty miles was definitely not enough to keep this history lover away from his monthly meetings and annual festivities at these two places where he served on the committee of each.

Danny continued his hurried trek into Ashtabula and East Fifteenth Street. His anxiousness to arrive there promptly had less to do with him not wanting to keep the movers waiting as it did with him not wanting to leave his precious cargo inside the moving van unsupervised. Danny was a huge collector of antique furniture. Everything, such as his antique dresser and desk, as well as his vintage 1870s Birdseye triple-mirror maple vanity—not to mention his exquisite Victorian rosewood etagere – was on that van. The thought of these priceless treasures sitting in the van in a strange neighborhood awaiting his arrival was a bit unsettling, to say the least. Danny, who was an old-fashioned throwback to a far earlier time, also had many valuable antique photographs on the van. Authentic photos of Presidents William McKinley and Rutherford B. Hayes and other famous Ohioans from nearly a century past had graced his walls at his home down in Niles and were being transferred to his new place in Ashtabula. He had some of them with him in his car, as well as his rare coin collection, but much of his collection had to be put into the moving van. He would not rest easy until he was reunited with his priceless treasures.

Danny's fears were allayed as he reached his new address and pulled into the driveway and found that he had arrived ahead of the movers. When they pulled in a few minutes after he did, Danny was already inside of the partially furnished house clearing the way, preparing a wide path for them in order to help them bring in his valuables unscathed. After a couple of hours, the job was promptly and professionally finished with not a single scratch to any item.

After the movers were paid and had departed, Danny began to feel hungry. He decided that he had better drive around the area and find something to eat before he took on the task of unpacking and rearranging all his stuff. Acting on a tip and directions from one of his new neighbors, Danny headed back to Columbus Avenue and headed south a couple of miles toward the city's downtown area to a Greek-style diner called Garfield's. There he enjoyed a plate of fine diner fare that included one of the biggest and juiciest cheeseburgers he had ever eaten in his life. Danny always enjoyed a delicious burger, but with Garfield's addition of fine Greek seasoning included into the mix, it was one of the tastiest ones he had ever experienced.

Heading out of Garfield's parking lot for the quick jaunt back to his new digs, Danny was treated to a treasure of classic Americana. He swung around the block and gazed directly face-to-face with the famous Flying Saucer Gas Station. The quaint relic from the '60s displayed a large flying saucer atop the little pay window office booth that had spiraling, flickering lights that attracted motorists from blocks away. The saucer itself resembled the *Jupiter 2* spaceship from the old television show *Lost in Space* from the 1960s. It was a glorious sight to behold for the relic-loving Danny. Although he had enough gas in his old Buick, he pulled up out of sheer appreciation and topped off his tank for a couple of bucks. His old but well-maintained Wildcat fit in nicely with the scene and drew a few thumbs-ups from the other patrons of the unique station.

After he topped off his gas tank, Danny decided to quickly find a grocery store in order to stock up on some food for home. When he was finished, he drove home and started unpacking and rearranging his fine antique furniture. Later he went for a quick and refreshing stroll through his new neighborhood. Much later, after toiling all evening moving and cleaning his treasury of antiques, he had a snack then decided to call it a night. His first day in his new adopted city was in the archives. Danny soon was fast asleep for the night.

The next morning, on Sunday, Danny decided he would get in his classic car and explore the sights of Ashtabula. First on his agenda was a return trip across town to Garfield's to enjoy a divine omelet breakfast. While there enjoying the fine Greek-style fare, he had a friendly chat with a patron who, when Danny told him that he was new in town, offered a few suggestions about places for Danny to check out. He gave Danny quick directions on how to get to the historic harbor area to view the famous lift bridge after he had let the patron know how much he appreciated local history and how involved he was in the

Niles area historical institutions. The man also offered him directions to Lake Shore Park on the city's east-side shore.

After breakfast and the nice chat were finished, Danny heeded the directions and headed straight down Lake Avenue for the harbor. He was more than pleasantly surprised when he saw the sign to turn right on Bridge Street and headed into the harbor district. Old-style alehouses and seafood places, as well as old bookstores and antique shops, greeted the enthusiastic newcomer. It was like taking a trip back to an old New England whaling town. As he drove a few more blocks downhill toward the Ashtabula River at the nadir of the harbor, Danny's eyes lit up as he came upon the famous lift bridge. The historic Bascule Bridge, with its massive concrete counterweight that is manipulated so the span can be tilted upward almost fully perpendicular as to let watercraft in and out of the harbor's river marina, was built in 1925. The bridge's talented designer, New York City engineer Thomas E. Brown, had also designed the Eiffel Tower elevator.

So enamored by this impressive structure was Danny that he promptly pulled into a nearby parking lot to get out and walk around and see it on foot. The bridge was only one of two just like it that still remained in Ohio. After feasting his eyes and senses on the bridge, he decided to walk back up the hill and peruse the many fine store and saloon fronts that occupied this unique hillside harbor.

There had been a couple of antiquated, tough old bars still remaining from the town's old shipping days. Some newer, family-friendlier sports bars were also onsite, as well. Danny had listened intently as the patron from Garfield's had told him that this was once one of the nation's busiest ports. He had explained to him how even back just a few years prior that Ashtabula was a great two-way port. Iron ore was shipped from the upper Great Lakes in huge ore boats to the harbor, which in tun were unloaded and then transferred into many railroad hopper cars for trips southward to the hungry blast furnaces for the steel mills of Youngstown, Pittsburgh, and Wheeling. Once unladed, the train cars were stuffed with the rich coal from Appalachia and sent back up to the harbor for transport by ships in return to the upper Great Lakes – a great reciprocal industry for the hometown port.

Danny ambled slowly up and then back down the sloping harbor areas, taking in the sights and watery aroma of this old-style Lake Erie waterfront town. Although it was Sunday and most of the shops were closed, he was still in full enjoyment as he let it all soak in. His amazement hit its zenith when he passed by the Harbor Antique Emporium and gazed from the shop's old-world picture window to view the priceless wares inside. Danny vowed that during the coming week, one day after work, he would return when the shop was open and check out the charming antique store. By the looks of it, it appeared that it might be able to help him add to his impressive Victorian-era furniture collection.

When he was done looking around, Danny asked a passerby about directions to Lake Shore Park. The friendly denizen gave him quick and simple instructions, and soon Danny was off. He motored across the lift bridge, which spanned the mouth of the river, in full view of the massive arched waterfront coal conveyor into the east side of town, and then continued on the shore road for about a mile or so. Soon, he reached the entrance and turned left into the scenic park.

Danny drove through the winding and picturesque entranceway and reached the shoreline parking lot. He got out and strolled around the beautiful coast, taking in the wonderful scent of the gentle breeze-tossed water. From his vantage point, he could see the harbor silhouetted by the immense coal conveyor. Harbor boats littered the surrounding waters near the port's entrance. Scores and scores of railcars, some empty, others fully laden with black coal, sat motionless, others jostling, awaiting their next assignment. Off in the distance stood the impressive lighthouse. It was situated atop its sturdy foundation, jutting out from the northern end of the western breakwater. What a fascinating sight for this history buff to enjoy.

Danny strode along the beach shoreline towards the smaller eastern breakwater and paced atop the massive rocks that led out a short distance into the lake. Danny looked around and was enamored with the sights and sounds of the beachfront with the seagulls bellowing and the breeze-propelled waves gently crashing as they met the shoreline. The wonderfully placid sounds of nature intermixed with the machinations of the harbor's industrial life was music to Danny's ears. He stood virtually motionless for a few minutes while drinking it all in.

He continued his shoreline stroll, pausing occasionally to absorb the early autumn sky extending down the sunny horizon, offering an amazing reflection upon the slightly choppy water. Danny thought that he was beginning to grow fond of his newly adopted town. He suddenly began to feel somewhat melancholic, however when he began thinking of how nice it would be to have a sweet young lady in his life to share it all with. Although being single had its advantages, it would just be a great thing, he mused, to have someone at his side to enjoy his new life with.

Danny walked around for a bit more and then decided to head back home and finish the task of moving in. On the way back, he turned left onto State Road and drove through the heavily industrialized section of town. As he ambled up the street and over multiple railroad tracks, he read the names from the sign of the different factories he passed. It suddenly occurred to him that he wasn't too far from where his new job was located. When he reached East Twenty-First Street, it was confirmed. He took a right-hand turn onto the road, and within a few seconds, his new place of employment came into full view. He hung a left into the parking lot and rolled up to the security guardhouse and stopped his car.

Danny got out and introduced himself to the guard as the new quality control assistant manager while simultaneously producing for him his company identification badge. The sentinel offered a hearty handshake and gave a quick tour of where Danny would park and which building to enter the following morning for his first day on his new job. After the quick orientation, Danny got back into his car and zipped down East Twenty-First Street to Columbus Avenue, turned right, and drove six blocks down to East Fifteenth Street and landed back at his new abode.

Danny puttered around and rearranged his antique furniture. He set up his old rolltop desk and armoire in the front spare bedroom, which he planned on converting into a den. He tidied the place up a bit and then made himself something to eat. He spent the rest of the evening relaxing and watching some old television shows. He arranged his clothing for his first day on the job in the morning. He set his alarm clock and drifted off to sleep. So ended his first weekend in Ashtabula.

The next day, Monday morning, Danny arrived at his new job. He had been with the company as a lab technician for twelve years at its Niles facility. When the position for senior technician opened up in Ashtabula, his experience as a certified sonic inspector, as well as with performing tensile strength testing and titanium metal heat treating and hydrogen analysis—on top of his time working with the company's metallurgist in metal etching in various acid solutions and ammonium bifluoride—sealed the deal for his getting the job and transfer. It was a good move for him financially. He just had to get used to the new surroundings. Being single, a new town and a new position portended a nice fresh start for him.

His initial day went well. He met his new coworker, Richie Kelleher, who astutely oriented him to his new surroundings and showed him the ropes on a couple of operations in which he had never experienced back at the Niles quality control lab. It was both a fruitful and enjoyable first day for Danny. He and Richie hit it off well and had a lot of things in common. They enjoyed the same old music and appreciated old cars, as well as a deep affinity for history.

After work, Richie offered to buy Danny a beer or two at the East Sixth Street Café. He and Danny shot a couple of games of pool while sipping on some suds. The two of them naturally talked about work and their respective futures there. They also chatted about the usual guy things—cars, football, and of course, women. Danny tendered that he would like to meet a special lady up there and someday settle down.

Richie soon tagged Danny with the nickname "Wildcat" because of his spiffy car. "Look, Wildcat, why do you want to settle down? You're too young yet," he razzed. The two continued their billiard game. "Roy mentioned at work today that you are involved in the historical society down in Niles," Richie chimed as he sank the ten ball into the side pocket.

"Yes, I am," Danny retorted. "The McKinley Memorial Library, also," he added.

"We have plenty of history up here, as well," Richie offered. "The Ashtabula Maritime Museum, for example, and the Civil War monument near the downtown area."

"I'm very big into the Civil War!" Danny replied. "I'm into that whole era."

Richie informed his new pal with a great deal of civic pride in his voice that Ashtabula was the northern terminus for the Underground Railroad, as well. "The houses are still standing where they hid the slaves before helping them sail across the lake into Canada and freedom."

Dany boasted that President William McKinley had been born in Niles. Richie missed his next shot. Danny eyed the table to line up a good shot for himself.

"In fact, I've studied that whole era from the Civil War up to 1901 when McKinley was assassinated," Danny added as he took a crack at the two ball narrowly missing the pocket.

"We've had a couple of famous people born here, as well," Richie shot back with a snicker as he prepared his next shot.

"Like who?" Danny grinned.

"Remember Father Guido Sarducci from *Saturday Night Live*?" he quizzed.

"Yeah, you mean Don Novello?" Danny answered.

"Yeah, he's from here, and that lady from the 1950s who hosted some kind of horror movie show or something – Vampira… Maila Nurmi was her name – she was born in Finland but grew up here," Richie gushed.

The two finished their game and had one more beer for the road while chatting for a few more minutes at the bar.

"This one's for the Kaiser!" Danny shouted as he raised his beer bottle high in the air.

"What was that for?" Richie asked as he laughed.

"My Grandpa Ed used to do that all the time. He was in World War One," Danny replied with a chuckle.

Richie hoisted his bottle in response. "Here's to the Kaiser."

When they finished their beers, they both headed for home. Danny got home and had a bite to eat and then just relaxed. Thus ended his first day at his new job.

The following day after work, a few of their coworkers joined them at the cafe for a few beers and more than a few laughs. It was still early in the game, but Danny started to feel like he had made a good career choice with the move. Afterward, he drove to Garfield's and treated himself to his favorite cheeseburger. Danny was quickly starting to fit in with the regular gang over there, as well. The old-timers really took to this young throwback from another era. They also took a liking to his old car. He stopped for a quick shot of gasoline at the adjacent Flying Saucer Gas Station, where he was also fitting in well with the gang over there, when he was done at Garfield's.

The rest of the workweek continued to go well for Danny. On Thursday, after a quick beer at the East Sixth Street Café, he took a quick jaunt to the nearby harbor to finally get a chance to check out the antique shop he saw on Sunday when he was walking around there. From the second Danny walked inside the weathered, aging emporium, he was instantly enchanted. He found the walls and tables graced with old railroad and Great Lakes shipping artifacts. Old lanterns, photos, and vintage glassware from maybe a century past bedecked the archaic, musty interior of the building. The relics from the once-glorious harbor life ignited his passions and piqued his appreciation of the great historical significance of the whole region. He exchanged pleasantries with the elderly white-haired attendant who was manning the cash register.

In the back of the structure, there was some antique furniture. As Danny walked toward the furniture, he paced by some old photos, trying to see if he recognized any of them. There was a photo of the old Swedish Pastry Shop with its kitschy sign in front of it. It looked to be from maybe the early 1950s. The pastry shop was still operating on the city's west side. Danny ambled to the back to gaze at the old furniture. The elderly attendant asked Danny if he needed any help finding anything. Just as Danny assured him that he was fine and was only browsing, he turned and saw it. As soon as he laid his eager eyes upon it, it had him mesmerized, and he stood frozen, beholding its beauty.

It was a large walnut Victorian pier mirror standing immaculately at about seven and a half feet tall.

The attendant quickly perceived Danny's hypnotical attraction to it and hurried to his side. "That's the original finish," the man boasted. He introduced himself to Danny, informing him that he was the proprietor of the shop.

"It sure is stunning!" Danny answered as he shook the elderly shop owner's hand. The man pointed to the mirror and eloquently described it as if he were a Cadillac salesman praising and assessing his fine wares.

“As you can see,” he proudly submitted, “it is graced with pressed acanthus-leaf crown molding on top, with picture-frame molding.” He continued to train his flowing hand and elaborate on the elegant egg-and-dart molding and turned drop finials beneath the incised carved faces on each side, as well as on the top. He expertly described the original beveled glass mirror and the scrolled sconces with beautiful block rosettes that possessed skillfully turned three-quarter columns extending down the sides.

If he were trying to do a sales job on Danny, he needn’t have bothered. Danny was already sold and definitely smitten by it. He inspected the mirror’s backing and found it to be in very good condition. It was all in very good condition, very well preserved. An illegibly inscribed tarnished brass plate was fastened to the backing of the mirror that was figured to be the brand name or possibly one of the previous owners’ names that had been engraved upon it.

“I’m sold!” Danny gleefully exclaimed, “This will be the crown jewel in my antique furniture collection!” When Danny asked him what year the mirror was made, the shop owner replied that it was definitely post-Civil War era. His educated estimate was that it was from around 1880, possibly a year or so before. The mirror was selling for $550, but the owner of the shop let Danny have it for an even $500 because the item had been sitting in there for a very long time. Besides, he was taken by the way Danny appreciated the fine antique and was honored to give him the discount.

Danny thanked him and lamented that he had no vehicle large enough to bring the mirror to his house. Danny offered him a deposit on it and promised the owner that he would come by the next day with his coworker's pickup truck and complete the transaction. The kind elderly man honored Danny's humble request, receiving a check from him for half of the amount, with the other half receivable upon pick up the next day.

Danny flew home and immediately phoned Richie and explained his dilemma. Richie assured his new buddy that he and a couple of coworkers, Lucky and Wild Bill from the shipping department, would go with him after work the next day and help him bring it home. The following day seemed to drag, as Danny wished to hasten its end so he and his friends could get the mirror to his house. The anticipation was driving him mad. Finally, the day and his first week there drew to a close. Richie, along with the other two, met Danny in the harbor and helped him load his newly purchased treasure into the pickup truck. Danny closed the deal with the shop owner by giving him the remainder of the money he owed him, while Richie and the other two carefully, at Danny's heartfelt pleading, buttoned everything up securely. They drove slowly and gently to Danny's new residence.

The two helped Danny and Richie muscle the impressive and bulky mirror into and around the house, and the four of them strained to stand it up in the front spare bedroom den. Richie remarked that it was a good thing that those old houses had been built with nice high ceilings to accommodate such a tall piece of furniture. Danny positioned his newfound treasure just right, angling it in the corner. He pointed out to Richie the tarnished brass nameplate on the back, telling him he was going to use brass compound to try to lift the engraving to the surface. He beamed as he stared proudly at his newly acquired masterpiece. It was the *coup de grace*, the *piece de resistance* of his already grand antique collection. It was the capstone to a great first week in his new life, his new town, and his new job.

Little did Danny know at the time, but that post-Civil War era antique mirror he had just purchased for $500 would be the best investment he had or would ever make.

2

November 1984

It was early November and Danny had been working at his new position for a little over three weeks. He was starting to grow comfortable with his new functions and duties, as well as with his new coworkers. After work one day, a few of the guys invited him to go with them to the "Six," their nickname for the East sixth Café, for a few beers and some billiards. Danny had to decline because he needed to get straight home and get ready to head down to Niles for his meeting at the Niles Historical Society. He would actually have preferred to stay up in Ashtabula and hang out with his friends, but he was not only a member of the society but also served on the committee. It was crucial for him not to miss any meetings. He also needed to be present because that evening at the meeting, it was going to be announced what time and what type of party they were going to put on for the public at their annual spring reception.

On his drive down Route 11 to Niles, Danny pondered the reception he was about to receive from the other committee members after the little tumultuous rant he'd given them at the previous month's meeting. He had rather aggressively voiced his strong displeasure at some of the other committee members' absurd proposals to make changes to some historical sites in town. Some of them posited that the old slate tile roof on the 125-year-old governor's house be replaced with new roofing material to prevent its weathering. Still others proposed to carpet the old oak floors as well, with the idea that it would help preserve them. They had already kind of gotten the ball rolling by discussing the projects with the city council.

"What!" Danny had responded to their rash logic. "That's like trudging down to Arlington, barging in, and laying down linoleum on Martha Washington's kitchen floor!" That rant drew a few icy glares. When it came to historical homes or artifacts, Danny hated when people tried to change or update them. He wanted to preserve everything in its original form. He felt it would alter and harm the historical significance if it was trifled with. He didn't mind something being repaired out of necessity, but he abhorred when they wanted to modify the antiquity of something.

As he continued motoring south through Ashtabula County's beautiful countryside, he began to recall the previous meeting at the McKinley Presidential Library and Museum two months prior, as well. Not unlike the committee at the Niles Historical Society, this committee was also proposing changes. They wanted to apply for state funding in order to reconfigure the spouting's drainage system on the top of the atrium in the memorial's front portico. It ran under the cornice and channeled the rainwater, therefore allowing it to run out the mouths of the semicircular grouping of lion-faced gargoyles that adorned the perimeter. The perimeter rested high above the courtyard. In its midst, a statue of President William McKinley stood gracefully, situated among a carefully maintained flower garden. Some members feared that visitors might get wet from the open drainage or slip and fall while traversing the sidewalk to and from the library when it rained. This preposterous bit of bad logic also caused Danny to opine vociferously against their ideas. He argued that such an ill-advised move would compromise the architectural integrity of the classic Greek- and Roman-themed design. This also touched off a verbal melee of sorts.

Danny continued driving toward Niles as he chuckled out loud to himself, thinking of the stern rebuke he had received from one particular elderly woman who sat on the committee.

"Well, we don't want to have a lawsuit on our hands now, do we, Mr. Dubenion?" she'd chided, causing Danny to snarl sarcastically and say, "Maybe we should try to get funding for some foam padding to wrap around the memorial's classic Greek marble columns so nobody gets hurt on them, either."

Needless to say, his sarcasm didn't engender much good will between himself and the rest of the committee.

Danny was by far a throwback from a previous era. He loved the old historical aspect of Niles, the city he had grown up in. He didn't want anything to change. That's why he'd joined the committees of both groups in the first place. He figured the main function of a historical society was to keep and maintain the original historical significance of the particular town. That was his stubborn desire, anyway – to love and preserve the past. This stubborn desire would produce one fruitful accomplishment in his eyes. About a year or so prior, he'd had a battle with the mayor's office, as well as the city council. The city contracted a paving company to resurface the roads in the area where he lived. His street, however, was still lined with the original brick from almost a century past. He became somewhat of a local urban hero when he successfully led a petition drive on his street to avoid the road renewal intrusion from taking place on his block. That portion of his street would remain brick. Every time he drove down that block or passed by it, like he would be doing that evening to go to the meeting, he smiled broadly for a victory over the establishment and for history lovers everywhere.

After about a fifty minute drive, Danny arrived in Niles and soon after pulled into the parking lot of the Niles Historical Society. The stubborn and preservation-minded Danny drew a couple of sneers from some members as he strode into the building. The first item on the agenda was the announcement of the theme for the annual March reception for the public. The annual festivity coincided with the March 3 birthday of Ohio's statehood. The theme for the upcoming celebration in 1985 was going to be "Saluting Famous Ohioans from the Past." It was going to be a costume party for people to dress up as their favorite famous Ohioan. This announcement drew cheers from everyone inside, including an appreciative Danny, who agreed that it was a great way to honor the past heroes of their fair state. After the applause died down, the regular items on the agenda followed, finances and future projects being the two main issues. The latter issue, of course, drew the usual jeers from Danny.

When the meeting was finished, Danny chatted with one of his fellow members in the parking lot. They exchanged brief pleasantries until Danny begged out because he had to head back up to Ashtabula. The acquaintance half-jokingly asked Danny why he was always so sarcastic to his fellow committee members. Danny apologized and told him that he was just really adamant against changing and altering such great local historical treasures.

"Maybe you just need to meet a sweet, old-fashioned young lady," he suggested to Danny.

"Those kind are difficult to find," he shot back.

"Well, at least there will be some who will be dressed the part in old-fashioned costumes at the reception next March," he declared. The two shared a laugh as Danny shook his hand and then took off.

Danny drove out and briefly stopped to see his parents. They made him promise to come over for Thanksgiving in a few weeks. His mother reminded him that his grandfather was going to be there, and he really missed seeing and talking to him. Danny's grandfather shared a great love for history with him. The two of them always had some really wonderful and sentimental chats together anytime they got together. Danny told his mom that he would be looking forward to it all. They chatted for a little bit, and then Danny insisted that he had to get back up to Ashtabula. His mother insisted that he have a bite to eat before taking off. Danny graciously accepted and had a quick bit of food and then took off north to his new town.

The next few weeks leading up to the Thanksgiving holiday weekend found Danny in his Ashtabula routine. He was performing some very critical sonic testing and hydrogen analysis for a very important jet engine contractor who sold them to the government for military application. This customer, as well as other ones, represented very lucrative contracts for his company. It was very imperative that the quality testing was done accurately and also on a timely matter. Danny was fast earning his nice new and improved salary.

Most typically, however, was the after-work routine. He and a bunch of coworkers now almost daily patronized the "Six" for a post-work libation or two and a few games of billiards together as they shared both laughs and typical job frustration and complaints. In the evenings when he was alone, when the other guys went home to have supper with their families, Danny often made his way to Garfield's for what he considered to be the next best thing to home cooking he could find.

One day after work, Danny went downtown to view the Civil War monument. He wanted to check it out and be able to describe it to his history-loving grandfather when they got together for Thanksgiving. He also made a mental note to view the war memorial by Ashtabula Harbor High School, which honored three generations of locals who gave their lives for this country. Danny's grandfather Edward Dubenion had served in World War I in Europe, and Danny had always admired and respected him for that. The stories that he told about it were legendary and heroic, and Danny wanted to let him know that he'd gone to these two Ashtabula sites to honor the soldiers.

A few days before Thanksgiving, Danny stopped down at the harbor to visit the antique shop where he had recently purchased the mirror. He was still eyeballing the kitschy photo of the old Swedish Pastry Shop he had seen there that day. He had half a mind to purchase it, but since had already spent $500 on the Victorian mirror, he decided to hold back from any unnecessary spending for a while. Still, he enjoyed just looking around, admiring the treasures of Ashtabula Harbor's glorious past.

As he looked around, the elderly proprietor came over and had a pleasant chat with him. Danny listened intently as the kindly old gentleman verbally revisited his childhood days. He told Danny of the many times as a kid growing up near the harbor when he would spend countless hours watching the shipbuilders construct Great Lake vessels or watch the big Hulett machines unload the massive ore boats from the docks and load the contents into the railcars for shipment southward to the big steel mills. He spoke sentimentally of the old Woodland Beach Park. When he was young, he would ride the rides there and swim at the bathing beach. He asked Danny how he liked the lift bridge that spanned the river by the marina. Danny answered enthusiastically. The elderly gentleman informed his newfound student of Ashtabula history that before they built the lift bridge there, a swing bridge was in operation at the site. It pivoted around to let vessels in and out of the mouth of the river. Danny thoroughly enjoyed the history lesson. He was getting a growing respect for the proprietor with each old memory that he shared about living through the Great Depression, his service during World War II, some of the tough jobs he labored in when he was younger, and so on. This fine man, who was about seventy five years old, had really made Danny's day in a very special way.

*

Thanksgiving Day had finally arrived. Danny had been looking forward to seeing his beloved grandfather ever since he moved to Ashtabula some seven weeks prior. He was fondly anticipating the long talks about Civil War history and the old stories from World War I. He often spoke of the hardscrabble life during the Great Depression. Now Danny could share with him the heartfelt stories that the antique owner had passed on to him of the same era. Danny's grandfather was a widower for nearly five years. He loved Danny tremendously, and since he was his only grandchild, he immensely enjoyed the time he spent with him. Danny felt terrible that this would be the first time that he would see him since he'd moved. He was really looking forward to making up for lost time.

When Danny arrived at his parents' house, they had already picked his grandfather up and brought him there. His eyes beamed when Danny walked in. They embraced each other warmly and instantly laughed as they shared their usual jokes with each other. His grandfather's eight-six-year-old body was growing frail, but his mind and wit were as sharp as ever. As they were getting ready to eat, he displayed his strong memory as he vividly retold a story to Danny about his participation in the Battle of Meuse-Argonne in 1918. That struggle would later be known as the largest offensive in United States history. He related to him that it was all part of the Allies' one-hundred-day offensive. Danny beamed proudly at his valiant grandfather as he loudly professed that this particular offensive ultimately led to Allied victory and the end of the war.

"We put on one of the greatest advances of the war!" he boasted as he winked at Danny. Danny returned the wink with ringing approval.

Danny told his Grandpa Ed about the historical society's planned public reception coming up in March. When he told him that the event was going to honor famous Ohioans from the past and that people were to come as their favorite famous Ohioan, Grandpa Ed asked Danny who he was going to go as. Danny replied that probably more than a few would go as U.S. Grant or General William T. Sherman. Most would go as Niles native William McKinley. Danny wanted to be unique. He told him he would probably go as Rutherford B. Hayes or James A. Garfield. Grandpa Ed generously offered to lend Danny his old antique pocket watch and fob to wear to the occasion that his own grandfather and father had passed on to him many years prior. Danny thanked him vigorously and remarked that it would great with the old period suit and vest that he had purchased years ago for his collection.

*

The rest of the afternoon went quite well. The dinner and conversation were both fantastic. Danny enjoyed himself magnificently. Then his parents dropped a bombshell on him that put a damper on the festivities: they told him that they had been actively looking for condos in Florida via a realtor down there. They were dreading the thought of spending the rest of their lives fighting the harsh winters of northeast Ohio. His dad, who was sixty-two years old, had recently retired and announced that moving south was the best thing for the two of them to do. Danny protested. He told them that he would hardly ever see them again. He scolded them for wanting to leave Grandpa Ed all alone. He was visibly upset with them for their suggestion. They apologized for upsetting him but insisted that it was what was best for them. They assured him that his grandfather would be well taken care of. Needless to say, Danny and Grandpa Ed were soured for the rest of the evening.

Later on, that evening, Danny drove his Grandpa Ed home. He promised him that either he could live with him in Ashtabula, or he would help him find a place to rent close by him up there. They enjoyed a nice little talk. Before Danny took off back to his parents' house, Ed gave Danny the antique watch and fob so he could wear it at the historical function in March. Danny thanked him and gave him a big hug. He promised to see him at Christmas or sooner, and then he took off.

*

Danny was spending the next couple of days with his folks. He had made arrangements to hang out with his former coworkers at the Niles facility. They planned on going bowling, having a few beers together, and hanging out and watching the football games.

In between trying to talk his parents out of moving to Florida, Danny had a blast the rest of the holiday weekend with his old workmates. They'd missed him at work since he'd left; they always had a good time together while he was there. Although it had only been about seven weeks or so since he'd transferred up north, it was still nice catching up with everyone.

They had a blast trying to bowl while everyone was making each other laugh the whole time. It was nice just sitting around talking and having a few beers together.

On Sunday, they got together again at a local sports bar and watched the football games. By this late in the football season, many Superbowl predictions abounded among the group. "It looks like the Dolphins and the '49ers this year," one of the friends chimed.

"I can't see anyone beating the '49ers," added another coworker, beer bottle clutched firmly in his hand.

"Unless the Raiders get in there and intimidate them like they did to the Redskins last year."

*

When the holiday weekend was over, it was back to business as usual for Danny. A whole lot of product testing needed to be done as the year began to draw to a close. With just about everybody having scheduled time off for the upcoming Christmas holiday, there was a rush to stay ahead of schedule. At the same time, a great attention to detail and taking one's time to do things qualitatively was also imperative. Danny had a couple of busy weeks ahead of him. Besides working some overtime to help the lab keep up with the demand, he had to drive to Niles for his committee meeting at the McKinley Memorial in early December.

Even though the Niles Historical Society's annual public reception was still about three months away, Danny drove across town one day after work to the novelty store in order to find a fake old-fashioned beard to go with his period outfit. He had decided to go as Rutherford B. Hayes instead of Garfield because he felt that since Garfield had been assassinated, it would be disrespectful, not to mention downright creepy to dress up as him. It took some looking, but he was finally able to find a replica close enough to President Hayes' long, mid-sternal-length, 1870s-style beard that would also match the era of his clothing. Once he had gotten home from the novelty store, he decided to try out the bottle of brass rubbing compound on the plate in the back of the mirror. After a period of firm rubbing, he was able to see an outline of a letter that he had brought to the surface. He went to the kitchen drawer and pulled out a magnifying glass. With the magnifier, he was able to view the letter *T.* If he was going to lift the name that was buried under the tarnish, he realized it was going to take a lot of time, patience, and elbow grease. He had just enough curiosity about it to apply all three. Sooner or later, he would know to whom it had once belonged.

*

It was now early December, and Danny again found himself attending the McKinley Memorial committee meeting. Since most members in attendance were also members of the Niles Historical Society, a reminder of the annual March 3 public reception was tendered as the first order of business. A report on the finances were of course the second order of business, followed by the reading of the prior meeting's minutes. Danny was pleasantly surprised when the new order of business was proffered, and it was mentioned that no progress had yet been made on the proposal to reconfigure the classically elaborate spouting system that he had strongly argued against at the last meeting. "I move that we end that whole foolish matter," he said sarcastically, to the consternation of some of the other members, and he received his expected share of icy stares. After that remark, Danny pretty much survived the rest of the meeting without further conflict. It was time to head back up to Ashtabula.

*

For the next two weeks, Danny was super busy at work. The end-of-the-year rush was upon them. Titanium plates that needed sonic inspection and tensile strength analysis seemed to stream into the lab interminably. Samples that needed heat treating and hydrogen content testing were piling up to the ceiling. He found himself working overtime almost every day. He scarcely had had time to run down after work to the "Six" with the guys for a beer and game of pool. The regulars at Garfield's were starting to wonder where "the guy with the 1965 Wildcat" had been lately. Only once in those two weeks did he find a few minutes to drive down to the harbor to look around and visit his elderly buddy at the antique shop.

On December 15, after work, he decided to get a quick meal and look in on the regulars at Garfield's. Going a couple of weeks without his favorite burger was killing him. It was good seeing everyone again. On top of that, his taste buds were revived again. There was nothing like Garfield's famous Greek-style burger to cure one's blues. He stayed for a bit and made small talk with the folks there. He needed to get home. He wanted to try on his Rutherford B. Hayes look in the mirror to see if it needed any adjustments or any additional pieces of clothing while he still had over two months to fix anything with it. He also wanted to do some more polishing on the tarnished brass plate. *Oh*, he thought sarcastically, *the fast-living life of a lonely man in Ashtabula.*

First Danny stopped off for a quick topping of gasoline at the Flying Saucer, and then he sped home to ply a little elbow grease on the brass plate. Afterward, he washed up really well, dried off, and then pulled out the period clothing from the closet to try on for the reception. He separated everything neatly and orderly on the bed in his room. He was a stickler for details and wanted to do this right to a tee. He wanted to make a unique impression on everybody at the reception. His Victorian gentleman's collection was a unique assemblage of genuine articles of fine clothing that he had meticulously garnered overed the past fifteen years from different antique clothing emporiums all over northeastern Ohio. Every piece was the real article. His close-fitting black double-breasted wool frock coat was one such genuine article that he had purchased a few years earlier at an old estate sale. With it came the matching double-breasted waistcoat vest. His matching black cashmere trousers, as well as the Victorian-style shirt and red cravat, were purchased from a collector's shop. He loved everything about that era. He especially appreciated the gentlemanly and integral attitude of the men from that time period. He had collected such an outfit in hopes of one day getting the opportunity to publicly emulate them, or at least be able to dress the part. He had even managed to corral a pair of black lace-up boots that fit him at one particular emporium near Cleveland some time ago. Now, with his Grandpa Ed's antique watch and fob to tie it all together, he would be a fine, well-dressed Victorian gentleman from head to toe, just like his hero President Rutherford B. Hayes of Ohio. He went over to where he had President Hayes's picture hanging on his wall, and while he was looking at it, it hit him that he didn't have an old black top hat that the president was sporting in the photo. The following day, Danny sought to rectify his oversight by hurrying to the antique shop to see if there were any old hats that somewhat matched that style from the 1870s.

Upon entering the shop, Danny urgently made his request known to the owner. The obliging gentleman immediately led him to the area where he had previously purchased the mirror. There, sitting on a shelf right behind where Danny's prized Victorian mirror had once stood, was just what his historical wardrobe was lacking. Propped up and displayed right in front of him was a deluxe black felt John Bull top hat.

"This might fill the bill," the man declared. "It's hand blocked, hand sewn, five inches tall, with a saddle brim and flattop crown." He turned it over to show Danny the fine white satin inner lining. He told him that back in the 1870s, it was considered a fancy but less formal type of gentleman's headwear. He mentioned that the hat was brought in there a few years back, and he didn't think anyone had any interest in it, so he would give him a discount on it. He figured he may as well make a couple of bucks from it. Plus, since Danny had purchased the antique mirror from him, he considered him a good customer. Danny thanked him vigorously and made the purchase.

Danny drove home and brought the entire outfit, along with his new purchase, into the den so he could put everything on in front of his grand Victorian mirror. It was now late evening. He carefully put on every article of clothing. He tucked in and tied everything neatly and sharply. Then he adeptly connected the pocket watch to the fob chain so it would fashionably dangle from the best pocket. It turned out that it was all unnecessary, trying everything on nearly three months early in case something didn't fit or was out of sorts or in need of any additional items. Everything fit smartly. He looked as sharp as a tack. Now that he was in possession of a classy top hat from that era, thanks to his elderly friend from the antique shop, everything was complete. He stood tall in front of the mirror motionless, taking it all in. The mirror's reflection made him look taller than his actual five-foot-ten-inch frame normally projected. He figured he would stand out even taller at the reception in March. All he needed to do now was to see how he looked wearing the beard. He went over and brought it into the den. He held it to his face to get a good look but didn't have the right angle. He placed the beard on the dresser and stooped down to pivot the huge, heavy mirror a bit so as to get the perfect view. He held the beard up to his face but decided he didn't look quite right with it. Besides it was the only article in this ensemble that wasn't authentic, so he put it aside.

Danny then walked over to his dresser where he had placed his top hat. He retrieved the hat and ambled up to the mirror. "Now for the topper," he declared audibly to himself. He proudly and pompously placed the hat upon his head and gently cinched it down over his slightly wavy sandy-brown hair, trying the look and feel of a couple of different angles.

Then something strange started happening to him, something perplexing. A sharp glint of moonlight caught the mirror at just the precise angle and reflected acutely into Danny's eyes. It set him back a step. He started to feel dizzy. There was a ringing in his ears. The mirror seemed hazy. The glass appeared to become foggy, even smoky. He felt like he was under a spell. Danny stumbled somewhat as he groped for the spare bed to sit down upon. He began to perspire. His heart began to race. The room started spinning. He lay down on the bed. After a few moments of trepidation, Danny kept his eyes firmly closed and eventually drifted off to sleep.

3

Danny had drifted off into a deep sleep. Soon he would be in dreamland. While dreaming, his subconscious began to replay his conscious thoughts in a way that only dreams can do. He dreamed that he was at the historical society's reception. Everyone was milling about and mingling in their period costumes. He was having trouble recognizing anyone. Most of the ladies were probably guests of the members, and he would not have known them, anyway. He figured the men had been so authentically disguised, he was having trouble properly identifying any of them. He decided to make his way to the back of the room to see if he could recognize anyone. He was however, receiving friendly greetings and inquisitive glances from many of the costumed attendees. As he ambled across the room, he went to tip his hat to a group of authentically old-fashioned-dressed ladies, but as he reached for it, it was not on his head. He figured that he must have left it in the car.

The strange part of the dream was that the reception wasn't supposed to be until March. Also, it wasn't being held at the usual reception hall that it took place at every year. In fact, the place didn't resemble a reception hall at all. It was a long, narrow room. He got to the back of the room and exited through the narrow doorway and into the darkened late-evening air. He walked across a metal platform with a chain-link guardrail for a few feet and into another long, narrow room. After a few seconds, he realized where he was. The reception wasn't taking place at any reception hall at all. He had just walked across an old gangway connector, the passageway between two railroad passenger cars. It was being held on a passenger train—an old-fashioned passenger train, at that.

Danny marveled as he gazed around at the ornate, mahogany-covered walls with their elaborately carved paneling. He stood in appreciative awe as he glanced up and eyed the skillfully crafted pressed metal ceiling with the classic clerestory roof just like the trains he'd seen in the old western movies where the center of the ceiling extended up higher than the surrounding area with narrow windows lining the length of it for more efficient lighting and improved ventilation. Patrons were laughing while enjoying drinks seated in the parlor car's plush, luxurious, burgundy-upholstered chairs with elaborate brass fittings and mahogany inlays. The tables bore amenities like frosted glass lamps and pendants. Everybody seemed to be having the time of their lives. Such a vivid imagination. Was it Danny's love and appreciation for the old trains at the harbor and in the old movies that his subconscious was playing out in his visions?

He ambled over to the side of the car and opened the custom curtain that adorned the windows. It was pitch dark outside. He could make out the dim traces of gently falling snow out there. He looked at his grandfather's pocket watch. It must have stopped. It read a little after two o'clock. The eerie part was that suddenly, the train was moving. He could barely make out the unrecognizable landscape that seemed to be racing by. He walked carefully through another gangway over into the next car, which was not as luxurious as the day coach, slid down into a booth chair, and looked around in utter confusion. He wondered why he was in an old passenger train, dressed up in his period clothing at the reception that was supposed to be nearly three months away. What a strange dream, indeed.

The next event the illusion had in store made it extremely interesting. As Danny was sitting back in the booth pondering everything, a beautiful, dark-brown-haired young woman approached him. She appeared to be maybe in her late twenties. She was very attractive. She was bedecked in a stunning floor-length dress in steel-gray taffeta and pale pink. Its smartly tapered waistcoat hugged her shapely and well-proportioned figure. However, it was not lewd or tacky. It was tastefully adorned with a gray silk knotted fringe line that loosely swaddled her below her waistline just above her blanketed knees. A conservative, petite, carnation bustle-era hat crowned her head, which highlighted her beautiful yet unassuming face—a face that carried with it a beautiful smile to match. An accoutrement of frilly lace adorned her high-neck collar, which underlined that beautiful smile. The stylish accessories that complemented her attire bore full decorum to this gorgeous and smartly dressed woman who apparently shared his wont for strict attention to detail.

She very femininely walked up to Danny and introduced herself to him. She was a bit shy in the most innocent sense, not tastelessly coquettish. "Hello, friend," she said as she extended her petite and gentle hand to him. "My name is Eva Lindfors. How are you today?" Her gentle but straightforward voice matched well with the tenderness and sweetness of her personality.

"I'm Danny… Danny Dubenion," he answered back with a receiving hand gently engulfing her own.

"Danny?" She politely chuckled. "Do you mean Daniel?"

"Ah, yes, my given name is Daniel," he confirmed as they both shared a laugh.

"I never just walk up to a man like this," Eva professed, "but sitting there as you are, all dressed up, you reminded me of someone that I once knew." Her tone grew hushed as she finished speaking.

Danny politely smiled at her. "I… uh… I hope it was a good memory," he answered back, not knowing what to say.

"Yes, it was… once, a very good… a very sweet memory," she responded without hesitation. "It was… he was… a very fond memory."

Danny nodded understandingly. If this was his subconscious calling, then this was his definite longing for such a tender-hearted, old-fashioned young woman answering the call.

Danny invited Eva to sit with him and talk. She had a Swedish-sounding name. Her dialect betrayed the fact that she was not an Ohio native. She told Danny that she was from Chicago, and she had been in New York City visiting her older sister and brother-in-law for Christmas. Danny questioned her as to her reference to her Christmas visit as being in the past tense. He didn't realize that Christmas had been over. She politely giggled as not to embarrass the befuddled Danny. "You are silly," she said with a chuckle. "It was over a few days ago." A puzzling dream he was experiencing, indeed.

Danny complimented Eva on her beautiful attire. He made her blush when he also told her how beautiful she was. She possessed a true modesty, without the slightest display of false humility. Her radiant smile had Danny captivated. He was truly enjoying their small talk. She in turn complimented his handsome attire, telling him that he dressed very well and was a fine-looking gentleman. Danny smiled. He was very smitten by this strikingly attractive young lady. She seemed to be adorned with a timeless beauty. She could have walked up to him out of any era – ancient Egypt, the genteel antebellum South, or even from off the screen during Hollywood's golden age of the 1930s and '40s. She had an old Hollywood actress quality about her, like a Greta Garbo or an Ingrid Bergman. She was all at once a big-city girl, laced with an old-world and easy yet spry, folksy charm. He surmised that this all must be a dream. Such a beautiful woman with an equally beautiful personality could not possibly be attracted to him, he thought. But this was a dream, his dream, and it was all playing out like he always desired. "I would tip my hat to you, but I left it in my car," he confessed with a grin.

"Oh, which car are you staying in?" she queried. "The drawing car, or one of the sleeper car berths?" Her inquisitive reaction puzzled him.

Danny asked her about her family. She told him that her parents came here from Sweden before she and her sister were born. Her ancestors had come from the southern part of the country, thus her dark hair. Her father was an investment banker in Chicago. He was quite successful. He had made quite a bit of money providing capital for many business endeavors along the Great Lakes, particularly in the shipping and transportation industry. "He invests money and supplies money to others to provide them capital for growing or starting up businesses."

Danny was impressed. He could tell that she was well educated. He was also very enamored with the fact that, although her father was fairly wealthy, she remained a kind and humble young lady. Her feet seemed firmly planted on the ground. Most importantly, as unbelievable as it seemed, she was unspoken for, suitor- or husband-wise.

Her father had studied business and economics at Uppsala University and furthered his training in Lund in southern Sweden. Those were two of the oldest and most prestigious universities in Europe.

"Do you know who else studied at Uppsala University?" she proudly asked him. "Anders Celsius, the Swedish astronomer and physicist," she boasted, not giving him any time to ponder an answer.

She asked Danny about his situation in life. Trying to talk to her while remaining undistracted by her lovely Swedish-Chicago accent was proving to be a very difficult task. He explained to her that he was living in Ashtabula and was working in the titanium business. He told her that he was a lifetime resident of northeast Ohio. She remarked that she had never heard of titanium before. He told her it was okay, that not many people outside of the towns he worked in had ever heard of it either. They both chuckled over each other's responses. When he revealed to her that he was also unattached, she reached over and gently touched his hand and returned a sweet smile in his direction. When she responded by telling him that she didn't know why some fine girl had not already grabbed him up, he knew for a fact that he had to be dreaming.

If Danny were dreaming, then he sure dreamed in very telling detail. Eva not only had that beautiful southern Swedish, shoulder length, dark brown hair but also possessed many other wonderful Scandinavian features, as well. She was graced with a very distinctive mouth. Her lips were wavy and sort of tapered at the sides, very cherry red in color. She had a full, youthful face, very attractive full cheeks. He was smitten by her bluish-gray eyes, which were fashioned like almonds. They were very fetching. Her nose was very distinctive, as well. As the two of them talked, the light reflected off her nose in such an attractive way. Danny had to fight back the urge to just stare at her. He did not want to ever wake up from this dream.

Eva asked him if he had ever been to New York City, and Danny said no. She described it to him in full detail and encouraged him to someday take a trip there. She told him how beautiful Manhattan was, especially around Christmastime. She told him how nice the neighborhood her sister and brother-in-law—who was also an investor—lived in. Danny sat enthralled, hanging on every word that came from her beautiful lips. She told him that her sister had taken her to Stewart's Marble Palace Department Store on Broadway and East Ninth Street to shop for clothing. She described Stewart's beautiful Italianate marble exterior and the large glass windows with the stunning Christmas displays in them. Her gorgeous Swedish eyes danced when she described the falling snow wafting against the display windows, creating such a wintertime Christmas pageantry. She told Danny that when she was at Stewart's, she purchased a wonderful gift for her mother for her and her father's wedding anniversary coming up that week. She didn't tell him what she had bought for her. She told him she would wait for the next stop to show it to him. It was packed in a wooden crate in the express car. He responded by telling her that if she had picked it out for her mother, then it had to be something very beautiful. She blushed and thanked him.

There was a short pause in their conversation. Danny looked out of the window again to view the landscape. He checked his grandfather's pocket watch once more. The watch read a little further past two o'clock. His watch was moving. He asked her if that was the correct time. She moved over to get nearer to him.

"Yes, it is," she said. "I'm usually not up and dressed this early in the morning."

"It's two in the morning?" he asked, very puzzled.

"You are silly," she chuckled. "Of course, it's two in the morning; we've been riding since ten last night."

Danny just sat and pondered. Together they sat close and stared outside into the chilling night air. They could dimly see the snow still falling. They were mesmerized by the hypnotic snowflakes as they appeared to fall and then get swooped up in the air again. What a romantic sight to behold as the train rumbled up the Hudson Valley countryside in the cold, dark, wintery night.

After a few quiet moments of enjoying the bucolic snowfall, Danny asked her if she also detected a kerosene odor. She said of course she had. She motioned to a cast-iron heating stove across the floor. She smiled and elbowed him and jokingly asked him what he thought was keeping the coach so nice and warm. Danny chuckled. He was a little embarrassed. He claimed to her that he was aware of the stove. Then she pointed to the kerosene-fed lamps on the tables. She playfully asked him what he thought was so smartly lighting the car. She smiled again at him. Danny realized that he was dreaming a very old-fashioned dream. After a few more quiet moments, Eva asked him if he would like to come over and sit with her in the parlor car, explaining to him that it would be much more comfortable and a little more private for them to talk to each other.

"Of course I would," he enthusiastically responded. "Let me hold your hand when we walk across the gangway. It's been snowing a little, and the train is moving."

"Of course it's moving, silly," she chuckled. "You may hold my hand, and I'll hold tightly to the chain railing with the other."

Danny gladly followed her to the parlor car and soon found it to be less crowded and far more luxurious than the day coach he had been sitting in. They sat and talked for a while, with Eva tenderly leaning on his shoulder. What an incredibly strange dream this was becoming. He was actually dreaming that he was dozing off. As Danny napped, Eva had awakened and headed to her drawing room to freshen up in her washroom and lie down on her bed. Danny woke up after a little while. He sat there trying to relax, wondering where Eva had gone. Soon enough, she had also awakened and returned to his side.

For a few moments, which seemed to last for hours, the two of them cuddled in the corner of the plush parlor seating, staring out of the window, watching the wispy snowfall through the darkened night. They talked about life's general things. She mentioned Chicago and her mother and father. She held forth fondly of her Christmas in New York City with her sister, Annafrida. She said how fond she was of long train rides. She enjoyed seeing the countryside. Danny leaned comfortably against the side of the train next to the window and gathered her warm stories into his being. He absorbed the warmth of her body as it cuddled against his. He was falling in love – the fact that he was dreaming all this, notwithstanding.

Eva apprised him of her life growing up with fairly wealthy parents. "Mother told me when I was sixteen and at a 'marriageable age,' I needed to train in the social graces and become 'accomplished' and learn all the proper etiquette. They sent me to Miss Porter's School in Connecticut. It was a one-year program. I learned academics and athletics, as well. I also went to a school in Manhattan to learn the talent of writing in Spencerian script. Father wanted me to learn it for business correspondence purposes. He employs me to inscribe his business lettering. Mother has me apply it for elegant personal letter writing and for her societal functions—you know, writing correspondence and invitations."

Danny was very familiar with the uniquely artistic, oval-based, looping penmanship from his experience with the historical societies. "That is very impressive," he extolled her. "So much beauty and so many brains."

After a few more moments, after they had finished talking, Eva began to gently and beautifully hum and sing an ancient Christmas hymn. Her voice was the sweetest and most lyrical he had ever heard. It was as though the angels were performing. He listened contently for a while and then closed his eyes and drifted back to sleep. Eva gently touched the side of his head, gently stroking his hair. She continued humming the song as Danny slumbered. A better and lovelier vision no one could ever have.

The voices of two men talking loudly stirred Danny out of his brief sleep. Eva was still gently leaning on his shoulder. The two men, one of them being the porter, were overheard talking about the train's approaching arrival at Albany, where it would stop and split into two trains. What a vivid imagination inside of Danny's brain was being summoned by his subconscious. *Why Albany? Why this detail?* he asked himself, even though he knew he was dreaming. *Why am I riding in a train to Albany, New York, with a gentle snowfall and a pretty, young lady named Eva Lindfors from Chicago? Why such vivid details?* Danny, whether he was dreaming or awake, returned to staring off into the snowy, dark countryside.

Eva told Danny that once they stopped in Albany, they would have the opportunity to take a short walk together and get some hot tea to go with some dry goods she had purchased at Stewart's in New York for the two of them to eat inside the train station. "The men were saying when the train stops to split, there will be plenty of time to get off and stretch out. Afterward, we are going to head west toward Syracuse, and the other half will be picked up by locomotives and head north to Saratoga Springs and Schuylerville on its way to Vermont. This will give us time to enjoy a nice bit of food that I brought from the city and go for a walk together in the cool, dark, air." She smiled and gave him a mischievous wink. Danny returned the smile and wink in kind.

A short time later, the announcement was given that Albany Station awaited just ahead. The train would be slowing soon. If anyone wanted to go to his or her respective compartments or berths to get anything for temporarily getting off the train, this would be the time. They were to be in their seats while the train rumbled to a stop. Eva took Danny by the hand and led him toward her drawing car. He again carefully escorted her across the gangways between the cars. "Wait here," she bade him, "I need to get my coat out of my compartment before we stop at Albany."

Danny realized that Eva was definitely a privileged young woman. To have a drawing car meant spending a lot more money than just booking a smaller compartment on a standard sleeping car. The drawing car allowed for quite sizable sleeping quarters, as well as a private washroom—far better than being packed into a car with about thirty other passengers in separate tiny compartments and a single washroom. She was privileged indeed, he thought. *Daddy's little girl.* But amazingly, she was so kind and temperate. He smiled as he pondered her many fine qualities. Within a moment, she emerged with her sturdy but fashionable wool frock coat in tow.

The train was nearing Albany where, as they had heard, it was going to split. Half of the train would be picked up by two locomotives and head north through Saratoga Springs and Schuylerville. Then it was to continue past Lake George and then up to Burlington, Vermont and beyond. The other half, the half the two of them would remain on, would continue its westward trek. The high-pressure steam whistle bellowed. Its potent warning echoed on high, reverberating through the upper Hudson River Valley, signaling the train's imminent arrival. Eva and Danny returned to their seats and waited for the train to slow down for its approach to the Albany depot. Eva told Danny that when the train stopped to split, before they got off to eat and have hot tea, she wanted to show him something in the express car. They would have plenty of time for her to show him what she had gotten her mother for her anniversary.

Soon the wheels began to screech as the brakes were rigorously applied. The train bean to slow. It thundered up next to the station. Soon, it would come to a halt. They stood up, and Eva took Danny by the hand and led him outside to the express car. "We have to make sure that we go to the right express car," she instructed Danny as he followed behind. "One of the cars is ours; the other is going with the Vermont train."

The two of them reached the express freight car, and Eva asked the porter to help her find the crate that she had brought on board from New York. Usually, passengers were not permitted inside the baggage or freight cars, but the lovely and persuasive Miss Lindfors was not easy to resist. Upon his request, she produced her bill of sale for the item, as well as the freight ticket that proved that she paid for the added cargo, as well as to confirm the ownership of the item. He led them in and helped her locate it.

She begged the porter's assistance, along with that of the baggage man, to help to open up the long wooden crate. When it was ready to open, Eva excitedly asked Danny's honest opinion if her mother would absolutely love the gift she had purchased for her. As the men assisted Eva in opening the wooden lid, the train jostled. Danny was jolted, losing his balance, and falling to the floor. He stood up and took a step back. "Daniel?" an alarmed Eva queried. "Are you alright?" As he had stood up in a hurry. Danny rocked back and stumbled. He began to feel dizzy. His ears began to ring. The voices sounded muffled and hollow as Eva and the porter asked him of his well-being. Everything grew hazy. Everything was getting foggy. He stumbled forward and fell, hitting his head on the crate, receiving a cut above his brow. "Daniel!" she screamed, being alarmed. "Are you all right?" That was all he heard. It was repeated over and over again. "Daniel, are you alright? Daniel, are you all right?"

*

Danny woke up in a cold sweat. His heart was racing. He was on his bed, at home, in Ashtabula. He hadn't gone to the historical society reception. That wouldn't be until March. He wasn't on any old train. There was no Eva Lindfors. It was all a dream, albeit very realistic, but still a dream. He looked across the room and saw his felt hat sitting on the floor in front of the mirror. He got up and took off his period outfit and neatly put everything away. Then he took a relaxing shower. It was already nighttime. He made himself something to eat, and then he went straight to bed. He lay there for a while with his eyes open. He marveled at the eerie realism of the dream. Did he love the old trains down at the harbor so much that he had dreamed about being on an old passenger train? Was finding the perfect woman for him always on his mind as well, that his fantasy of such would play out in his sleep? He lay there and thought on his dream further. After many minutes of pondering, he chalked it all up to him just dreaming about two of his beautiful passions – old trains and the girl of his dreams. In the case of this particular dream, that girl's name happened to be Eva Lindfors.

The next morning and the whole time at work, he pondered his lucid dream. He couldn't stop thinking about Eva. He wished that she was real and not just pure reverie. When he was able, he kept to himself at work that day. Even when he met the guys at the "Six" and they asked him what was so visibly bothering him all day, he didn't share the dream with them. He kept the whole matter to himself. What a most remarkable night vision it all was.

4

December 1984

Christmas was only a few days away. Danny was at home getting dressed for his department Christmas party that was hosted by his boss, the supervisor of the quality control department. Danny had taken a few vacation days off from work, and coupled with the paid holidays, he was now off for the remainder of the year. He wanted to dress up and look nice for the occasion. He was taking one of the ladies from the spec certification office as a date—more like an experimental date, in Danny's mind. Maybe she was that special woman, maybe not. Her name was Maureen. He had met her about a month before when she had come over to the lab to confirm some testing results from the manager. Danny was in the office at the time, and they were introduced. Danny, who had been hoping to meet a nice girl for some time now, decided to give it a chance.

Danny was putting his tie on in front of the mirror. Ever since he had that strange, albeit delightful dream about a week earlier, he had approached and looked at his curious antique very differently. He wondered what part of the whole episode was fantasy and how much was reality. The strange hazy aura that emanated from the face of the mirror when the moonlight had hit it, the feeling of dizziness he experienced… was that just a dream? Had that been all a part of it? Maybe he fell asleep before he looked into the mirror and it was all part of the eerie vision. Or did gazing into the mirror precipitate the whole fantastic state of reverie? He wondered just what kind of mirror this antique shop had sold him. What sort of imagery did it project? With, as the proprietor had pointed out, it's "pressed acanthus-leaf crown molding and its elegant egg-and-dart molding and turned drop finials." He learned forward to tighten the knot in his tie. He secured the knot and leaned back. He stood there motionless, staring at the peculiar, old-looking glass. *What about the girl?* he thought to himself. *What about Eva? Was she just a dream?* He knew that his subconscious mind was playing out his desire for such a sweet girl. But everything was so detailed, so vivid. He could feel her touch. He heard her words, her precise Chicago dialect, layered with her learned Swedish accent one would pick up from immigrant parents. He had his share of evocative dreams before, but this one was completely different. This was by far the most realistic of any.

As Danny was driving to pick up Maureen on the way to the Christmas dinner, which was being held at a really nice steak house in nearby Saybrook Township, he began to think that maybe it was all a prophetic vision. Maybe a girl just like Eva was waiting for him in the near future. Maybe it was the very girl he was taking to the dinner that evening. Maybe the dream, or the mirror, was trying to show him a happy glimpse into his future. He smiled at the thought of it all and then dismissed it all as pure fantasy. It was all just pure reverie, just one big, contorted dream. The girl, the train ride the flashing moonbeam in his mirror—it was all just a grand illusion that his subconscious mind was playing in response to his desires. He reasoned that since he had moved to Ashtabula, all he had been thinking about was finding that type of girl. He enjoyed going to the harbor to watch the trains He loved the history of the old trains. He certainly had not been able to get his wonderful Victorian walnut antique mirror off his mind since the day he'd bought it. The more than a century-old priceless relic was the crowning glory of his lifelong collection. He figured since he usually went to bed with all those things on his mind, the only natural result would be to dream about all of them.

Danny picked up Maureen and drove her to the Christmas party He was hoping he could put those incessant images of Eva Lindfors out of his mind long enough to have an enjoyable evening with her and have a nice time with his fellow workers. The party was nice. It turned out that Danny had a great time with everyone, including Maureen. It was nice to enjoy a festive time outside of work with all the employees from the lab, not just with the guys who met him at the "Six". The boss took the time to give a hearty toast to the excellent job everyone had done throughout that whole year. He praised their teamwork and gave everybody due credit.

"It was a great year we all had!" he lauded. "But don't get too comfortable—next year is going to be even busier."

The party lasted until after midnight It was really enjoyable. Danny took Maureen back to her house and dropped her off. Then he drove himself back home. He had a nice time with her. She was definitely a nice girl, but on the way back home, those images kept coursing through his mind. Would she be the girl of his dreams? Would she be like Eva? He sat idly at a red light, his obsession taking hold of him. *No one could be like Eva,* he thought. He drove onto East Fifteenth Street and ambled up his driveway. He turned off his car and sat motionless in the chilly December night air. *This is insane,* he told himself. *She was just a dream. How can I be in love with a dream?*

A couple of days later, Christmas Eve morning, Danny decided to stop off at Garfield's for a quick breakfast and a cup of coffee. He also wanted to wish all the folks he had gotten to know there a merry Christmas. He received plenty of holiday greetings himself as he enjoyed his delicious morning fare. He answered in the affirmative when they asked him if he was going to down to Niles to spend Christmas with his folks. One of the patrons who always complimented and admired his old Buick asked him if he was going to drive a winter car for the next couple of months and leave the old classic in the garage. Danny responded that it was his only car; he didn't own a cheap car to drive in the winter. He added that it should fine. When Danny tried reassuring the guy that he had driven the car in the winter for a couple of years down in Niles without any problems, many of the patrons there briskly chimed in. They informed him in no uncertain terms that Niles had never seen winters like Ashtabula. They chuckled and warned him that, as a first-year denizen of Ashtabula, he was in for a real treat. They proceeded to offer some heavily laden stories of past blizzard experiences from bygone and more recent seasons and seemingly endless winters throughout their many years up there. Danny sighed as he finished his breakfast. Then he admitted that maybe he should look into getting a winter beater car to drive until spring. One guy quipped that Danny should plan on driving the beater car until mid-May, when he could be sure the snow would be gone. Everyone laughed, including Danny. He wished everybody in there a merry Christmas and then got in his car. He scurried over to the Flying Saucer and filled up his tank for the trip to Niles.

*

Christmas Day had arrived. Danny had spent Christmas Eve at his parents' house. He made it his first priority that morning to drive over to his Grandpa Ed's to pick him up and bring him back to the house. His grandfather couldn't drive that well anymore. He got around his apartment fairly well, but they arranged for him to have a nurse's aide stop over a couple of times a day to help him with meals and with doing his chores. One thing was certain: he may have had some physical problems, but his mind was as sharp as could be. The second that Danny helped him get into his car, Ed was already giving him a Civil War history lesson. By the time they got to the house, he would already learn all there was to know about Pickett's Charge.

Once they got back to the house and all the Christmas greetings were exchanged, Ed and Danny monopolized each other's time. After about a half an hour of discussing the Civil War, Danny paused and asked him if he knew of any historical significance about Albany, New York. Ed at first was a little puzzled about Danny's asking about Albany. After a little reflection, Ed was able to relate to Danny what he had once studied about the New York State capital. He was able to inform him about it being a Dutch colony way back in the 1600s. "They built Fort Nassau and Fort Orange, I think. A lot of fur trading they did back then."

Danny listened and nodded his head out of respect. "Grandpa, I mean did anything more recent than the 1600s happen there historically?"

Ed chuckled, not knowing what Danny was driving at. "I know Andy Rooney is from there. He was a reporter during the war in the early '40s, you know. He worked for *Stars and Stripes*, I believe."

Ed asked him why he wanted to know so much about Albany. Danny thanked him for trying, telling him that he was just wondering. Danny blushed when Ed asked him if he had a girlfriend who lived up there. Danny knew that William McKinley had gone to Albany Law School and lived in the city for a while. He began to wonder if the train splitting in Albany in his dream was a revision of how he had divisions with the other committee members at the McKinley Library over certain matters. Boy, was his mind really playing tricks on him in dreamland, he thought.

Danny was the only child of a father who was an only child. He was Ed's only grandchild. Danny's mother, on the other hand, had a few siblings This gave Danny plenty of cousins on her side. After dinner, his mother's sister, her husband, and a couple of cousins stopped over to visit. Danny had a pleasurable time with them all. He didn't get to see them that often lately. It was a great visit. They had a lot of catching up to do. Grandpa Ed fit right in, as well. It was a very pleasant Christmas.

By late evening, Danny drove Ed back to his apartment. Danny helped him to the door. He bade his grandfather a merry Christmas and gave him a firm hug. Before Danny started to walk back to his car, Ed motioned for him to come up to his apartment. "Come in a minute, Danny. I've got something for you."

Danny followed him up to his apartment. When they got in, he handed Danny a wrapped package. "This is for you, son," he said as he handed it to Danny. "The nurse wrapped it for me."

Danny thanked him and unwrapped his gift. It was a hardcover Civil War book that Danny had mentioned before that he wanted. What made the moment really touching was when Ed told him to open the cover and read the inscription that he wrote to him. Ed had written a touching and heartfelt message to him on the title page. It was basically about how he loved and appreciated Danny and his shared affection for history and how much he esteemed him as his own son. Danny read it as tears began to well up in his eyes. He gave his grandfather a tremendous hug and thanked him wholeheartedly.

Ed turned around and reached for one more gift to give him. It was a small item, and he handed it to him. "She wrapped this, too," he said with a beaming smile on his face. "I want you to have and treasure this. Merry Christmas, son."

With a tear in his eye, Danny accepted the gift from his grandfather. Ed put his arm around him as he opened it up. Danny had a look of stunned silence. It was his grandfather's World War I US Army bronze infantry collar disc bearing the crossed rifles. Danny didn't know what to say. He knew how much his grandfather treasured his old army uniform. This gift was saying to him what words could never say. Speechless, he embraced Ed, fighting back his tears.

Danny returned to his parents' house. He showed them what Ed had given him. His mother reaffirmed how much his grandfather loved him. His dad replied that he was all that he talked about when they visited him or brought him over to the house. Danny had a little more to eat and then settled back with his parents and watched a Christmas movie on television. Danny really didn't pay any attention to the movie. He couldn't take his eyes off the infantry uniform disc he had received. When he did take his eyes off it, it was only to read and then reread his grandfather's inscription on the inside of the book he had given him.

*

The following evening, Danny had again made plans to meet his former Niles coworkers out on the town. While he was getting ready to go, his mother made mention of the cold weather. This led to his parents mentioning their earnest intent of selling the house, buying a condo, and moving down to Florida. Danny tried to dissuade them by telling them that they and his Grandpa Ed were all that he had up there. He asked them who would help take care of his grandfather, being that he himself lived almost an hour away in Ashtabula and Ed was having a difficult time getting around. His parents tried to assure him that they would assist Ed in getting a full-time nurse to take care of him. Danny wasn't buying it. He tried to dismiss their wanting to move south as pure fantasy. He finished getting ready and then drove out to meet his friends.

Danny and the gang met at a local pub where they enjoyed some chicken wings and a couple of beers. Of course, the main topic of choice was pro football. The general consensus by now was that the San Francisco '49ers were going to win the Superbowl in a few weeks. Without exception, the whole gang touted that Montana, Roger Craig, Wendell Tyler, and Ronnie Lott were just about unstoppable by any other team in the league. Later that evening, they enjoyed a few games of bowling, followed by hanging around and talking about the old times they'd had together when they had just started working together years prior. Danny always enjoyed going out with the gang. He promised to meet everyone in the spring and do it all again.

The next day he was at his parents' house, getting ready to head back up north. Once again, the minor argument ensued about what Danny referred to as their unwarranted decision to want to move to Florida. They stuck to their case about needing to get away from the harsh winters of the area. Danny reasserted his claim that he would try to find a retirement apartment up in Ashtabula for his grandfather. He was still a little upset at them for leaving his dad's father here by himself. The point was moot; they were totally in earnest about the relocation.

*

On the drive up Route 11, it began to snow slightly. It was a gentle snowfall at first, which reminded him of his dream of being on the train. He began to think of Eva Lindfors. She was only a fanciful vision, but her features and personality were so lurid and lifelike. He wanted to meet and marry a girl just like her. He began thinking about Maureen. He thought that maybe when he got home, he should call her and ask her out for New Year's Eve. Maybe she was the one for him. She was cute and friendly enough. She was a little old fashioned. Maybe she would end up being the girl of his dreams. As he drove farther north into Ashtabula County, the snow started to get heavier. By the time he hit Jefferson, about ten miles from his place, it was so heavy that he could barely see the road. He slowly crept home the rest of the way. His windshield wipers started to freeze up. The flakes were the size of golf balls. When he finally made it in, he phoned Maureen and had a nice chat. She told him she would be delighted to go out with him on New Year's Eve.

They had a great time on New Year's Eve, but as nice as Maureen was, to Danny she was just a friend. Maybe he was just setting the bar too high for the kind of woman he was seeking. She just didn't seem like the right one.

A week or so later, he went on another date. It was with a girl he had met and talked to at the grocery store. Again, he had an enjoyable time with this date, but she just didn't capture his heart. Danny did not want to be with a girl unless he was certain he would want to marry her. He was old fashioned in that way as well. Again, this made him think of Eva. He knew it was not healthy to obsess over anything, let alone over a dream. The quite bothersome fact was, however, that Eva, although just an imaginative illusion, was now the measuring stick for any other woman he would meet from now on. Unfortunately, nobody else seemed to measure up to her. A psychiatrist would have a field day with him, he presumed.

*

It was now the middle of January. The Ashtabula winter was turning horrendous. It snowed heavily on an almost daily basis. The ice-cold air whipped furiously off Lake Erie and right through his bones. Temperatures were hovering near zero degrees at night. It got to be that the hardest part of his busy work schedule was just driving to and from work every day. It was a laborious struggle negotiating the snowy and icy roads, and he only lived a little more than a mile from work. He was lamenting the regrettable fact that he had omitted getting a winter car to drive. His precious classic Wildcat should have been stored in the warm garage for the winter, like the guys at Garfield's had heavily recommended. Even though he had lived his whole life in Niles before moving there, and it was only fifty miles away, he had never experienced such a harsh winter like this.

One particular Saturday, while he was relaxing in the warmth of his home, his mother called him on the phone. She spoke in a near-frantic tone when she explained to Danny that his dad was shoveling snow and slipped and fell on the icy driveway. She said that he had badly hurt his knee and was about to drive him to the emergency room. Danny said he would drive down and meet them there. He assured his mom that he would stick around down there for the rest of the weekend and help out. She expressed her immense gratitude to him and then hung up in a hurry. Danny washed up quickly and got ready for the car ride to the hospital near Niles. When he got to his car, it was snowing a little bit. It was also starting to get a lot colder.

After about an hour, he arrived in the parking lot of the hospital. The girl at the front desk directed him to where his father was being attended to. He was in some pain and quite grouchy. His mother greeted him with a hug.

"Thank you for running down here," she said.

His dad greeted him with a snarl and a gruff, "This is why we are moving to Florida!"

After another hour or so, Danny's father was released to go home. Danny went back to their house to help him get in and around and to aid his mother in taking care of him for the weekend. Danny halfheartedly submitted to their reasoning about moving. He begrudgingly admitted that it might be the wise thing for the two of them to do. Before he headed for home the next afternoon, his dad cheerfully thanked him for all his help.

All the night before, the thermometer had been steadily dropping. It had hit a low of fifteen degrees below zero. The high temperature that day had struggled to achieve only a reading of five below. By the time Danny was heading back to Ashtabula, it was already on the decline. It was almost ten below and falling. As he motored closer to the Ashtabula County line, the snow naturally picked up momentum. The hard-hearted wind was furiously churning, as well. Plowing through the icy hard snowdrifts that had wafted onto and formed across the frozen highway was as surreal as anything Danny had ever experienced while driving. He didn't know if his poor car or he himself would be the first one to shatter every time he crashed through one of them. Having a ragtop roof as insulation from the extreme cold was not a great feeling of relief, either. To say that his belabored car heater was straining hard would be a gross understatement.

When he finally and painstakingly arrived home, he promptly jumped into a steaming-hot bathtub to defrost his frigid bones. Needless to say, for the next couple of weeks, other than going to work or to the store to buy food, he dared not venture out into the fierce winter landscape of this bitter frozen tundra.

*

It was a typical early February morning in Ashtabula. Danny, who had just plied his trusty snow shovel the afternoon before, digging himself into the driveway after work, now was again shoveling himself back out to go to work. This was practically his routine for the last couple of weeks. The guys at Garfield's had been spot-on correct when they warned him of winter's powerful punch up there. Not only was Old Man Winter getting very old and tiresome, he was grouchier and crankier than ever. It seemed that every night six or eight inches of snow would fall. He would have to dig himself out in the morning. Then during the day, maybe six or more additional inches would fall, and he would find himself digging his way back in. It had snowed so much up until then that the snowplows had nowhere else to put it. Snow was already piled up so high by the variety of snow removal machines that it nearly crested the telephone poles.

Each morning when Danny was finally able to dig himself out of his driveway, it only represented half the battle. The treacherous, snow-covered roads presented the usual challenge of getting to work on time and in one piece. It was truly like a frozen tundra, like everybody there called it. The most frustrating part of it was that when Danny got into work one day after another tussle with winter's fury and murmured about the endless snow, ice, wind, and subzero temperatures that had pummeled him thus far all winter, everybody stared at him and laughed. A couple of coworkers bellowed out in unison that winter was not even half over yet. Everyone laughed in response, much to Danny's consternation. To say that the Ashtabula winter of 1984-85 was merely brutal would be to suggest that Caligula was merely dysfunctional.

Danny promptly went over to the sink and thawed out his freezing hands in the warm water. He quickly shook off the outside coldness and got to work preparing some titanium test samples for critical analysis. He was on a project that required the product to meet certain hydrogen content levels in order to pass specification. It was all part of the company's massive and lucrative commercial jet engine manufacturing contract. After he settled into his routine, Danny decided to go get a quick cup of hot coffee to help warm himself up.

While he was in the office getting coffee and making small talk, the phone on the clerk's desk started to ring. The clerk picked up and answered her phone. "Ah, sure, he's right here," she said and then handed the phone to Danny. "It's for you, Danny."

He shook his head, hoping his dad hadn't fallen on the ice again. "Dubenion here," he said into the phone. There was a pause. The pale look on his face boldly announced that something was terribly wrong. His dad hadn't fallen. It was he who had called Danny. He sadly informed Danny that his Grandpa Ed had just passed away. Danny slumped into a nearby chair that was in the office and sank down into it. When Danny ruefully asked what had happened to him, his dad explained that he was walking to supper last night and just fell down. The doctor at the hospital said it was a cerebral aneurysm. They physician had explained to his dad that it was a quick death and assured him that he didn't suffer at all.

Danny sat there, frozen in shock. He couldn't believe the tragic news. Everybody in the office instantly knew that something had gone tragically wrong for him. His boss encouraged him to get home right away and get ready to go Niles to be with his family. He prodded Danny to take a few days off. He knew how close Danny was with his grandfather. Danny's boss assured him that everyone would pick up the slack while he was away. Danny humbly thanked him and everyone for their sympathy. After exchanging a heartfelt embrace with the clerk, he bundled back up and sadly trudged back out into the cold, heartless Ashtabula winter.

5

February 6, 1985

Danny hurried home and quickly got ready for his trip to Niles. Within two hours of his father's phone call, he had already arrived at De Sante & Volpe Funeral Home on the west side of town to meet him there to help make arrangements. He joined his dad in the unenviable task of choosing the casket and vault for his Grandpa Ed's burial. He assisted him in picking the floral arrangement for the funeral director to order from the florist. His dad gave him the honor of writing the obituary. After confirming reservations for the after-funeral dinner for friends and family, the two of them headed to Ed's apartment to sort out any of his belongings that they wanted to keep for mementos. His dad would also gather any unpaid bills that Ed had collected to take them home to settle the debts.

At the apartment, Danny's dad offered to let him keep Ed's army uniform that he had carefully packed away in his closet. He suggested that Danny take as many of his history books with him and as many old photos of his grandparents as he wanted to. He assured Danny that his grandfather would want him to have them, knowing how much he had treasured them. Danny graciously accepted them. He grabbed an empty box that his dad had brought along for the bittersweet occasion. He sadly gathered his precious mementos while he mournfully and methodically took a look around the apartment. His mind flashed back to Christmas Day six weeks before, when he'd driven his Grandpa Ed back home from his parents' house. He fought back a few tears as he recalled his beloved grandfather's gifts to him—the book with the heartfelt inscription he had written inside of it and the bronze collar disc from his infantry uniform that he had fondly and proudly given him. He was surely going to miss his old friend and confidant. He was going to miss him an awful lot.

A couple of days later at the service, Danny was greeted by family from his mother's side, as well as some of his dad's friends. Richie and a few of his Ashtabula coworkers, as well as his old Niles ones, stopped in to pay their respects as well. Danny had the honor of delivering the eulogy for his grandfather. He related some of the humorous stories his grandpa used to tell him about the old days. He mentioned the fond memories of his Grandpa Ed and his father taking him up to Cleveland Stadium when he was a teenager in the mid-1960s to see the Browns and Indians play, and how enjoyable and fun it all was. He recounted for everybody there the long talks about history and the Civil War he'd had with him and how he had meticulously taught him a lot of interesting aspects and details of nearly every battle. Danny began to well up. A few years back when his grandmother passed away, he'd gotten a few tears in his eyes. Those tears were partly for his grandfather, who was in pain over losing her. This time, he was outwardly and visibly in tears. His Grandpa Ed had surely meant the world to him.

He went on to hold forth about Ed's courageous and loyal service to his country during World War I. He proudly boasted of his participation in the crucial Meuse-Argonne offensive on the western front in 1918. He was part of General Pershing's Expeditionary Force that pressed the war to its end. Danny could not overstate his grandfather's brave and heroic actions for the people in attendance. He mentioned to everybody there about Ed's prized infantry disc that he had given to him. "He entrusted it to me as though it were some sacred fraternal pledge … and indeed it was," he humbly said. He told of how Ed survived the Great Depression and about Ed's job as a tough ironworker in the 1930s through the 1950s. By the time he was finished speaking, he was struggling to hold himself together. This was the only funeral that he had ever truly cried at. His Grandpa Ed meant that much to him.

Everyone at the service afterward gave Danny a hearty embrace. They knew he was hurting and wanted to give him some small degree of comfort. Later, at the cemetery, Corporal Edward Dubenion, US Army infantryman, was given a full military ceremony. It included the folding and presenting of the United States burial flag and the playing of "Taps." He also received the traditional twenty-one-gun salute. After the service, Danny's dad gave him the flag to keep. He held it firmly in his arms across his chest. Danny then took a rose from the funeral director, who was handing them out. He closed his eyes and slowly raised the rose to his face and took a long, pensive smell. He placed the rose gently on the casket and bid his grandfather a fond farewell. He then quickly turned around so as not to let anybody see him weep. Then he hastened back to his car and got in.

Later on, that evening, back at his parents' house, the three of them sat and talked quietly of their fond memories of Ed. After a while, Danny wondered aloud of what they were going to do with the rest of Ed's stuff that his dad and he didn't retrieve from the apartment. His mother answered that they could probably have an auction to sell anything that remained from what they didn't want to keep. Danny suggested that there really wasn't enough stuff left over to really pay an auctioneer to sell it.

However, for Danny the other shoe was about to drop. His parents informed that they would combine their stuff with Ed's and have one big auction. When Danny questioned what the two of them were getting at, they replied that they had recently put a bid on a condo in Tierra Verde Beach, Florida. Although he knew it was inevitable, Danny was still stunned. Not only had he lost his dear grandfather, but soon he would be a thousand miles away from his parents. He paused for a moment and then sighed that at least he wouldn't have to worry about his grandfather being left alone down there anymore once they moved. Needless to say, the next morning's drive back up to Ashtabula on the cold and desolate highway would be a long, lonely trip. He pondered the fact that very soon he would be devoid of his close family members in any proximity. His beloved Grandpa Ed was gone. He couldn't just visit his parents every time he was in Niles anymore. What if something happened to one or both of them? He wouldn't be able to just hop a flight to Florida on a whim every time. It had been a cold, dark, introspective last few days in his life.

He also began to wonder if he was being too choosy when it pertained to finding a good woman for his life. Maybe he should give Maureen another chance. She wasn't perfect for him, he surmised, but who would be? He was certainly far from perfect. All kinds of thoughts were racing through his befuddled head. He again began to think of his dream he'd had weeks before. He couldn't get Eva out of his thoughts. She was just a dream, he kept trying to reason with himself, but she was so vivid, so lifelike. He was being so choosy because no one could compare with Eva. He was driving himself mad.

He arrived home around 11:00 a.m. He was scheduled to go back to work the next morning. He ate a light lunch and lay down on the sofa. He stared at the ceiling, pondering his life's next move. He assured himself that throwing himself into his work and into his obligations on the two historical committees in Niles would do him good. It would all help him refocus his priorities and help him get his mind off not having his three loved ones in his life any longer.

The following week, he busied himself in order to keep his mind from his depressing losses. He came into work a little early every day for a little overtime to help the lab keep up with the massive workload. On Monday, his first day back, everyone extended their sympathies to him, while at the same time allowing him to keep pretty much to himself. They all knew how much he was hurting inside. It seemed like a very long day for him.

After work, the gang took him down to the East Sixth Street Café for a couple of beers and some billiards. They succeeded with their proper good humor in cheering him up for the time being. Once he was back home alone every day, he took long, pensive walks in the chilled air along Fields Brook through old Swedetown, dealing with all the agonizing thoughts swirling around in his head.

Wednesday after work was his meeting at the Niles Historical Society. This was an important meeting. The committee, in tandem with the McKinley Memorial group, was going to put any last-minute finishing touches on the public reception that was just a couple of weeks away on March 3. The reception, with the theme of "Saluting Famous Ohioans from the Past," gave Danny a refreshing sense of purpose and belonging. He was thrilled that he would be getting the chance to relive the old days—days of yore that he sometimes wished he could go back to, days of a politer time, a refreshingly more civil and chivalrous era when men of upstanding behavior and character carried the day. Women were old-fashioned and graceful. At least for a couple of hours on March 3, he could pretend to live it, he reasoned.

Wednesday after work, he left for Niles a little ahead of time. He made it a priority to go visit his Grandpa Ed's gravesite. This would be the first time he would be able to be alone with him. He could talk to him. He couldn't do that with the crowd of people at the funeral. All the way down the snowy drive through Ashtabula County, his thoughts were zeroed in on his grandfather. He wanted to tell him that he loved him and to thank him one last time for all that he had done for him throughout all the years. Danny doubted that he would be able to keep himself together at the cemetery. He hoped he didn't walk into the meeting all flushed and misty-eyed. As he headed south into Trumbull County, the snow had started to abate. The roadway was clearer. He picked up speed in order to get to Niles and the cemetery quicker. He wanted to have plenty of time to visit the grave before the meeting started.

Danny reached the Niles cemetery with plenty of time before the meeting started. He turned into the entrance and made the long, sinuous drive to the back, where the veterans' section was located. Danny parked his car along the edge of the narrow cinder roadway. He got out and walked slowly past numerous war veterans' grave markers. He paused and viewed several of the heroes of past conflicts who had been buried there. Some were World War II participants. A few were from the Vietnam conflict, as well as Korea. There were several from the First World War, including his beloved Grandpa Ed. He quickly located his grave, as it was the only fresh one in the section. Nothing was more of a sadder sight for Danny than a fresh grave, piled high, inundated with a heap of withering flowers. He slowly and sadly made his way across the wet, snow-melted grass toward the grave.

Danny stooped down and talked to his grandpa. "You're with grandma now," he said audibly as he looked up at the gravestone that bore both names, albeit without his grandfather's date of death yet engraved on it. He put his hand gently on the stone and glanced down at his grandmother's grave that had long since settled with the ground. "Take care of him, grandma," Danny gently pleaded with her. "He was really missing you." Danny thanked his Grandpa Ed for always being there for him and all that he had done for him throughout his life. He told him how grateful he was for all that he had taught him about life and history. He said that he wished he could have taken him around historic Ashtabula Harbor and showed him the sights and sounds of the old port city. He assured him that he would have surely enjoyed it. Danny said a prayer for the two of them and then slowly rose up. He looked around and saw the new veterans' war monument in the back row over against the woods that bordered the cemetery.

The memorial was fairly new. Danny hadn't had the chance to really view it before. It was dedicated to all who had served in foreign wars. He reverently walked up to it to pay his respects. On the face of the monument was an engraving of John McCrae's solemn poem "In Flanders Fields." Danny took a moment to read the beautiful work that McCrae had written after seeing his best friend get destroyed by a German shell at the Second Battle of Ypres in May of 1915. He wept as he read the poem. His Grandpa Ed used to recite it to him years before. As Danny read the poem to himself, he could hear Ed's voice in his mind, reading it to him. He couldn't hold back his tears. He stood in front of the monument for a few minutes, just revering the moment. Then he realized he had to get going to the meeting. He paced back over to view his grandparents' grave one last time and said goodbye to them.

Once Danny arrived at the meeting, he could not pay attention. His mind was stuck back at the cemetery with his Grandpa Ed. The poem by John McCrae was incessantly coursing through his brain. He couldn't shake it. He was just going through the motions during the entire course of the proceedings. His face was still red from his weeping at the monument, and he felt embarrassed. He couldn't wait for everything to wrap up so he could get out of there. Eventually, the important part about getting the final preparations in order for the public reception was addressed. When everything was finalized and the meeting was finished, Danny left with all haste.

All the way home, Danny recited the beautiful poem in his mind. He couldn't get the horrible images of the Great War out of his head. The first line of the hauntingly majestic poem kept coursing through his mind: "In Flanders Fields the poppies blow between the crosses, row on row …" As he neared Ashtabula, naturally, the snowfall started. He arrived home, got something to eat, and went to bed for the night.

*

February continued with its brutal weather. For the remainder of the workweek, Danny employed a bunker mentality. He had stocked up on groceries to last a while. Other than working, he stayed at home. He didn't even go to the "Six" with the guys or even to Garfield's for his favorite cheeseburger meal. It was somewhat boring. He watched a lot of old television shows. He took a few extra naps. He also took some time out to apply more brass polish to his antique mirror's brass nameplate. After using a bit of muscle on it, he was able to see an outline of another letter that was brought to the surface. He again got his magnifying glass and was able to get something accomplished while sitting at home waiting out the harsh Ashtabula winter.

On Saturday, he received a phone call from his parents. It was a call he had expected, albeit not so soon. They told him that the seller of the condo down in Tierra Verde had accepted their offer. They had contacted their realtor up here and told him to proceed on the selling of their house in Niles. Danny was saddened. He understood that it was the right move for them, but he was still going to miss them badly. He didn't know how often he would be able to go down and see them. Plus, once they moved, he would never be able to visit the house that he had grown up in. As sentimental as he was about it all, thought, he was happy for them. After experiencing his first Ashtabula winter, anybody's wanting to move to Florida was beginning to get his ringing approval.

The following day, Sunday, Danny drove down to their house to help them organize a little. They were going to have to get rid of a lot of accumulated things they had amassed in the house throughout the many years, and they were going to have an auction in order to minimize what they had to haul down to Florida. They wanted Danny to come down and take whatever he wanted from the house before they either sold it or packed it for the move. He found his old record collection of 1950s and '60s music, which was boxed up in the basement. He also found his old *Life* magazines from the 1940s and '50s that he had amassed from collector shops throughout the years. They were valuable to him, so he wanted to make sure to hang on to them. He stayed a bit to help them pack some things. He loaded up his car with his collectibles. He promised to stop back plenty of times in the ensuing weeks to help them get things ready for the move. Then he headed back home.

On the final weekend of the month, he went out with Maureen one last time. Again, they had a nice time. She was friendly and sympathetic to his streak of bad fortune. They shared a few laughs together as she tried to brighten things up for him. Still, Danny didn't feel the special connection to her that he had hoped for in a woman he could fall in love with. As nice as she was, he would have to keep on searching. He dropped her back to her house when the date was over and then went home to relax.

Danny sat down and gazed out the window. It was snowing pretty hard. February was finally and painstakingly coming to an end. He stared out into the dark, cold, late evening and wondered when the hard stuff would quit falling, literally and figuratively. It was the most difficult month in his entire life. He had lost his grandfather, who was his lifelong friend, mentor, and confidant. His parents were moving a thousand miles away and he would hardly ever see them again. He couldn't seem to find the right girl to share his life with, which was something he wanted desperately to do. His job was even starting to get a little mundane and repetitious. The winter of 1984-85 was wearing on him, grinding him down. It was definitely taking its toll. He took a nice hot shower and crawled into bed early in advance of Monday's workday.

March 3 had finally rolled around. Spring and warmer weather were hopefully around the corner. It was nearly seven o'clock. This was the big evening. Danny stood in front of his mirror, putting the final touches of his period costume for the historical society's public reception. This was the real thing. It was not just a dress rehearsal like when he was trying it on back in December. He wanted very much to look sharp. He wanted to give old President Rutherford Birchard Hayes from Delaware, Ohio a good send-up. He had already put on his double-breasted wool frock with its complementary waistcoat vest. His nice, clean, white Victorian-style shirt was neatly tucked into his black cashmere trousers. His black felt top hat lay on the sofa alongside the fake beard, adjacent to where he was standing in front of the mirror. The only thing he needed to do to look like an 1870s gentleman was to fashionably adorn himself with his bright red cravat.

Before he put on the cravat, however, he ambled over to his filing cabinet. He unlocked the metal drawer, opened it, and pulled out a small cache of genuine antique money from the 1860s and 1870s from his valued collection. He had a couple of old five-dollar demand notes and some five-dollar United States notes. He also had a twenty-dollar National Bank note from 1875. He wrapped them around some one-dollar legal tender notes from the 1860s. He tucked them into his antique sterling silver money clip and inserted the money in his trouser pocket. He wanted to impress everyone at the reception with his astute attention to detail. He figured if he was going to be President Hayes for the evening, he would play the part totally and completely. Just to make sure that he wasn't leaving out any detail, he also put some coins he had collected from the same period into his vest pocket. Then he leaned into the mirror to apply his bright red cravat. When that was neatly in order he gazed over at the sofa and again decided to nix the unattractively fake beard. He went over and grabbed the black felt top hat. He faced the mirror, standing all proper and straight. With great circumstance, he carefully fitted the elegant hat onto his head.

Suddenly, the mirror reflected a glint of evening moonlight from the window, just like it had in December when he'd been in front of the mirror trying on the period suit. He started to come under a dizzying, hypnotic spell again. The sharp light penetrated Danny's eyes and blinded him for a few seconds. Again, he started to teeter back and forth. *Not again!* he thought. *This isn't happening again!* Danny's ears started to get that familiar ringing inside of them. He made his way to the bed, staggering, and plopped down upon it. Everything grew hazy. Danny's head grew foggy. Within a few moments, he drifted off to sleep.

6

"Daniel! Are you all right, Daniel?"

Danny was lying on the floor, a bit shaky.

"You fell, Daniel. Do you feel all right?" It was Eva.

Danny slowly rose to his feet, assisted by her and the porter. She brushed the dust from his black frock coat and trousers.

"You fell, Daniel. Are you hurt?" she repeated, alarmed, as he was helped to his feet.

Danny asserted that he would be okay. He had his hand pressed against his forehead, near his eyebrow. He was feeling a little dizzy. Eva adjusted his mussed-up red cravat and firmly but gently hugged his arm. Danny was dazed not just from his fall but more from the eerie notion that it appeared his dream that he experienced months ago had picked up right where it had left off. He was back on the train with Eva. They were in the express car at the Albany stopover.

The crate with the opened lid was lying near where they stood. He remembered that she was showing him what she had bought for her mother for her parents' anniversary. He was about to look inside the crate, but that's when the train jostled, and he fell. He remembered getting dizzy and hitting his head on the crate. That's when the dream had ended, and he had awakened from it on his bed in the spare bedroom.

"Daniel!" Eva shrieked as he took his hand off his forehead. "You have a cut over your eye. You poor dear."

"I feel okay. I must've hit my head when I fell," he replied.

The porter told them that there was a physician on board, a Dr. Penwalt. He said he would summon him to come and take care of his cut. Within a minute or so, the porter walked back into the express car leading the doctor to where Danny was seated on the crate. Eva was sitting next to him, making sure he was all right. The doctor cleaned his wound and bandaged him up in quick time. Eva made sure he sat for a moment to make sure his dizziness had ceased before he stood up. Danny seemed fine. He thanked the doctor and the porter for their kind help. With Eva's tender but firm assistance, he rose up.

"I'm sure I'll be fine," Danny assured them all. He put his arm out to Eva to escort her out of the express car. Together they strode toward the door, escorting each other as they went. Danny again reached for his head. "What's the matter, Daniel?" Eva asked in a troubled manner.

"Oh, it's nothing. I was just reaching for my hat, but it's not there. I wanted to tip my hat to a beautiful lady." He grinned.

"But, Daniel," Eva replied, blushing, "you said that you left it in your sleeper car."

Eva and Danny exited the train to find a place to sit down and eat. It was about three o'clock in the morning. It was dark and still gently snowing outside. It wasn't long before they found a café inside the train station house. The two of them snacked on the dry goods that Eva had brought along from New York—walnuts and roasted beans—and enjoyed a nice hot cup of tea purchased from the station. "This is not much," she admitted, "but it's the only food that I've eaten since before we departed New York last night."

"It's just fine."

"Did you get any sleep on the train since we left?"

"A little bit," he replied. "Did you?"

"I slept a couple of hours in my drawing room, plus a little nap with you at our chairs in the parlor car."

The two of them talked for a little while as they ate their humble meal and sipped their tea. Outside, the snow had started to pick up a bit. "We can grab some real, hot breakfast when we arrive at the Syracuse station," Eva pointed out.

"This should hold us over until then," Danny added.

When they had finished eating what Eva had brought along, Danny instinctively reached into his pocket to pay for the hot tea. Once again, he was overcome with an eerie feeling. He pulled out the antique money that he had put in there for the reception. His dream sure had some uncanny detail. What was stranger yet was that the café employee accepted the old antique one-dollar note as payment and then returned the change to him in old coins. Danny was puzzled. This was a very realistic dream, not to mention a perplexing one. When he implored the attendant to please keep the change, the attendant thanked Danny profusely as though he had offered him a fortune.

Needing some fresh air, he suggested that the two of them go for a short refreshing stroll around the station house grounds. Eva asked him if he was feeling well enough to walk around in the cold and snow, as she gently felt his bandaged eyebrow. Danny assured her that the cold air would be good for him and would help him clear his head. Eva concurred. They took each other's hand and strolled together in the darkness and through the winter air around the outside of the station house. The two of them talked and enjoyed each other's company as they took about a ten-minute walk. With his slightly foggy head and the snow blowing around the dimness of the night, Danny didn't even notice the markings on their train. The inside of the train seemed old-fashioned to him. Again, he chalked it up to his mind replaying his talk that he'd had with the antique shop owner about the old trains in the harbor and his love for the old passenger trains of the old West. After all, he thought again, this was his dream. It would be dreamed his way.

Soon after, the call came forth to board the train. He helped Eva step back on, where she proceeded to her drawing room to put her coat away and freshen up. Danny had his bandage checked by the physician, Dr. Penwalt, who proceeded to clean his wound and replace his bandage. Then they proceeded to the parlor car, where they sat back down in their plush seats. Another one of the grand old cast-iron potbellied heating stoves cast a warmth on their chilled bodies. The kerosene lamps had remained lit but had been dimmed by the porter. When they were outside walking, the train had been repositioned. It had additional coal and wood loaded on it for fuel. It also took on water for its boilers and tenders, as well. The whistle blew, echoing on high with full force. The engines roared. The volatile steam vents blasted away nearby snowdrifts into oblivion. The two locomotives began chugging, tugging the train westward in the snowy early morning air toward its next stopping point, Syracuse.

The two sat in the plush parlor seats near a window. Eva gently leaned against Danny's sturdy shoulder as the two of them peacefully drifted off for a brief nap. Danny awoke first, a few minutes before Eva. This, of course, afforded the pleasurable opportunity to give her delicate beauty the once-over.

Eva soon awoke, rubbed her eyes, and gently massaged the stiffness out of her neck. "Were you staring at me?" she asked bashfully.

I was just admiring you. I'm certainly smitten by your exquisite Swedish features." Danny went on to explain to her that he had known a few people of Swedish descent, and they all had blond hair and blue eyes, as well as fairer skin. She repeated to him that her dark brown hair and bluish-gray eyes, as well as her slightly darker skin tone, were traits more common to people of southern Swedish lineage.

"Where did your parents and ancestors come from?" he asked.

"My parents and forebears are from Uppsala, a city a little north of Stockholm, in southern Sweden."

"Well," he stated rather matter-of-factly, "I do believe that Swedish Americans—especially southern Swedish American women—are truly the most beautiful." He winked at her as she wryly but playfully slapped him on the shoulder.

"Do you say this to every lady whom you meet on a train?" she queried jokingly.

"I don't know; this is the very first time that I've been on a passenger train, and you are the very first dark-haired Swedish girl that I have ever met."

She smiled as they both stared out of the window into the darkness. It was a little after four o'clock in the morning. The warm glow cast off from the heating stove amid the dimness of the trimmed lamps caused them to open and close their eyes sluggishly, intermittently inducing brief sleep.

Eva's eyes popped open as she fought off the urge to doze off again. "Do you know who else was a beautiful Swedish American woman?" she abruptly quizzed him to help them stay awake. She went on to educate Danny about the wonderful beauty and talent of Jenny Lind, the Swedish-born opera star who came to New York in 1850 at the express invitation of master showman P.T. Barnum. "She was an angelic soprano. She was known as the Swedish Nightingale. She sang in Sweden and all over Europe before coming to New York."

"You sing quite beautifully yourself," Danny complimented. "That hymn you sang to me earlier was angelic also. You should be called the Swedish Angel. I really mean it."

His boasting of her talented and heavenly voice caused her to blush. "Mother always told me about Jenny Lind when I was a little girl. She is the whole reason that I became interested in singing and taking voice lessons."

"Well, it really paid off magnificently," he added, unable to take his eyes from her.

The methodically rhythmic clattering of the iron wheels against the rails, along with the warmth from the heating stove, was making it difficult for both of them to not drift in and out of slumber. As they had taken their initial hour-long nap after boarding from Albany, the train had adeptly steamed past Schenectady and then onto and beyond Amsterdam. As they sat and talked, drifting in and out of their brief respites, the train, unnoticed by them in the shrouded early morning air, was steadily working its way toward Utica and the bucolic Mohawk River Valley.

"Do you know who else was from Sweden?" she asked, continuing on the subject as if uninterrupted by the short sleepy lapses. "The famous John Ericsson."

"John Ericsson… hmm… that name sounds familiar to me," Danny pondered aloud.

"We probably wouldn't be riding on this fair train right now without the brilliance of Mr. Ericsson," she proudly exclaimed. She explained that Ericsson was very instrumental in developing and designing the steam locomotive in the late 1820s and early 1830s. "Father taught me all about him."

"Yes, of course, John Ericsson," Danny piped. "He was a major contributor with the design of the USS *Monitor*. He helped to save the Union's naval blockading squadron from destruction by the Confederate ironclad during the Civil War. Brilliant man, that Ericsson."

"He was another in a great line of fascinating Swedes," she boasted.

"Well, that great line leads me to this fascinating and very beautiful Swede," Danny assured as he pointed to her and took her by the hand again, causing her face to redden.

After a brief pause, she declared her feelings on the horrors and sharp divisiveness that the war produced. She told him of a friend of her family and associate of her father who had lost a son, a young officer, late in the war at the Battle of Walkerton in Virginia in 1864. "It was a horrendous loss," she lamented. "Such a fine gentleman." She reiterated the fact that a lot of people in her area had experienced grim loss one way or another.

After telling Danny about the familiar slain young officer and his upstanding family back in Chicago, the conversation turned to some of the battles of the Civil War. She conversed authoritatively about the siege of Vicksburg and Sherman's burning of Atlanta, as well as his ensuing march to the sea. Danny was certainly impressed by her astute knowledge and accuracy of the dates of the discussed battles.

"You know General Sherman was an Ohio boy?" Danny crowed proudly.

"Oh, right." Then, after a short pause, she declared, "You and General Sherman—two heroically dashing Ohio boys!" He actually blushed and she chuckled.

He was falling in love. Her beauty and charm, her warmth, the way she carried herself were becoming too irresistible for him. He mentioned Gettysburg, and she kept pace with him in all the details.

"The war was all dreadful," she concluded. "But alas, it was also necessary. I tend to agree with Mr. Lincoln. I agree with the cause he stood up for – emancipation."

Danny, convinced by her staunch conviction, nodded firmly in agreement.

"It is most terrible what they did to him," she said emphatically.

Referring back to the merits of the Civil War, Danny assured her that it was a just and noble cause. To add a small bit of levity to the somber discussion, he added that General Grant was also an Ohio native.

"Yes, Daniel, he was," she fired back without hesitation. "But it wasn't until he moved to Illinois that he rose to prominence." The two of them shared a laugh. She was definitely becoming irresistible.

Danny emphasized the important fact that Ashtabula was very notable for its prominent and beneficent Underground Railroad activity toward the abolitionist cause. "People would hide the runaway slaves in certain designated houses at great risk, and the boat captains in port would convey them across Lake Erie to Canada and freedom."

Eva responded by suggesting that Ashtabula sounded like a wonderful town. "I can't wait to meet Father there this evening. You must join us and show me around your fair city."

Danny readily agreed to do so.

Danny sat quietly for a few moments, fiddling with his suit and cravat. "By the way, Miss Lindfors, what is your educated opinion of Mr. Rutherford B. Hayes?"

"Well, Mr. Dubenion," she answered, playing along, "I think he is a very good man. I think Mr. Hayes will make a very fine president starting in March. Father really respects him."

"Well, I'm a very big fan of the man myself," Danny said unequivocally. "You know, it's the native Ohioan thing."

Eva reacted to Danny's sense of humor with a smile as she shook her head. "You are impossible, Daniel from Ohio. But yes, I do like Mr. Hayes."

Danny sank down comfortably in his chair and drank in a good look at the exquisite Miss Eva Lindfors. For a brief moment, he wondered why such an exquisite woman was yet unmarried. He was definitely happy that she wasn't. He closed his eyes and mourned the fact that it was too bad that this was all just a dream. If Eva were real, however, how his Grandpa Ed would have adored her. How he would have approved of her to be Danny's wife. Only if he were still around. Such a beautiful and smart young lady who had such a grasp on the

Civil War and presidential history. Being as kindhearted and respectful as she was, she would've easily garnered his utmost admiration. But alas, Danny grieved, she is but a thing of the imagery of his yearning and longed-for dreams. His Grandpa Ed was no longer alive. He opened his tiring eyes and looked again upon Eva. He reached over and gently took her by the hand, softly caressing it. She gazed at him and smiled. Together, they soon drifted off to sleep.

After a while, Danny again woke up a little before Eva. He checked his pocket watch. It was about 6:20 a.m. The train was now a little west of Utica. Eva woke up and rubbed her eyes and stretched her arms.

"Eva, I've been selfish having you sit here with me. You must be uncomfortable. Why don't you go back to your drawing room and lie down for a little while? I'll walk you there."

"No, Daniel, I'm quite all right. I enjoy sitting with you and talking. After we stop at Syracuse, I'll go in and lie down a while. It's nice staying out here with you." She slid over and leaned her shoulder into his. Danny melted right with her. "How is your forehead feeling?" she quietly asked as she fought off a yawn.

"It hurts a little," he responded. "I think a nice hot breakfast at the Syracuse station house next stop will do me a lot of good."

Eva smiled and just shook her head.

"What is it?" he wondered out loud.

"Nothing. You just go right back to sleep so you can dream about having a nice hot breakfast at the Syracuse station," she laughed as the perplexed Danny sat there and sighed.

Needing to get up and stretch his legs, Danny politely excused himself and took a short stroll around the parlor car and across the gangway into the smoker car. People were beginning to stir from their sleepers and were starting to mill about. The smoker car was just like Danny remembered from watching old western movies. There were tables for card playing. There was a counter that served as a makeshift bar. Danny made a little friendly small talk with some of the folks who were up and about. There was a couple from Buffalo who had been visiting New York City and expressed their eagerness to get back home. A family from western Indiana near Chicago, with two small children who were rambunctiously scurrying around the car, exchanged pleasantries with him, as well.

After a few minutes, Danny returned to Eva's side.

"Daniel, you must accompany Father and me around Ashtabula tonight and tomorrow morning to the station before we depart for Chicago."

'I don't know," he said hesitantly. "I would probably just be in the way of you two."

"Don't be silly. When I tell him how bravely you tended to my safety and well-being during the whole trip, he will be delighted to meet you. I'm positive he will want to invite you to dinner tonight at the hotel."

“Don’t the two of you have a lot of business to attend to?”

“No,” she insisted. “Father has already attended to everything—the bank, the harbor offices, the paperwork, everything. He just wants to show me everything that he has invested for me. Also, he just wanted to meet me there so he could accompany me back home.”

“I still don’t know. Don’t you want to spend some time alone with your father?”

“I insist, Daniel; I won’t accept any other reply from you.”

After a little further cajoling, he capitulated.

Eva told Danny that she felt badly about her father going out of his way like that to do all this for her. She made the point clear to him that her father was an extremely busy man with much business to tend to and many important people to meet and deal with back home. She reiterated that it was the reason he could only be in Ashtabula for only one full day. He had made all his appointments there for that day, Friday, the twenty-ninth. He would have to leave the next morning to get back to Chicago as soon as possible. “I so urgently want you to meet him; this is the only opportunity,” she exhorted.

“He sure sounds like a very important man,” Danny said respectfully.

“Oh, he is, he is,” she assured him. “You have no idea of how many people he has to meet with and plan things with on a daily basis throughout the year.” On top of some of the very prominent businessmen and bankers, she enlightened him on the fact that he often had to convene with politicians from around the state of Illinois, besides Chicago. "He's attended meetings with Senator John Logan," she boasted, "as well as Senator Oglesby."

When Danny pointed out that those two names sounded familiar to him, she remarked that both senators had been Union generals during the war and were both very honorable men. "He's also had vital conferences with Governor Beveridge last year, and Governor John Palmer a few years before that. "Governor Palmer was also a Union general."

Danny sat enthralled as Eva regaled him of her tales of when she and her sister visited the statehouse in Springfield with their parents at the express invitation of Governor Palmer a few years prior. She boasted about the ornate Greek revival structure and them attending dinner in the governor's reception room. "We toured Representatives Hall, the senate chamber, the law library, and the state library. Mr. Lincoln's desk from decades ago still resides there."

If Eva wasn't proud enough of her well-connected father's political ties, she launched a few names of industrial magnates he had come into contact with since being in business in Chicago. "Mr. Cornelius Vanderbilt, the gentleman in New York who founded this New York Central Railroad we are majestically traversing the countryside on, has met with Father on one occasion," she gushed. She explained to Danny that, seven years earlier, when Vanderbilt was taking over the Lake Shore and Michigan Southern Railway, thus enabling him to run his line from New York to Chicago, her father and other investment brokers met with him and participated in the transaction. "Oh, he did business many years ago with Cyrus McCormick, the developer of the reaping machine, from when I was just a little baby."

Eva's parents, Gustav and Ingar Lindfors, emigrated from Sweden in 1843. Soon after, they came to Chicago as they rode the gathering wave of Swedish immigrants to the city. Annafrida, Eva's elder sister, was born to them in 1845, while Eva, the younger, came along three years later in 1848. As an early investor and manager in the region's embryonic development of the railroads, in 1849 Gustav would be doing business with McCormick, the pioneer of the mechanical reaper, by helping him expand to a wider distribution of his much sought-after machinery to various distant markets outside of Chicago via rail transport.

Throughout the ensuing years, as Gustav's investments in the railroads grew, he formed his own investment brokerage and became quite successful. Now, after time, with no sons of his own to bring along in the investment world, and Annafrida already well taken care of, thanks largely to his help, he was seeking a stake in the next viable region—the fledgling Ashtabula rail transportation industry—for his beloved Eva as a way of setting her up to be financially well off.

Now, as her train was rolling westward past Rome and then skirting the southern shore of the calm and chilly waters of Oneida Lake through the town of Canastota, it was pressing for a stop in Syracuse. There it would again reload coal, wood, and water for the boiler and tender, as well as take on and release passengers. Then it was to proceed onward through Batavia to Buffalo, Erie, and finally, to let her off in Ashtabula by early evening, where she could then behold her glorious and generous financial endowment. She was a benevolent father's dutiful little girl but well-grounded and pragmatic. Yet, as realistic and graphic as this all seemed, it was all just part of Danny's fanciful and imaginative dream.

They were now only a few miles outside of Syracuse. Through the morning light they witnessed the increasing snowfall. Eva and Danny stared out of the window, eager to get out and stretch their legs and have a little breakfast at the depot.

"The snow is really growing heavy," Eva observed.

"Heavy or not, I need to get out in the fresh air, walk around for a minute, and then go to the station for a little food," Danny replied.

As Eva stared outside, she smiled and gave a small chuckle.

"What's so funny?" Danny begged.

"Oh, looking out, thinking of our train … it reminds me of when I was a little girl, maybe six or seven years old. Father bought me a toy locomotive with its tender attached. It was made in Germany out of pressed metal, tinplate. He, of course, loves trains. I would sit on our hardwood floor and push and pull it along. Father would stoop down and help me pull it across the floor. He would make the loud chugging sound with his deep voice, and the loud steam whistle sound, much to Mother's consternation. He would make me laugh. I would try to mimic Father's sound but didn't have the powerful voice that he possessed. It was my favorite toy as a child, partly because I loved the locomotive, but mostly because it came from Father. It meant the world to me. Father bought Annafrida a wood-and-paper train. She kept it on display in our home for many years." Eva held a distant look in her eyes as she smiled fondly.

"I'd wager that you were the absolute most adorable little girl in the whole wide world," Danny proffered.

"You are quite the flatterer, Mr. Daniel Dubenion," she playfully scolded.

"It sounds like your father really adored you."

"When I was little, he used to call me 'little Eva Gustafsdotter.' That means 'the daughter of Gustav.' He would tell everybody that this was my name."

Danny sat and smiled as she told him all about it.

"You see, Daniel, it was as to say, 'Father's little girl.'"

Yes, indeed, Danny thought as he doted fondly on her. *Definitely Daddy's little girl.*

They sat back down together, waiting for their any-minute arrival at the Syracuse depot. Hand in hand, together they watched the charging snowflakes as they assaulted the surrounding area outside.

*

It was now about 8:00 in the morning. The steam whistle once again shrieked its high-pitched advance warning. Soon the train was pulling up to the Syracuse train depot to pick up and let off some passengers and again pick up coal, wood, and water. Eva and Danny were staring out of the window at the ever-increasing snowfall that had started to pick up heavily since the early morning the farther west they had proceeded.

As they stared, a voice bellowed out, "Miss Lindfors, I thought that was you! How is your father doing these days?"

Eva spun around to notice a familiar face. "Why, Mr. McCarthy! How are you, sir?"

The well-dressed man, who was about in his mid-fifties, took Eva's hand and gave it a gentlemanly kiss. Eva introduced him to Danny.

"Daniel, this is Mr. McCarthy from back home in Chicago. He does business with Father. Mr. McCarthy, this is Daniel Dubenion from Ashtabula, Ohio."

The two men shook hands and exchanged pleasantries.

"Your father is a very fine man, Miss Lindfors. I've done very well with my investments with him. How have you been, my dear?"

"I was in New York, spending Christmas with Annafrida and her husband," she replied.

"Are you heading back to Chicago?"

“I’m meeting Father in Ashtabula first. He is setting me up with some railroad company investments there. Daniel, Mr. Dubenion here, is kindly accompanying me there. Then Father and I will continue on home to Chicago.”

“Delightful, my dear, delightful. Believe me, my lovely Miss Lindfors, your father is a true expert in setting one up for good and wise investments.” He turned and asked Danny, ‘And what do you do, young man? What business are you in?”

“Umm, I’m in metals … special metals, in Ashtabula,” he answered awkwardly.

“Delightful! Just delightful!” he replied with a thunderous roar. That is a very lucrative business to be in. Eva, you hold onto this fine young man!”

“I will, Mr. McCarthy, sir,” she replied with a chuckle. “You can bet I will.”

“Are you two young folks getting off for some breakfast at the station house?”

“Yes, we are,” they answered.

“Well, enjoy. I’ll see you two back on board later,” he bellowed as he again eagerly shook Danny’s hand.

While Danny had a pretty fair idea of what general era his dream was taking place in, he wanted to narrow it down closer to the year. He asked Eva if she had ever heard of the telephone. She replied that she had. She told him that the peculiar innovation occurred a few years back but that it had just recently been made available to the public. "Soon, more people, including our home in Chicago, will have one." When she asked him why he had asked her that particular question, the historically astute Danny answered that he wanted to have a little fun with the boisterous and jovial Mr. McCarthy. "By the way," he added, "the word *telephone* comes from the Greek language. It means 'traveling, or distant sound.'"

"I am quite impressed," she returned, flashing a broad smile.

Amid the hustle and bustle of the crowded station house, and above the roaring din of voices and clattering coffee cups and metal plates, Eva and Danny tried their best to ingest the eggs and cold beans while trying to gulp down the stale coffee that the depot had to offer.

"Well, at least the coffee is sort of hot," Danny muttered as he attempted to choke down a sip.

"Well, Daniel, I know it isn't much, but it is your standard railroad station house fare. I've eaten worse before while traveling," Eva informed him as she picked through her cold beans.

"Well," Danny replied with a sigh, "maybe lunch in Buffalo later will be better."

"I wouldn't count on it." She giggled as she shrugged her feminine shoulders. Her dancing, bluish-gray Swedish eyes, not to mention her sparkling, wavy Scandinavian lips, electrifying him as he sat enamored in his chair. "The next good meal any of us will get to have will be in downtown Ashtabula, at the hotel Father is staying at, after we get off this train."

They continued quietly trying to ingest their station house meal. Then Eva asked him, "What was it that you and Mr. McCarthy were discussing as we were exiting past the smoker car?"

"I was just giving him a very pertinent investment tip." Danny told her that he advised Mr. McCarthy that soon next year he would be wise to buy into a new avant-garde company called Bell Telephone Company. When Eva quizzed Danny on the details of this new cutting-edge company, he raised her eyebrows, as well as her curiosity, as he held forth to her on what seemed like a prophetic discourse about the future necessity and importance of this new and unusual invention. This also in turn caused Eva to chuckle a bit in disbelief and accuse him of jesting. "No, I'm very serious about this!" he affirmed.

"Well, what did Mr. McCarthy say about all this generous and prescient information?"

"Well, naturally, he said, 'Delightful! Delightful!'" he answered, as Eva roared with laughter while Danny aptly imitated him, gestures and all.

Again, they quietly attended to their dubious meal. There were a few moments of awkward silence. Finally, Danny inquired, "Earlier, when you first saw me, when I was sitting in the day coach, you came up to me and mentioned that, sitting there, I reminded you of someone … some memory from the past."

Eva hesitated and then looked at Danny. "Yes, Daniel, you did remind me of someone." Eva paused.

Danny quickly sensed that she was reticent to discuss it. If you are not comfortable, we don't have to talk about it," he offered.

"No, it is okay, Daniel. It's only fair. I'm the one who brought it up first when I saw you sitting in the day coach."

"Well, I can only guess that something bad happened between the two of you."

"You are right, Daniel. He and I… I choose not to mention his name… were engaged a number of years ago when I was younger. He was a lot like you in many ways, Daniel. He possessed the many fine qualities as you do. He was kind, very intelligent, a true gentleman. He came from a very upstanding family."

Eva appeared troubled. Danny sat motionless as he listened raptly.

"Our two families knew each other well for many years. His father, like mine, was an astute man of business. In 1863, I was scarcely fifteen years of age. He was twenty-three and a lieutenant during the war. He was serving out west, so fortunately he didn't see too much hostile fighting. Two years later, he returned to Chicago whole and in good health. I was just returning from school in Connecticut. That is when we started courting. We fell in love. I was seventeen." Eva halted and stared blankly out at the station house wall.

Danny could tell that she was very saddened talking about this unpleasant episode in her life. He again offered for her to refrain. She politely declined and painstakingly continued. "After a couple of years, we became engaged. Sometime before the marriage was set, in 1868, he traveled out west to help his brother and sister-in-law manage and help prop up the nearly played-out family mine operations in the Comstock Lode. The two of them had been out there for some time before he arrived to help out in the family's once lucrative claim. He would send me letters and tell me that he loved me and that, upon his imminent return, we would be married."

Danny knew enough about old western history to not only know where she was talking about but the perils that both miners and claim owners faced on a daily basis. "What happened?" he asked her, alarmed. "Did he have some sort of accident?" Danny listened intently, awaiting her response. He gently rubbed her shoulder as she continued to stare off; a pained look had swept her weary eyes.

"An accident would have been less heartbreaking, Daniel," she replied as her misty eyes began to well up. He could see that this was becoming all too upsetting for her to go on about it any longer. He leaned over and held her in his arms and reached his head to gently kiss her shoulder. After a few moments, she managed to show him a strained smile.

Eva stared out of the station house window. Not wanting to cast a dark cloud over their time together, she tried to brighten up and change the subject. "Oh, this most dreadful weather—it's growing worse. As we sit here and speak, it's growing worse."

Danny nodded in agreement, his head again aching somewhat now that he lifted it off her shoulder.

"I can scarcely wait for springtime. Springtime and summer in Chicago are so lovely," she said, daydreaming. Danny sat back and gingerly rubbed his forehead, entranced, allowing Eva to do most of the talking. "Hopefully this spring and summer, Father will take me to the Twenty-Third Street grounds like he did last year to see more National League ball games." When Danny inquired about these National League ball games, she promptly told him about last year's inaugural season of the very first major league of baseball. She explained to him that the new league was founded that previous February in Chicago, by Chicago businessmen William Hulbert. "Mr. Hulbert also owns our local team, the Chicago White Stockings," she declared.

"Do you mean the White Sox?" Danny pressed.

"No, silly, not the White Socks—the White Stockings," she reiterated while finishing her now cold cup of stale coffee. "Father knows Mr. Hulbert. They've done business together. He invited us to three ball games this past season." She went on to let Danny know that the White Stockings were the champions that year, the new league's very first. They finished immediately ahead of the Saint Louis Brown Stockings and the

Hartford Dark Blues. “Annafrida and her husband cheer for their team in the new league, the New York Mutuals. They didn’t do so well, though.”

As the two continued to work on finishing their food, Eva pressed on about baseball. “The White Stockings won all three games Father and I attended with Mr. Hulbert. We beat the Louisville Grays and the Boston Red Caps, and when Annafrida visited in the summer, we beat her New York Mutuals.” She held forth about the local ball club’s rising stars. She spoke glowingly of Ross Barnes, Deacon White, Albert Spalding, a new arrival named Cap Anson, who played very well, and a giant hitter by the name of Cal McVey. “Albert Spalding announced his plans to open a sporting goods retail store in Chicago soon; he is a great ballplayer, and I just hope his new business venture does well, also.”

“Albert Spalding?” Danny asked vociferously. “*Spalding?*” he emphasized. “In the sporting goods business?”

“Yes, Daniel, Spalding.”

“Don’t worry, I think he’ll do quite well,” he assured her with a mischievous grin.

What manner of woman is this? Danny thought with amazement. *One minute she is confiding in me about something very deep and personal, very heartbreaking. The next minute she is talking baseball.* Danny cast an admiring glance at her, not knowing what to say next to this beautiful dream. There was another brief moment of awkward silence as they finished their so-called breakfast.

"How is your head feeling, *min söta*?" she asked him as she tenderly touched his bandage.

"What did you call me?" he chuckled.

"It means 'my sweet' in Swedish. Mother called me and my sister that always when we were children," she answered.

"Well, I guess I'm your little child." He laughed. "It's hurting a little."

"I was hoping we could hurry to the express car and I could show you what I bought for Mother."

Remembering what had happened back in Albany when she had opened the crate, he begged off. "Ah, I'd really like to," he claimed as he gently caressed his forehead. "Maybe I should just go back to my berth and lie down a little bit."

"Come on, *lilla bebis* – that's another name Mother called us when we acted like a little baby," she said as she took him by the hand in haste. "Let's go get the porter to let us into the express car to look in the crate – then you can go lie down." The snow was coming down heavily. The wind was whipping the frigid air all around the boarding area platform outside of the train station.

Danny reluctantly went along with her and the porter to where the crate was being stored. Eva, though a delicate young lady, could also be quite spry as she dashed across the landing in the driving snowstorm, Danny in tow. With the assistance of the porter and the baggage man once again, Eva enthusiastically opened the lid, claiming that Danny was going to love what she had purchased. Within a split second, as the lid was being opened, Danny abruptly woke up from his sleep. He rubbed his eyes and arose back to reality.

What a marvelous dream, he thought. It had been about three months since he had first dreamed of Eva and the train. It had inexplicably picked up and continued right from where the first one had left off. Danny wished to himself that he could have that dream every night. He gazed at his pocket watch. It was about 7:15. He had only been sleeping for about fifteen minutes. He had plenty of time to neaten himself up and drive to Niles for the reception.

*

Danny arrived at the hall just before 8:30. He cordially greeted and shook hands with everybody and made the regular small talk. People were still asking him how he liked living up in Ashtabula. As he had expected, a fair number of the men were dressed up as President William McKinley. A few others appeared as Presidents Garfield and U.S. Grant. Some guy even attended impersonating one of the Wright Brothers from Dayton, replete with leather aviator cap and goggles. Some of the men were just dressed up in elderly clothing without any specific character identity. Danny was the only one who came as Rutherford B. Hayes. He made quite a convincing appearance as the nineteenth US president, displaying all the fine traits of the well-polished, latter-nineteenth-century gentleman.

Danny impressed many at the reception by producing his antique money holder with all the equally antiquated paper dollars and coins. They were also very taken by his grandfather's generations-old pocket watch. The women in attendance were all equal to the task. They fit in quite well, adorned in the raiment of the various periods of Ohio's famous females from the past. Many of them were, of course, arrayed as Ida Saxton McKinley, the president's wife. There were a couple of Annie Oakleys, from Darke County in Ohio, on hand. There was even one young lady who sported a spot-on Lillian Gish look.

Everybody appeared to be having a pleasant evening. Dany took to meandering around the banquet hall. He enjoyed observing everyone while he politely waved and nodded to the friendly greeters as he passed. It felt very strange to Danny. With many of the men sporting top hats and frock coats from a long-gone era, and quite a few women clad in Victorian apparel, he was gripped with an eerie kind of expectancy. Most of the people were dressed like the ones on the train in his dream. He partly felt that at any moment, a shadowy figure from his dreams would inexplicably emerge from among the crowd of attendees and take him by the hand, and together they would walk out, arm in arm, in the gathering moonlight and forever be together. Regrettably, he knew that it was an impossibility, a pure fantasy.

He stuck around for a little while, mixing and rubbing elbows. Then, as stealthily as he could, he slipped out the front entrance and took off for home. Back to his real world, in his old house on East Fifteenth Street, in Ashtabula. Back to his ever-growing lonely existence.

7

March 1985

It was now the middle of March. The persistently harsh Ashtabula winter still had Danny hemmed inside of his place. Again, other than going to and from work and grocery shopping, he pretty much stayed put. One more item of persistence was his obsession with his second dream about Eva on the train. Although it had been almost two weeks since his splendid reverie of her, the vision of her was still indelibly etched in his psyche. While at home during the harsh weather, Danny frittered his time away by watching old movies on his VCR, reading, and occasionally applying a little brass polish in an attempt to decipher the mysterious engraving on the back of the mirror.

When the weather turned fair and the roads were cleared of the deep snow, the cooped-up Danny would venture out to Garfield's or to the newly discovered Swedish Pastry Shop that had been in its west-side location for decades to purchase their doughnuts and legendary coconut bars. One particular day after work, he finally got the chance to resume his routine of hanging out with the guys at the "Six", where he was also becoming well known and liked by the usual clientele. Having a beer with everyone at the bar, Danny again bemoaned the seemingly endless winter. For the umpteenth time, he would hear the ribbing from everybody that it was only halfway over. Richie promised him that sometime in the following month he would take him fishing in the nice cool spring air. Every April, Richie rotated between spring walleye or steelhead fishing in the Ashtabula River and angling for perch off the break wall of Lake Erie in nearby Conneaut. He conveyed to Danny the tremendously relaxing feeling of fishing after the long, brutal winter finally comes to an end every year up there. He told him that he had plenty of gear for the both of them and would supply him with whatever he would need. Danny, although a novice, readily accepted the future invitation.

As March slowly faded to a close, Danny found himself to be a very busy man. Overtime at work continue to pile up. He attended both historical society meetings. He again began to grow weary of both committees as they renewed their respective thrusts to implement the changes that he so vehemently despised. He began to feel jaded with them all. After the usual vain arguments he would have with everyone involved, he pondered the idea of quitting them both. He began to feel as though he was now becoming a seasoned citizen of Ashtabula. After all, he had survived his first winter living there. He thought that maybe he should start getting involved in the local history up there. Besides, with his parents getting ready to relocate to Florida, maybe it was high time to extricate himself from Niles once and for all.

In fact, it was his parents' pending move that would help keep his plate full for the next several weeks. He would make the fifty-mile trip a few times to help them pack and move bookshelves and furniture to the garage for their upcoming property and asset auction. He would also help them throw away a lot of stuff into the huge Dumpster they had rented to help lighten their load for the move. They just kept the necessities with them until they could move them with them to Florida.

He found time during his Niles visits to go and see his grandparents' grave. While there, he once again viewed the "Flanders Fields" veterans' monument. Once again, he read the poem inscribed upon it. As was the case before, it elicited a few tears. He wandered over to where his grandparents' gravesite was located. Like he did on his last visit, he bid a fond and tearful farewell to his Grandpa Ed, his mentor and dear friend. He was gone. His parents were leaving. He had no siblings with whom he could share his sadness and the void he had in his heart. He was growing tired of his stale membership in the thoughtless and contentious historical societies. Even his job was growing mundane and wearisome, with its repetitious and endless product tests and scarce time off. He couldn't seem to find the right girl to be with. His sense of personal loss was accumulating.

On the drive home, he didn't even listen to his old music on his cassette tapes. He didn't even turn the radio on. He just stared out into the open space as he drove down the highway, with its shapeless and empty terrain. Life was passing him by. It was slipping by, being wrested from him. All that he had now was a dream. All he had in that dream was Eva. It was a dream that he painfully wished was recurrent, if not real – one he could dream about every night. Then at least when every empty day had ended and he laid his head down on his pillow to sleep at night, he could be with her every night, all the time.

*

At least he had a good friend in Richie to hang out with. On a nice, cool, fifty-degree early April day, he was taking Danny to Conneaut for a nice perch fishing excursion out on the rock pier that extended about a hundred yards or so into the cold, choppy waters of Lake Erie. After what seemed like an interminable winter up there, the two thought they would make the twelve-mile trip from Ashtabula to relax, have a couple of beers, and pull in a few fish. The lake water was still frigid. With the breeze blowing, it would be very cold; the boys would have to dress warmly, but that mattered little to them. They had the day off. It was finally spring. The winter had been long and treacherous. They had been working a lot of hours back in the lab. It was time for them to relax and enjoy the sport of angling. Danny was more of a novice fisherman. Being from Niles, he hadn't gotten the chance to fish all that often. Richie was more of the crack fisherman. Living by the great lake all his life had given him the opportunity to hone his skills.

After they had gotten all their gear set up and settled into their fishing spot out on the huge boulders of the breakwater, the two of them naturally lapsed into conversation about work—specifically about a few of the women at the workplace. When Richie pressed him about finding the right girl, Danny responded by saying he would like to meet a nice Swedish young lady. Richie offered that blond hair and blue eyes were always his favorite. Danny told him that he would much rather prefer the dark hair and bluish-gray eyes common among the southern Swedish girls. Obviously, he had Eva, the girl both figuratively as well as literally of his dreams, in mind. Richie chimed in that he never knew that Swedish women had dark hair. Danny informed him that southern Swedish women did possess that beautiful quality. He offered Greta Garbo and Ingrid Bergman as the exemplar quality of his type of Swedish girl.

"Wow!" Richie beamed sarcastically. "Garbo and Bergman—you're not asking for too much." He punched his buddy squarely in his arm.

"I'm just saying," Danny retorted with a sneer. "I would just enjoy the company of a beautiful southern Swedish babe."

As the boys continued fishing, Richie more successfully than Danny, the conversation moved to old classic cars. As they were chatting, Danny took a long, circuitous look around the lake and the surrounding area. He took in a deep breath of the cool lakefront air and commented on how much he was enjoyed living up there now that winter was finally over. Soon the talk shifted from cars to some of the famous people who hailed from the area. Then Richie told him of the other fine places he had gone fishing. He told him of how a couple of years prior, he and a friend went down to North Carolina on a fishing trip. He encouraged Danny to come with him for a few days the next time he went down. Danny told him that it sounded like a great idea. He said now that his parents were getting close to moving to Florida, and his grandfather was gone, he would be freer to go on trips like that since he would have nobody up here to look after anymore. Richie offered his regrets about Danny's family members but added that it would be good for him to get away, nonetheless.

As Richie was describing his trip to North Carolina, he was reminded of an old urban legend from down there. He described a place called Mystery Hill. "It's one of those zero-gravity hills where you get to the bottom of the hill and then the car unexplainably begins to roll back up the hill on its own." When Danny expressed his disbelief, citing some optical illusion as a rational explanation, Richie swore up and down that it was true. "I experienced it myself, bro! My car was literally rolling backward up the hill, about fifty or sixty feet. It was really freaky!" Richie added that the legend held that many years ago, a young mother and her toddler were driving down the hill when her car stalled at the bottom. She got out of the car and tried to push it and the toddler out of harm's way when a truck barreled down and killed her. The legend said that from that point, when anybody is at the bottom of that hill, her ghost pushes that person back up the hill, out of harm's way. Again, when Danny expressed his doubts about the legend, Richie told him that once after a man was pushed back up the hill by the ghost, he applied some baby powder to the hood of his car and discovered a set of female handprints on it. He explained that in the small town of Boone, nearby the gravity hill, they had this house as a tourist spot where you fall uphill and lose your balance on an even floor. He said one could set a ball on the ground and it would roll uphill on its own. Danny insisted that if he ever went down there with him, it would be a must-see attraction for him.

Soon the boys exchanged weird stories from their respective towns and the surrounding area. Danny told Richie of a young woman who was murdered a number of years before, not too far from where he lived. He said that the legend had it that if you went out to the old country road, late at night where the killing took place, you could hear an audible gasp coming from the quiet country air. It was said that it was the young lady's last gasp before she died, being heard over and over again. Richie asked him if he had ever heard of the legend of the Green Man of western Pennsylvania. When Danny indicated that he hadn't, Riche explained it to him. "When this guy was a kid, he got electrocuted by a power line or something. His face became disfigured and had a weird greenish hue to it. He lost an eyeball and everything."

"Man, that's crazy!" Danny responded.

"Yeah, his midnight walks around that area, scaring everybody, was definitely the thing of urban legend."

In awe, Danny observed that he had never heard of him before. Danny offered one more urban legend from a town near Niles where he grew up. He said there was a place called Crybaby Bridge. He told Riche that many years ago, a distraught young mother threw her baby off the bridge late one cloudless night. He said that if one goes to the bridge at the same exact time at night, you could hear a baby crying.

The two continued fishing, laughing and joking the whole time. When Danny asked him if Ashtabula had any urban legends or strange stories, Richie stared up and thought for a few moments. Danny's telling of the Crybaby Bridge story sparked his memory. Then he mentioned that he'd once read that the city's Chestnut Grove Cemetery was haunted and that many people had attested to that fact. Danny inquired as to how the graveyard was haunted. Richie said that voices and murmurings were heard by people visiting the cemetery through the years. When Danny asked him for specifics, Richie said that it had something to do with the great Ashtabula Bridge Disaster, and the people who had died in it and were buried there in a mass grave. Danny responded that he had never heard of the disaster. "It happened about a hundred years ago or so," Richie informed him. "The bridge collapsed, and a lot of people died. They are buried in this mass grave up in Chestnut Grove. They say that these restless souls whisper and moan their displeasure."

Danny was in awe. He told Richie that he wanted to go and visit this cemetery.

"There is a big monument for the victims," Richie explained. "One of these weekends when we are off, I'll show it to you." He said to Danny that since he was such a big history buff, he was surprised that he had never heard of it before. Danny assured him that he was positive he hadn't.

The two wrapped up their fishing expedition, with Richie snagging seven perch and Danny getting only two. Danny would end up giving his to Richie, anyway. They packed up their gear and headed the twelve or so miles back to Ashtabula and a quick stop at the East Sixth Street Café. The boys had a beer and a fast game of pool. During their beer, the talk of the haunted cemetery resumed. Danny was intrigued with the horror of the local tragedy as Richie explained it in greater detail. When he couldn't remember exactly what year it had occurred, someone at the bar confirmed to them that it happened in 1876. The man at the bar explained to Danny that a train was crossing the Ashtabula River gorge in the dead of winter when the bridge collapsed, killing about ninety-two people. He also told him about the monument dedicated to the victims at the cemetery. The man also echoed Richie's semi-humorous warning that Chestnut Grove was haunted. Danny, now really fascinated, impressed upon Richie that he wanted to go there and see the monument. Richie promised him that he would take him there and show him in the near future.

The two finished their beers and got up to leave. Danny stepped out to the parking lot and again savored the fresh, crisp, early springtime air. He hesitated as if he wanted to tell Richie something but held back. "Go ahead in your car," Danny insisted. "I'll walk the rest of the way home."

Danny strolled the nine blocks down to East Fifteenth Street. He had many urban legends on his mind. He wanted to visit the cemetery with Richie, but he couldn't get up the gall to tell Richie about the strange antique Victorian mirror he had purchased in the harbor—the bizarre, anomalous, dream-inducing mirror.

With the mysterious mirror on his mind all the next day at work, Danny made it a point to run down to the Harbor Antique Emporium after he got off to quiz the friendly proprietor as to the origin of it. Besides, ever since he had patronized the

Swedish Pastry Shop a little while back, he had been thinking about purchasing the old picture of it with its kitschy blue sign featuring a neon image of a quirky, toque-wearing chef.

The aforementioned workday dragged by slowly for him the next day. Fortunately for him, Danny managed to wiggle out of any unwanted overtime. He bolted out of work precisely at 3:30 and headed straight to the harbor, passing by and forgoing the "Six" in the process. When he arrived at the shop, he found the owner busy with another customer. They greeted each other as Danny strolled by and meandered to the back to seek out the picture and wait for the elderly proprietor to be finished with the lady he was attending to.

Danny reached the back and soon located the sought-after picture. Since had had gone to the pastry shop and had seen the sign up close, along with the fact that he had been working more than an ample amount of overtime, he figured he would spend the extra money and buy it for his wall at home. He was more than certain that he would find the right spot for it among his antiques that adorned his abode.

After a couple of minutes, the old shop owner walked up to him. "Ah, Danny, I see that you still like that picture," he enthusiastically said to him in greeting.

"I think I'm going to get it," Danny affirmed. "Ever since I went there a while back, I had to get this picture with its sign on it."

"Oh, yes, it is a great establishment!" the old man bellowed. "You should go there around the holidays. Their pumpkin and Christmas cookies are famous around town."

Danny attested that if they were as delicious as their doughnuts and coconut bars, he was in for a real treat with their other delicacies.

After a moment of small talk, the shop owner asked Danny how he was enjoyed Victorian mirror he had purchased form him months back.

"I absolutely love it!" he exuberantly roared. "It has added a splendor to the room and to my life that I could never have dreamed of."

The proprietor nodded in agreement, not fully knowing what Danny had meant. "Well, good. It sure is a lovely mirror."

"I'd like to ask you something about the mirror, though," Danny said hesitantly. As soon as he said that, however, the same lady customer interrupted them with a question about some item, thus pulling the owner away from him for a few minutes.

Danny paced back and forth, looking at some old, framed photos that were on the shelf as he attempted to occupy himself while he waited for the man to return. After a bit, the owner came back.

"Have you been to the marine museum yet, Danny?" he queried, forgetting about the prior conversation about the mirror.

"I've been working so many hours; I haven't really had the time."

"You should definitely go when you get the chance. There is a lot of interesting history down in this harbor."

"My friend from work is going to take me to the cemetery to see the bridge disaster monument from about a hundred years or so ago."

"Oh, yes, it was in 1876," the old man said in a somber tone. "It was a dreadful, horrible disaster. My grandfather was a kid, maybe ten or so when it happened. He used to tell me shocking stories about it." He informed Danny a little bit about the disaster. Danny humbly expressed his desire to view the monument and pay his respects to those who were killed and buried in the mass grave where the monument stood.

"Rudyard Kipling even mentioned it in one of his stories," the dour-looking owner informed him. "I believe it was *Captains Courageous*."

Danny and the elderly proprietor talked for a few more minutes. Finally, Danny had to get back home and have something to eat. He paid for the old picture of the Swedish Pastry Shop and then headed to his house. When he got inside, he set the picture down on the table. He noticed the light blinking on his phone message machine. He played it back. It was his dad, announcing the news that he and Danny's mother had just accepted one of the potential buyers' bids on their house, the house he had grown up in. It was now sold. Within a month or so, they would be gone.

*

The second weekend of May had rolled around. The weather was picture perfect. The cloudless sky was cobalt blue. The temperature was an optimal seventy-two degrees, resembling early June instead of an early day in May in northeastern Ohio. It was turning out to be a beautiful enough day to make one almost forget about the dreadful Ashtabula winter that seemed to have just ended. Danny drove over to pick up Richie at his house so he could show him around the cemetery and view the monument together.

Danny told Richie that he wanted to stop at Garfield's to get a bite to eat before heading to Chestnut Grove. On top of getting something to eat, he had promised all the regulars there from all the way back in October that when the weather was warm, he would show them his 1965 Wildcat convertible with the top down. The folks there were definitely very impressed with Danny's topless classic. He and Richie thoroughly enjoyed the company as well as the classic cheeseburger dinner there. They stayed and chatted with the gang for a while and then headed out for the cemetery.

Danny drove south on Main Avenue toward Grove Drive, just north of West Fifty-Eighth Street and Plymouth Ridge Road. On the way there, besides girls and classic cars, they talked about their other favorite subject—music from the 1960s. A friendly argument ensued when Richie asked him whose version of "Twist and Shout" he liked better: the Beatles' or the Isley Brothers'. When Danny explained that he preferred the more soulful Isleys' version over the more raucous Beatles' rendition, Richie shouted that he was crazy. Then he went on to vociferously make his case on behalf of the Fab Four.

As they wound around the side street toward the cemetery, Richie explained more facts to Danny about the bridge disaster and monument. After a few moments, Danny pulled his car into the gravel parking lot of the foreboding graveyard. He turned off his car as they both started at the base of the cemetery from which it rose into a steep incline that ascended toward the main burial grounds. A group of old, uneven stone steps accompanied the hill to lead visitors to the top. Hundreds of aged headstones covered the precipitous hillside. They were all leaning forward as if they were to come tumbling down at any moment. "This is eerie," they both muttered as they got out of the car and started their arduous trek up the steep incline. Danny attempted to hike up the steps a little too fast and got a minor headache from it. He had to pause for a few seconds until it subsided. He shook it off and proceeded upward.

As the two friends arrived at the top, they quickly spotted a blue sign that pointed the way toward the monument. Danny submitted to Richie that the English word for cemetery comes from the Greek word *kemeterion*, which meant "a burial place." Richie sarcastically thanked his buddy for the pertinent information, addressing him as "Captain Obvious." Danny responded by telling him that he was just trying to teach him a little of the ancient culture, and he joked that next time he wouldn't bother him with any more educational facts. The heavy variety of shade trees that were at the top of the hill made it much cooler than the area below. The much cooler air up there made it feel like a late October day, adding to the surrounding eeriness.

The cemetery stretched north atop the ridge and then came to a sudden, sharp drop-off. The acutely sloped hill bore numerous tiny faded grave markers of the young children who were buried there from nearly a century past. On the other side of the ridge was a gradual downhill slope that emptied into a craterlike basin with a multitude of headstones that seemed to be a generation of two younger than the archaic ones at the top of the ridge. As they ambled down the easy slope and scanned around, Danny spied a large family stone that bore the name *Toomes* upon it. "Who's buried in Toomes' tomb?" he shouted sophomorically to Richie.

"Why, I think that Tommy and Tula Toomes are buried in Toomes' tomb," he shot back without hesitation. Danny rather matter-of-factly told him that he would not bother to inform him on the fact that the word *epitaph* came from the Greek words *epi* and *taphos*, which meant "upon the tomb." The two of them roared with laughter.

Danny strolled around a bit, but Richie stood motionless as he started in utter fascination at one particular grave. He called Danny over to where he stood in front of an oddly newfangled marker. He motioned to a square stone with a hollow recess in the center. In the recess, a long, shiny dagger was encased in acrylic. Richie was entranced by it and wondered out loud as to what may have happened to the twenty-seven-year-old man who was buried there, who had died on his own birthday. Danny stared at the stone for a few moments with equal wonderment.

Then he chimed in that the two of them should hurry up and locate the monument, as the place was starting to creep him out. the two of them strode back up the slope to the top of the ridge.

Back at the top, they came upon an aging mausoleum that entombed some of the city's early prominent families, as well as that of Charles Collins. Richie explained to him that Charles Collins was the designer of the poorly drawn up and ill-fated bridge. He told Danny that shortly after the bridge collapsed and all those people tragically perished, Mr. Collins, who was racked with tremendous guilt, took his own life.

"This is one of the sites that I read was haunted," he informed Danny. "People have documented that they've heard moaning sounds emanating from his tomb. Some have seen him weeping over the monument."

"Great." Danny sighed. "Let's just go see the monument and get the hell out of here."

Richie chuckled at his buddy's discomfort and motioned for him to follow.

After a few moments, the two arrived at the tall obelisk structure that kind of resembled the Washington Monument in its design. All around its base were inscriptions. On the front side, it read:

> TO THE MEMORY OF THE UNRECOGNIZED DEAD OF THE ASHTABULA BRIDGE DISASTER, WHOSE REMAINS ARE BURIED HERE.

On the side, it read:

DISASTER OCCURRED DEC. 29, 1876 AT 7:28 P.M.
MONUMENT ERECTED MAY 30, 1985

Richie remarked that the two of them were not standing far from where the tragedy took place, as he pointed northeast toward the river gorge. They stared at the monument silently for a few seconds. It was a moment of chilling reverence. Then they walked around to the back of the monument. At the base of the back side were inscriptions of the names of the known people to be among the unidentified victims of the tragedy. Mystified, they both stared and silently began to read the thirty names that were inscribed thereon.

A few moments passed. Richie stepped away to observe the gorge. Danny continued reading the names. It was then that he gasped and took a step backward in recoiled horror. He could not believe what his eyes were showing him. Perhaps his mind was playing tricks on him in such a morbid atmosphere. He stepped back up and reread the name. "Eva Lindfors!" he shrieked in stunned disbelief. He fastened his eyes upon the name to make sure he was not just imagining the whole thing and blurted it out again. The alarmed Richie double-timed it back to the side of the monument, only to discover that Danny's startled face had turned paler than the hydrochloric acid that they always used in the lab at work.

Richie asked him what the problem was. "You told me this place was haunted?" a trembling Danny frightfully asked his pal. "I think I just saw a ghost!"

When Richie asked him what he was talking about, Danny, with gaping eyes, pointed at Eva's name on the monument. "So what? That woman's name was Eva Lindfors. What's the big deal?"

"That's the name of the beautiful girl I told you that I've been dreaming about!" he shrieked.

"Well, so what?" Richie tried to rationalize. "You've probably seen her name before and dreamed about it."

"I've never been up here before," Danny nervously claimed.

Richie reasoned that since Danny was such a history buff, he'd probably read about the disaster and may have seen her name mentioned. Danny protested to Richie that he had never read about the disaster and had never heard of it before until he had mentioned it while the two of them were fishing a couple of weeks back. Richie insisted that the name had to be in his subconscious memory from hearing it before somewhere. He was trying to convince Danny that the whole thing must have some rational explanation. Danny vehemently denied ever hearing her name before, insisting that it was altogether possible that the Eva Lindfors on the monument was the Eva Lindfors he had dreamed about.

The two of them walked along the ridge to head back to Danny's car. Richie was convinced that his friend was blowing his dreams way out of proportion. The two reached the old uneven stone steps that led back down to the parking lot. Richie slowly and carefully descended the archaic stairway, while Danny stood frozen at the top, staring up into the still, cloudless sky. Richie implored him to snap out of it and forget the dream, as he was driving himself crazy from it. Danny didn't move a muscle. He just stood there and continued to stare off into the sky. He pivoted around to face the direction of the monument. Eva's inscription on the monument was etched in his brain. Danny reeled back and unwittingly nearly tumbled down the old stone steps. Once again, Richie insisted that it was all in his imagination. He insisted to Danny that he wake up and for the two of them to get going.

"Listen, Danny!" Richie hollered up to him. "If you want to know all about the Ashtabula Bridge Disaster, you can go to the library downtown and look it up in the local history section. I'll go with you sometime. But there has to be some sane reason why you had a simple dream with that lady's name."

Danny briefly shook it off and ambled carefully down the stone walkway. Richie promised him that it if would clear his mind of the whole matter, he would go with him to the library the following Monday after work. They got in the car and headed back home.

"But why Eva Lindfors?" Danny questioned. "That is not a common name, to say the least. This is more than just a mere coincidence."

Richie sat there silently for a moment, trying to calm his buddy down. "Look, man," he insisted, "maybe you were watching some old *Green Acres* episode and had Eva Gabor on your mind that night. Maybe you had eaten some anchovies that evening. You know, Eva and anchovies will give you some pretty crazy dreams."

Danny gave a halfhearted chuckle at Richie's kind attempt to make light of the frightful matter.

"Come on, Wildcat," Richie cajoled. "Lighten up, man. It's just a crazy dream."

Needless to say, Danny got very little sleep that night. If he wasn't lying still, staring at the ceiling into the darkened night, he was nervously churning in trepidation on his bed. He asked himself how he could have dreamed about somebody that he had never heard of or seen before, about an event he had never read of or heard about before. How could that person be on a monument dedicated to the known among the unidentified dead of the Ashtabula Bridge Disaster of 1876? He continued staring, wide eyed, into the blackness of his darkened bedroom for moments on end. Then suddenly, it hit him like a bolt of lightning. "It was December 29th!" he bellowed out loud to himself. "That's why she'd said that Christmas had already passed, and she was heading back home to Chicago." December 29, 1876. That was why she'd mentioned the new National League and all those strange baseball teams. She'd said it was the league's "inaugural season." The National League was founded in 1876. Danny's mind was racing uncontrollably. He reasoned that was why in the dream she referred to Rutherford B. Hayes as "a good man" in the present tense, saying, "I think Mr. Hayes will make a very fine president starting in March." Hayes was elected in November of 1876. All those people on the train. They were all dressed in clothes from that time period.

It wasn't a costume party. It was really 1876. All those other things she spoke about. They didn't make any sense, unless it was 1876. But why? Why was he dreaming of that train, on that day? Why was he dreaming about being on a train on December 29, 1876, with a woman who died in the disaster whom he had never before heard of? Why in such lurid detail? Danny could scarcely wait until Monday after work so he could research all of it at the library.

8

May 1985

Danny eased down West Forty-Fourth Street and slowed his Buick to a halt. He waited for the oncoming traffic to clear and then rolled it into a gentle left-hand turn into the parking lot of the Ashtabula Public Library.

"I can't believe that I'm doing this!" Richie sighed in frustration as he slumped back in the passenger seat. "I'm spending my Saturday—a *gorgeous* Saturday—not fishing… but going to the library."

"Hey, didn't I tell you how much I deeply appreciate you coming with me?" Danny reiterated.

"For what?" Richie begged for a legitimate answer, trying to make sense of it all. "Because you had a silly dream of some girl on a train?"

"*Two* dreams," Danny pointed out. "Two vivid, recurrent dreams. Just please help me look this up."

"What am I, your mommy? I gotta go with you to the library?" Richie joked.

Danny placated his buddy by promising him he would treat him to lunch at Garfield's when they were through, and he assured him that afterward he would have plenty of time to cast his line into the Ashtabula River and pull out all the fish his heart desired.

It had been an entire week since the two of them had gone up to Chestnut Grove Cemetery and he had seen Eva Lindfors' name on the base of the monument as one of the known to be among the unidentified dead of the bridge disaster. The world's ultimate understatement would be to suggest that he had merely a long, harrowing seven days as he was anxiously waiting to look up the facts about the Ashtabula Bridge Disaster of 1876. He parked his car and turned off the ignition and turned to Richie. "Just help me find all the facts. It's very important to me."

Richie let out an exaggerated sigh, and then he resigned himself to the task of helping his buddy out.

Seeing the name *Eva Lindfors* etched into the base of that monument of the known to be among the unidentified dead was etched firmly into Danny's psyche. All week it had shaken and stunned him. It had deeply disturbed him. He absolutely, without further delay, had to research and get to understand everything he possibly could about the disaster.

The two friends ambled into the front entrance and made it over to the information desk. They asked where the local history section was and if there were any articles on the disaster. The affable young lady at the information desk willingly led them to the local history section and showed the two the many articles written on the subject. She gracefully pointed to and swept her hand across the front of the sizable bookshelf that was amply stocked with the sought-after information as smoothly and eloquently as a game show hostess demonstrating the grand prize that was to be won in front of two fanatically eager contestants. They enthusiastically thanked her as Danny immediately plunged himself into the vast collection of writings on the matter.

They sifted through the vast material, searching for anything they could find. They came upon a blue, three-ringed notebook full of laminated newspaper articles from the time of the disaster. Some articles were from the local papers, while others were from all parts of the country. A locally written periodical from 1976, memorializing the one-hundredth anniversary of the tragedy, first caught their attention. It briefly summarized the accounts of that ill-fated evening. It went on to say that the early winter of 1876 had already produced three heavy snowfalls before the one that pounded the city all day on December 29. The heavy amounts of snow and ice were onerously weighing on the poorly designed bridge that spanned the precipitous Ashtabula River Gorge that led to the train station on the western part of town with tremendous stress. The article continued by stating that earlier, on the night of the twenty-eighth, the number 5 Pacific Express train had departed New York City on the New York Central Railway, heading for Chicago and points west. It was to stop in Ashtabula, among other stops along the way, where some passengers were to get off the train. By nightfall, as the train neared the bridge, it began to slow down, as the depot was just a short distance away. However, the article went on to explain, the wheels stopped, and a loud *snap* was heard. As the train began to sag with the buckling bridge, the alert engineers hit the throttles. The lead engine, Socrates, raced to the abutment and made it over the bridge. They second engine, Columbia, hit the abutment and briefly clung to the lead engine. The sinking cars behind it began pulling the engine, and the coupling broke, sending it and the eleven luxury cars behind it plunging into the deep, dark, icy gorge. Many were crushed to death, while many others perished in the ensuing conflagration started from all the tumbled heating stoves and kerosene-fed lamps that were on board. The brief article concluded by rightly opining that it was a catastrophe of the largest magnitude—the worst train bridge disaster in American history.

Danny's heart sank to his feet as he turned to look at Richie, whose face bore a stunned look. He informed Danny that though he had heard a little about the disaster years before, he had no idea how horrific it actually was. What had sickened Danny the most was not only was this a horrifying tragedy in and of itself, but there was actually a female named Eva Lindfors on board who had perished, as well. The distinct smell of kerosene in his dreams from the heating stoves and lamps jumped into his mind as well. It was all too real. He began to wonder how badly she had suffered before her tragic death. He wondered how realistic his dream may have been. He told Richie that it was very uncanny that in his dreams of Eva and the train, that it had departed from New York City the night before, and also, she'd mentioned that she was going to get off the train in Ashtabula to meet her father, who was going to make some investments for her in the local shipping and railroad business, and then accompany her back home to Chicago. He also explained how in the dream, the closer they traveled west toward Lake Erie, the heavier the snow picked up, just like in the article they just read.

Richie was at first taken aback by Danny's bizarre claim of the eerie reality of his seemingly prescient dreams, but after a few moments of rationalizing, he concluded that it was merely his subconscious playing out in his night visions. "Look, Wildcat," he stated very firmly, "you obviously were dreaming of the heavy snowfall because of the terrible winter up here that you had been agonizing about the whole time. The old train… you love old trains. You told me how much you love to go down to the harbor and see the big rail yard. Plus, you are always griping about not being able to find a nice girl. Obviously, you are going to dream about all those things. It's just your mind playing tricks on you while you sleep."

"Okay, wise guy," Danny fired back, "what about all those other accurate details? I have never heard of anybody named Eva Lindfors before. I've never heard of the disaster before. How would I know that it departed New York on the night of December 28 that year? How could my subconscious play back something that I have never seen or heard of before? Besides, this dream was tangible; I could feel Eva's touch."

"*Eva's?* You're on a first-name basis with this dream girl? Come one, buddy, a lot of dreams are like that. You are really scaring me."

The two of them resumed leafing through the notebook, digging for more articles. After a few moments, Danny came upon an article from the *Chicago Tribune*, dated December 30, 1876, the day after the disaster.

Danny proceeded to read the article. As he read, he recoiled at the ghastly details that the newspaper had reported. After he was finished, Richie asked him why he looked so disturbed. He slowly and deliberately quoted the article to Richie: "'The proportions of the Ashtabula horror are now approximately known,'" the story began. "'Daylight, which gave an opportunity to find and enumerate the saved, reveals the fact that two out of every three passengers on the fated train are lost. Of the 160 passengers who the maimed conductor reports as having been on board, only 59 can be found or accounted for. The remaining 100, burned to ashes or shapeless lumps of charred flesh, lie under the ruins of the bridge and train.'"

Richie gasped as Danny read the grotesque facts of the terrible incident. Danny's mind could only wonder and hope if the Eva Lindfors who perished in the catastrophe had at least died instantly and somewhat more mercifully rather than burning to death during the unthinkable conflagration.

Danny continued reading from the *Tribune*'s account: "'The disaster was dramatically complete. No element of horror was wanting. First, the crash of the bridge, the agonizing moments of suspense, and the seven laden cars plunged down their fearful leap to the icy riverbed; then the fire, which came to devour all that had been left alive by the crash; then the water, which gurgled up from under the broken ice and offered another form of death, and finally, the biting blast filled with snow, which froze and benumbed those who had escaped water and fire. It was an ideal tragedy.'"

Richie offered a suggestion that the people who were named on the monument as the known to be among the unidentified dead were probably those for whom the article had just mentioned as those who had either frozen to death or drowned in the icy-cold river. "That's probably the only way they were still maybe semi-recognizable," he said as Danny attempted to register and sort out the insanity of it all.

"Either way," Danny lamented, "they all suffered immensely." He couldn't even attempt to fathom the breadth and scope of it all, let alone how awfully Eva Lindfors, whether or not it was the same young woman in his dreams, had suffered a nightmarish and painful death.

As much as he was sickened by the account, Danny couldn't help but continue reading. "'The scene of the accident was the valley of the creek which, flowing down past the eastern margin of Ashtabula Village, passes under the railway three or four hundred yards east of the station. Here, for many years after the Lake Shore road was built, there was a long wooden trestlework, but as the road was improved, this was superseded about ten years ago with an iron Howe truss, built at the Cleveland shops, and resting at either end upon high stone piers, flanked by heavy earthen embankments. The iron structure was a single span of 159 feet, crossed by a double stack seventy feet above the water which at the point is now from three to six feet deep, and covered with eight inches of ice. The descent into the valley on either side is precipitous, and, as the hills and slopes are piled with heavy drifts of snow, there was no little difficulty in reaching the wreck after the disaster became known.'"

To break the morbid tension of the moment, Richie half-jokingly suggested that nothing had changed about Ashtabula's horrible winters all those many years later. Danny, whose only concern at the moment was the degree and severity of Eva's horrid death, really didn't hear Richie's ridiculous but well-intentioned comment.

It had become obvious to Danny that Richie was getting bothered by the gruesome details of the newspaper's account, so he read silently while his fidgety friend strolled around the rest of the library. The article continued:

> The disaster occurred shortly before eight o'clock. It was the wildest winter night of the year. Three hours behind its time, the Pacific Express, which had left New York the night before, struggled along through the drifts and the blinding storm. The eleven cars were a heavy burden to the two engines, and when the leading locomotive broke through the drifts beyond the ravine and rolled across the bridge, the train was moving at less than ten miles an hour.

Danny paused in his reading of the article to momentarily dwell on the uncanny fact that in his dream Eva had said that the train had left New York City on the previous night, the night of the twenty-eighth. He continued to be awestruck with the striking realism and accuracy of his remarkable dreams on the matter. He looked back down on the article and onerously continued to read.

> The headlamp threw but a short and dim flash of light in the front, so thick was the air with the driving snow. The train crept across the bridge; the leading engine had reached solid ground beyond, and its driver had just given it steam, when something in the undergirding of the bridge snapped.

Danny's heart raced, and he began to break into a cold sweat as he thought of all those poor souls on that train. Those poor souls who were crushed and charred and buried in a heap of a mass grave up in Chestnut Grove. Whether the Eva Lindfors, whose name was emblazoned on the monument as one of the known victims, was the same woman he had dreamed about or not, the mere thought of the horrific suffering she had endured made him cringe.

As Richie continued to pace the aisles, patiently waiting for Danny to be finished with his research, Danny resumed reading from the article.

> For an instant, there was a confused crackling of beams and girders, ending with a tremendous crash as the whole train but the leading engine

broke through the framework and fell in a heap
of crushed and splintered ruins at the bottom.

Danny looked up from his reading and could tell that Richie was growing uncomfortable, as well as a little bored with the whole thing. Although he hadn't finished reading the article, Danny walked over to the copying machine to get a replication of the story. He paid the girl at the information desk the ten-cents-per-page fee and then motioned to Richie for the two of them to move on to Garfield's for his promised lunch treat. The two of them somberly motored the couple of blocks to the eatery. While there, Danny reiterated to his pal that his dreams were awfully evocative to be just a mere coincidence. Richie tried to calm him down by echoing his former logical explanation of it all. "Come on, buddy," he reasoned. "Even the part where Eva's father was going to meet her in Ashtabula—that was just your brain telling you that when you do meet that nice girl you've always been looking for, you're going to be nervous about meeting her father. It's no big deal."

"Oh, what now?" Danny fired back. "Who are you? Sigmund Freud? The great analyzer of dreams?"

"I tell you what," Richie blurted, starting to get bored with the subject, "I wish Freud was alive and right here with us at Garfield's. He'd tell you to stop driving yourself nuts over this. Not only that, but he'd probably ask you some sexual question, like 'Did your train go through any tunnels?'" Richie roared with laughter. Puzzled, Danny asked him how he could make jokes about this dire matter.

To get Danny's mind off the subject, Richie suggested that he drive him home to pick up his fishing gear so the two could catch some steelhead in the Ashtabula River. Danny passed on his buddy's offer, stating that he didn't feel right about fishing right near where the train wreck occurred. It definitely wouldn't get his mind off it.

When Richie pressed him on the offer, Danny begged out of it. "Besides that, I have to go to the West Avenue Laundromat to wash my clothes."

"Oh, that sounds really fun," Richie mocked. "While I'm hauling in some tasty steelhead, you'll be fluffing and folding."

Danny ignored his friend's giggling retort and drove him home when they were through having lunch. Danny went home to pick up his clothes that needed to be washed to bring to the Laundromat. He also brought along the copies he had made of the article from the *Chicago Tribune* from the day after the horrible tragedy. While waiting for his clothes to wash and dry, he couldn't put the article down. He read and reread it. He was now totally obsessed with the gruesome and disturbing details of the whole matter. He was fully in the grips of imagining all those people who were traveling home from the holidays, from visiting relatives, or relaxing from a business trip, not knowing the horrific fate that literally lay ahead of them on the Ashtabula Bridge. All those innocent, unsuspecting folks of all walks of life unknowingly destined for such a horror. The unimaginable, engulfing flames. Mostly, of course, one passenger in particular—the one who he had mysteriously dreamed about. This eerie obsession was not about to leave him alone anytime soon.

So, while at the Laundromat, as his clothes washed and rinsed and tumbled dry, he sat and continued to read from where he had left off from the copy he had made from the *Chicago Tribune.*

> Notwithstanding the wind and storm, the crash was heard by people within-doors half a mile away. For a moment, there was silence. A stunned sensation among the survivors, who in all stages of mutilation lay piled among the dying and dead.

Danny drew back as he tried to absorb the graphic and brutal recounting of the horror. He morbidly marveled at the author of the article's thorough description. He realized that back in 1876, there was not radio and television to portray an audible or visual picture, so a writer had to give a complete and total description, no matter how dreadful, in order to fully and successfully embed the scene in the readers' hearts and minds. In a dark and disturbing way, the scene was not lost on himself.

Then arose the cries of the maimed and suffering.

> the few who remained unhurt hastened to escape from the shattered cars. They crawled out of windows…

Danny closed his weary eyes to picture the scenic and snowy countryside that he and Eva had gazed at through the window from their chairs in the parlor car and day coach in his dream as the two of them romantically held each other's hand while she trustingly and tenderly leaned on his shoulder. Now, shocked, he was reading of the terrified and panicked passengers that were screaming and currying to escape a horrid end through those same broken, flame-swept windows.

> …into deep and freezing water waist deep. Men, women, and children, with limbs bruised and broken. Pinched between timbers and transfixed by jagged splinters, begged with their last breath for aid that no human power could give.

Increasingly bothered by the piercingly unpleasant article, Danny stood up and sauntered to the dryer to see if his clothes were finished. He made a mental note to finish the article later that evening at home. It was just too much to digest all at once. He folded his clothes and set them in his laundry basket, tossed the article on top of the pile, and headed for home.

Once home, Danny put his clothes away and cleaned up around the house. Afterward, he decided to take a stress-relieving stroll around his old Swedetown neighborhood.

Walking was always a good way to clear his head. Still, as he walked around the back streets and along Fields Brook, his mind was anything but clear. His obsession with the bridge disaster, as well as with the monument, was growing epically. After his nearly half-hour stroll, he went back in the house. He got himself a nice, cold drink, grabbed the copy of the *Tribune* article, and ventured into the den. He was still perplexed as to why he had never before heard anything of this disaster of such magnitude until recently when Richie mentioned it to him while they were fishing. He turned on his reading lamp and settled down in his desk chair and began to finish reading the article.

> Five minutes after the train fell, the fire broke out
> in the cars piled against the abutments at either end.
> A moment later, flames broke from the smoking car
> and first coach piled across each other near the middle
> of the stream. In less than ten minutes after the catastrophe,
> every car in the wreck was on fire, and the flames fed
> by the dry varnished work and fanned by the icy gale,
> licked up the ruins as though they had been tinder.

Danny cringed as he read the part about every car being in flames. Hesitantly, he continued reading.

> Destruction was so swift that mercy was baffled.
> Men who, in the bewilderment of the shock, sprang
> out and reached to solid ice, went back after wives
> and children and found them suffocating and
> roasting in the flames.

It was almost unbearable for him to continue on. He got up to get himself another cold glass of water and to take a deep breath. He could only imagine the immensely excruciating pain and suffering that had taken place aboard the wreckage at that moment. Still, undoubtedly because of his dreams about being on an old passenger train and all the uncanny similarities between them and the reality of the disaster—and most definitely because of having dreamed of a young woman whose name was on the monument—he kept on reading.

> The neighboring residents, startled by the crash, were lighted to the scene by the conflagration, which made even prompt assistance too late. By midnight, the cremation was complete. The storm had subsided, but the wind still blew fiercely, and the cold was more intense. When morning came, all that remained of the Pacific Express was a row of car wheels, axles, brake irons, truck frames, and twisted rails lying in a black pool at the bottom of the gorge. The wood had completely burned away, and the ruins were covered with white ashes. Here and there a mass of charred, smoldering substance sent up a little cloud of sickening vapor, which told that it was human flesh slowly yielding to the corrosion of the fires.

As Danny pored over the remainder of the writing, he was relieved to see a brief abatement of the sickening account with a scanning of at least some good news from it.

> On the crest of the western abutment, half buried in the snow, stood the rescued locomotive, all that remained of the fated train. As the bridge fell, its driver had given it a quick head of steam, which tore the draw head from its tender, and the liberated engine shot forward and buried itself in the snow.

Just as quickly as any alleviation of the horror came, however, it was quickly revived by the stark, caustic terror that ensued.

> The other locomotive, drawn backward by the falling train, tumbled over the pier and fell bottom upward on the express car next behind. The engineer, Folsom, escaped with a broken leg; how, he cannot tell, nor can anyone else imagine.

The article went on to inform the reader that, as of the morning of the thirtieth, there was no list of the dead to report. The gruesome reality of it was there could be none until a list of the missing who traveled on board could be made up. It added that there were no remains that could ever be identified. Danny's only miniscule hope that he could even scarcely cling to was that the Eva Lindfors died a quick and painless death and was preserved in a dignity wherein she was able to be somewhat recognizable. Danny had a visible tear in his eye as he read the writer's summation of the entirely unimaginable, brutal ordeal.

> Old or young, male or female, black or white, no man can tell. They are all alike in the crucible of death.

Not surprisingly, Danny, whose head was overflowing with the image portrayed in the newspaper article, had much trouble sleeping that night. The next Monday at work, all through the day, he couldn't keep quiet about it to Richie or anyone else in earshot. After work, the two of them, along with a couple of other guys from the test lab, went down to the "Six" for a few relaxing beers and games of pool. Again, the entire time, the obsessed Danny could not quit talking about the disaster. A few nights later, even if it was not the kind of dream he had hoped for, Danny dreamed a bizarre revision of his visit to Chestnut Grove Cemetery.

It was dusk. Danny was standing all alone in the gravel parking lot. His car was not there. He pivoted and gazed toward the other side of the lot and caught a glimpse of an elderly gentleman dressed as a chauffeur tipping his cap to him. The man changed into the aged proprietor from the Harbor Antique Emporium. He smiled a gentle, toothy grin at Danny and then abruptly got into his limousine and sped off out of the cemetery, leaving him by himself in the desolate parking lot. As the limousine was nearing the exit gate, it turned into an old horse-drawn funeral carriage. The horse's prancing hooves and the wooden carriage wheels echoed through the evening air as it was being driven furiously up the street. Danny turned back around and beheld the archaic, narrow stone stairway that would escort him to the top of the ridge and into the burial grounds. Danny approached the stairs and began to slowly and deliberately ascend the clumsy steps. When he had made it almost halfway up, the ascension mysteriously morphed into an escalator. The outmoded escalator resembled the one from the old department store in downtown Youngstown that his mother used to take him to during the Christmas season when he was a kid during the late 1950s. Danny easily rode it the rest of the way to the top.

As he arrived at the crest of the ridge, it was suddenly pitch dark, as black as midnight. The grounds were somewhat familiar to him from when Richie had taken him up there. Toomes's tomb came into view. However, instead of a headstone, the family name of *Toomes* was displayed upon a large billboard with neon motion lights to illuminate it. Danny carefully roamed the area, edging toward the monument. Along the way, he chanced upon the mausoleum of Charles Collins, the designer of the doomed bridge. The archaic stone structure was surrounded by a grouping of haunted-looking oak trees. They were all knotted and twisted. As he sidled cautiously past it, he heard a doleful and bitter sobbing emanating from inside the ancient tomb.

Next, as if the vision wasn't quite macabre enough, out from the ancient, moss-covered structure and the grotesque copse of trees appeared 1950s television and B horror movie actress Maila Nurmi. She was bedecked in a tattered and torn cobwebbed Vampira costume that fit the ghastly television persona as the horror movie hostess from back in the day. The eerily provocative Miss Nurmi stiffly and straightly trudged up zombielike toward Danny. He remembered Richie telling him way back when he first went to the "Six" with him when he was still new in town that Maila Nurmi, who was born in Finland, had moved with her family to Ashtabula when she was two years old. After growing up there, some years later, she relocated near Hollywood, California, and eventually became an actress.

She approached and then halted a few yards from where Danny was nervously standing, facing him. She at first stayed silent, but the sobbing from the mausoleum persistently echoed from inside of it. She peered at him with her lips pursed and acutely angled. They were shrouded with a thick coating of jet-black lipstick. Then she muttered in her broken English, "Mr. Collins says he is sorry for hurting Eva. He says he should have known that the bridge was unfit for any train to travel over." She stood there motionless, her long, scraggly, tousled dark hair shimmering in the cool, flowing breeze. Her Scandinavian features, as well as Finland's proximity to Sweden, was obviously not lost on his subconscious dream machine.

Maila stood perfectly still and erect. Her face bore no emotion but an icy, soulless glare. She painfully and methodically raised her right arm, thrusting it outward. She extended her oversized, gnarled, arthritic fingers, pointing toward the distant monument. "Go forth and tell Eva Lindfors that Mr. Collins says that he is sorry. He should have built a better bridge. Go!" Danny's nightmarish illusion continued with him wheeling around and slogging toward the far-off, shadowy bridge disaster monument that bore the engraved name of Eva Lindfors.

As he inched ahead to the monument, it seemed to appear farther and farther away. In the background, Maila's voice grew faint and distant as she repeated her directive. "Tell Eva Mr. Collins is sorry." Her voice faded out. A thick, dense fog enveloped him.

The obelisk monument seemed to disappear in the misty distance. Danny felt as though he was moving backward. He was back on the escalator, descending to the bottom and the empty gravel parking lot. His back was to the lot as he traveled down, facing Charles Collins's ancient mausoleum. That's when he woke up, panting, and in a cold, drenching sweat. He realized it was all just a terrible dream.

"Where is Sigmund Freud when I need him?" he mumbled to himself. He got up and took a shower. He tried to shake the harrowing feeling brought on by his grim nightmare. He had some breakfast and coffee and then headed off to work. It was another workday filled with him keeping to himself as much as possible.

By May 27, Danny had taken a few vacation days off from work. He was going to Niles that day to spend one last night in the house he had grown up in before taking his parents to the airport for their one-way flight to Florida on the twenty-eighth. For the sentimental thirty-four-year-old, spending his last evening and night in the house he had grown up and lived in for the first twenty-two years of his life was, to say the least, bittersweet. After he had graduated from high school, he lived at home with his parents while he attended college locally. After getting his chemistry degree, it wasn't long before he was able to secure his lab technician position at the local titanium plant. For being single, the starting salary he was offered enabled him to afford to rent his own apartment nearby and live on his own. Even then, living just two miles away from his folks, he was always there for them and always felt that their house was always his home.

Now, as he wandered around his old neighborhood, taking a long, pensive stroll through the old side streets that he played street baseball on with all his friends as a youth, he mused about all the fun and frolic that he had once enjoyed on those byways. The miles and miles of endless bicycle rides on those brick-lined roads, the football games he ran so fast in, the many trips to the ice cream shop and five-and-dime store… those were the sweet ingredients he was taking in as he trekked past his old friends' houses reminiscing about his bucolic childhood. The bitter chaser, however, bubbled up to the top as he realized that with his parents about to be gone his grandparents deceased, his job fifty miles away, he questioned if he would ever really come back to Niles anymore at all after tomorrow, especially since he had just recently resigned his commitment and membership to both historical societies that he belonged to in town. He continued walking a few more minutes until he reached the former house of his onetime junior high school sweetheart, Michelle. He produced a quick, fond smile as he wondered what had ever become of her. He had heard years before that she had moved to Virginia and studied at Old Dominion University in pursuit of a criminal justice degree.

Danny did an about-face after pondering Michelle's old house and current whereabouts and began his trek back home. He spent the rest of the evening with his mom and dad, taking them out to dinner and one last night on the town before they left it for good. When they returned to the house, they chatted until late, recalling all the fond memories throughout the decades spent in it. Danny slept his last night there, using one of the sofas that his parents were leaving behind for the new owners.

In the morning, after breakfast, which Danny had picked up from a fast-food pickup window, he drove them to the airport, which was about ten miles away. Amid the heartfelt and misty-eyed farewells, the mutual promises and consolations of getting to see one another twice a year were brought to the fore. Before heading back to Ashtabula, Danny made it a point to visit his Grandpa Ed's grave. He didn't know when he would get a chance to visit it again. Afterward, he gassed up the old Wildcat and headed for home. His separation from Niles, his boyhood home, was nearly complete.

*

In the most rapid and devastating stroke of both symbolism and stone-hard, brutal reality, Danny's separation from the town he had spent thirty-four years in was made total and complete when a massive tornado angrily swept mercilessly and indiscriminately like a bulldozer through Niles, Ohio, just three days later on May 31, 1985, at a little after 7:00 p.m.

The herculean twister was devastating. Entire neighborhoods were wiped out. Some houses were shredded in half, their interior walls stripped bare and made to resemble broken dollhouses. Innumerable tons of debris and shattered glass were scattered citywide. Branches and trees were strewn and splayed across streets and yards. Incredibly, Danny's parents' former house was untouched, along with most of the houses on that block. Many of Danny's childhood and teenage haunts were removed from off the face of the earth in a matter of seconds. The roller-skating rink he used to frequent while in junior high school was eradicated. The old movie theater, places he used to go and eat and hang out with friends, were completely gone. The old bowling alley and many other businesses were left in ruins. Even the cemetery was mowed down. Fortunately, although the ground had been denuded of virtually all its trees, his grandparents' grave, as well as the entire veterans' section, apart from a few tilted headstones, was left unscathed. It was swift, staggering, and wide in scope. In one bold stroke, it would forever alter the city of Niles, Ohio.

Danny was shocked and deeply disturbed by the news of the destruction from the deadly tornado. The entire region had been under severe weather and tornado warnings the entire day of the thirty-first. Ashtabula County itself also had a tornado touch down around the same time that evening. It actually ran about thirty miles parallel to the one in Niles. However, the one in Ashtabula County swept mainly across fields and sparse country, and the damage was minimal, unlike Niles. It took Danny a long time to finally hear from former coworkers there that his old house and neighborhood had been mostly spared from the furious storm.

A week later, still reeling from the jolt of his old hometown's devastation, Danny returned to work. It was a mentally strenuous week for him, as the onerous weight of both the tornado and his strange nightmare from the other week continued to bear down on him. His job was becoming more and more repetitive, as well. He was starting to get bored with doing the same type of testing over and over again. Richie sensed that he needed a good cheering up, so he asked Danny to join Wild Bill, Lucky, and himself at the "Six" for a few beers after work. Danny agreed to go but really couldn't enjoy himself. Mostly he stayed quiet. He was really starting to feel the lonesomeness in his life. He wished he had that perfect girl of his dreams with him at all times. If he could only find her. He excused himself from his friends after just a short while. He went home, washed up, and went for a long walk. While walking, he thought back about the two dreams he had some time back about Eva and how he was falling in love with her in his vision of fantasy. He wished he could dream of her again, but there was no telling when he would be able to, if ever.

While out walking, Danny decided that he would go back to the library the next day after work. He wanted to check out the local section where he'd found the *Chicago Tribune* article for any additional information about the horrible bridge disaster he might have overlooked the last time. He wanted to find out any and every detail about it that he could.

9

The next day at work, Richie sensed that Danny was a mile and a half low. "You look bummed, Wildcat. Come on with us after work to the Six."

"I don't know, man. I'm not really up to it today."

"Come on, man. I know that tornado down there in your hometown has been eating at you. Come down there with us. We'll make Lucky buy us some beers. He won forty-two bucks in the lottery yesterday."

Danny only frowned. That was his only emotional display. After waiting patiently for a few seconds, Richie lit up. "Ah, man, you aren't still hung up on all that stuff you read in the library about the bridge disaster, are you?"

Danny remained quiet and just shrugged. Richie playfully gave him a punch on his arm. "I know the whole thing was brutal and everything, but it all happened over a hundred years ago, man. Come on, let's go drink one for the Kaiser!"

"I've just been having some really strange dreams lately. It's been kind of bothering me. I'm going to pass on the Six this time." Danny was becoming detached.

Danny eschewed the upbeat scene at the café bar with the guys in exchange for another quiet foray into the library. He went inside and breezed past the familiar young lady at the information desk. He waved to her on his hurried way to the local history section. He immediately delved into the blue three-ringed notebook where he had found the other articles, seeking some additional information.

After a few moments of intense scouring, he came across two pertinent items. One was another local author's take on the disaster. This particular write-up didn't offer Danny any facts that he didn't already know about, but it did add an interesting nugget that was immortalized about the disaster in classic literature. The author of the article cited a reference to it from Rudyard Kipling's 1897 definitive tale of a spoiled son of a railroad tycoon in *Captains Courageous*. He remembered the antique shop owner mentioning it before. Danny read the quote with much amazement:

> "You've heered talk o'Johnstown?"
> Harvey considered. "Yes, I have. But I don't know
> Why. It sticks in my head same as Ashtabula."
> "Both was big accidents – thet's why, Harve."

Danny was astounded. The great Ashtabula Bridge Disaster was forever enthroned in classic American literature.

Danny searched onward. He came across an article from an old Cleveland newspaper, the *Cleveland Leader*, from December 30, 1876. Again, although it didn't offer anything much different about the wreck from what the *Chicago Tribune* presented on the same date, it did contribute two pearls that were lacking from the Windy City's major news source. In fact, the priceless gems the *Leader* had tendered sent shock waves tingling down Danny's spine. Just like at the cemetery when he saw Eva's name seared into the base of the monument, he again now wondered if he had just seen a ghost. The first item described the train as departing New York City on the night of December 28. However, the Cleveland paper added this extraordinary bombshell:

> The fated train on the New York Central railroad
> Line made a stop in Albany, NY, where it would
> Effect a split off. The one part proceeding westward
> to Syracuse and Buffalo, while the other part, being
> picked up by two locomotives, would thus be heading
> northward to Burlington, Vermont.

Danny's eyes nearly jumped out of their sockets. *How in the world would I know that particular detail to accurately dream about that?* He frantically thought. He looked around the room. His eyes carefully scanned to see if somehow he were being accompanied by a ghost. If someone were to calculate the odds of such a coincidence, how probable would it be to dream that particular detail of an event that no one had ever previously heard about before? A million to one? Ten million to one? For the first time since he had the two dreams about Eva and the events on the train, Danny was starting to wonder if it was really something more than just fanciful dreaming. Was it possible that he was being visited by a vision from beyond? Now his next question became, why? And when would he dream about it again?

That night, Danny lay awake on his bed, wondering if it were really out of the realm of possibility to be more than merely a dream. But how? How could it be anything but a dream? What else could it be? It had to be a dream. Maybe Richie was right. Maybe somewhere, at some time, he had heard or read about the details of the disaster and just couldn't remember. Maybe he'd overheard a conversation about it. Maybe he'd seen a documentary about it. He was positive he hadn't, but that wasn't out of the realm of possibility, either. Still, he was totally amazed about being able to so accurately dream of the train's Albany split-off before reading about it in the old news article.

Danny tried desperately to fall asleep in hopes of dreaming about it again. He couldn't get to sleep. He couldn't stop thinking of the name Eva Lindfors and the astronomical odds of dreaming about someone with the same name on the monument. *Another ten-million-to-one occurrence?* Eventually, he drifted off to sleep. He failed, however, to dream about any of it – not the train, not the monument, and most disappointingly, not about Eva. Nothing.

*

Danny's workday dragged by as he began to inadvertently isolate and disengage himself from everyone. Again, other than going out to buy food and other necessities, he pretty much kept to himself at home, frittering away his time watching old television shows, playing solitaire on his kitchen table, and occasionally polishing the brass plate on the back of the mirror. It appeared to him that more of the engraving on the plate was beginning to be lifted into view, but he was even too listless to go get his magnifying glass to check it out. He was getting to the point where he was looking to get to bed early in a neurotic attempt to dream about Eva and the train. Again, he surmised that all the rich and descriptive details he had previously dreamed about everything associated with the fated train was far too unearthly to merely be a dream. But even if that were true, even if they were nothing but pure reverie, he still deeply wished he could at least continue dreaming it and visit and spend time with her in his very realistic and lifelike night visions—so realistic, in fact, that he could still recall the scent of the pleasant perfume she was wearing, as well as the sharp aroma emanating from the kerosene lamps and cast-iron heaters. Reading what he did about the horrible conflagration, the thought of the kerosene lamps now made him cringe.

Unfortunately, not only did he fail to have the desired dream that restless night, but he did not have it for the next few lonely nights either. The only time one of his dreams remotely resembled anything like his desired one during this time period was more in the form of his previous nightmare of being in the cemetery with Maila Nurmi.

Then finally, one particular night, he was drifting in and out of sleep. He had been lying in bed, racking his brain as to the circumstances he was experiencing leading up to and preceding his two previous dreams about Eva. As he was floating between consciousness and sleep, the idea jumped out at him like a frightened deer bolting out of the forest. It suddenly dawned on him that in spite of all his concentration and obsession of Eva and the tragedy, the only two times that he had the occasion to summon the dream were when he was in his old 1870s period clothes. Also, both times he was gazing into his antique mirror while standing in front of in the spare bedroom. It seemed that in each case, right after he was fitting his old top hat on his head, he would experience immense dizziness and be forced to lie down to sleep it off.

He went into the other room where his closet and mirror were. He lay down for a while and then sat up in the spare bed and gazed through the darkness toward his closet, its white door visible in an infiltrating beam of moonlight. He began to wonder what might happen if he were to get up and edge over to it and remove his old suit out and try it on in front of the mirror. He also wondered if he were beginning to go crazy by even contemplating such a nonsensical notion. He was starting to drive himself mad by letting his dream consume him. He continued staring at the closet for a moment. As he gazed at it and contemplated his wavering sanity, he convinced himself that either way, it was all going to drive him insane anyway. He spun around and rose up out of bed. He went straight to the closet and removed the outfit along with all the accessories. As crazy as it all seemed, he felt that if he could manage to reenter the dream, he could probe and test the reality of this fantastic vision.

Danny hastily threw on the outfit after turning on the light. He took time to carefully and neatly tuck everything in. He pointed out to himself that if he was physically able to enter the dream, he didn't want to appear shoddy or like a slob; he wanted to look sharp and gentlemanly for Eva. He smartly tied on his red cravat and then grabbed his black John Bull top hat. He carefully set it atop his head and stared at the mirror… and waited. He stood there for a while. Nothing happened. No dizziness, no ringing in his ears, no blurry vision… nothing. He continued to stand and stare longer with the same result. Finally, and disappointedly, he edged back into his empty bed. He took off his hat and lay down on his back. He laid the hat on his chest and stared vacuously at the blank ceiling in pronounced dissatisfaction.

He lay there for a while until he absolutely loathed himself. *What am I, a lunatic? Am I the most idiotic person on earth? What would people think of me doing this?* He imagined everyone at work laughing at him with scorn and derision for acting so looney as to be dressed up and waiting for a dream to occur. Danny was indeed questioning his own sanity. He was now sinking to an all-time personal low point. After some time, he again began drifting in and out of sleep.

As he lay there, a glint from the beam of moonlight struck against the mirror, creating an acute and fluttering flashing image against the wall. It seized Danny's attention, causing him to come bounding from his bed. He slowly inched up to face the mirror. Again, he started to see everything blurry. There was the dizziness as before. It seemed to him that the face of the mirror was becoming dappled and rippled, as if somebody had skimmed a flat, smooth stone across the surface of a pond. Danny stared deeply into the mirror, holding the stand to prevent himself from reeling over. He became overcome with vertigo, ringing ears and all. It was an all-too-familiar feeling. But this time, he didn't seem to mind. He knew what lay ahead for him that night. He stumbled over to his bed and collapsed into it.

*

Danny woke up in his sleeper compartment. He rubbed his eyes and gingerly felt his sore forehead. He checked his pocket watch. It was a little past ten o'clock in the morning. He had been sleeping for almost two hours. He freshened up and straightened himself out as much as he could and exited his berth. He made his way to the parlor car to see if Eva was up yet. He heard a raucous din coming from the day coach. He ambled across the gangway into the car to the sound of a group of people singing and clapping their hands. He wondered what was going on. The smoker car was crowded, as well. He spotted Eva, who had awakened about a half hour earlier, seated in the parlor car adjacent to the boisterous day coach. Danny noticed that Eva was wearing different clothes. She had on a three-piece bustle dress. It was gray with a trimming of dark blue velvet. It was very stunning on her. He grew confused. Maybe he was only dreaming. Maybe the details had changed, and it really was all a dream. But the train was still exactly the same. Everything else was unchanged, as well.

Eva spotted Danny wending his way through the crowd of people back to the parlor car and motioned for him to join her. She grabbed his hand and accompanied him to the entry of the day coach gangway. Danny saw a man strumming a guitar and leading the crowd in song.

"Daniel, this is Reverend Phillip Bliss!" she shouted above the merry singing voices. "That's his wife over there. They boarded in Syracuse. He is singing to everybody some wonderful hymns. Isn't it beautiful?"

"Why, yes, very," he replied as he was recognized and interrupted by the family with the two small children with whom he had made small talk with before Syracuse. They greeted him as they made their way to listen to the reverend sing the hymns. Everyone seemed in good spirits. Many people joined in the spirituals the reverend was singing. Everyone still seemed to be in the Christmas mood. The two of them sat and listened awhile, with Eva joining in, lending her angelic singing voice.

Danny urgently looked her straight in the eyes. "Listen, Eva," Danny said, attempting to talk over the soaring music. "I really need to talk to you about something."

"I've changed my dress, Daniel. It got all wet with snow at Syracuse. I put on a new one when I awoke from my nap. The bustle will prevent my skirt from dragging the ground," she interrupted.

"You look very beautiful. It looks very becoming on you. I just wish that I could find where I left my top hat."

"But you are inside, Daniel. Why do you need your top hat now?"

"Like I've said before, I always like to tip my cap to a pretty lady," he replied with a grin.

"You are quite the flatterer," she responded, returning the grin. She suggested that they move to the far end of the parlor car in order to be able to hear each other talk.

Frustrated at not knowing if all of this was pure fantasy or some sort of apparition, Danny had a multitude of questions bottled up in his head for Eva to answer, but he had no idea how or what to ask her. If this were all real, and he indeed has been receiving a vision from the past, he didn't want her to think he was a madman. Anytime he tried to allude to what he was and had been dreaming, she simply attributed it all to his head injury back in Albany. He no doubt was enjoying all the sympathy she was showering on him, but not being able to decipher and differentiate between dreaming something and experiencing a phantom specter was indeed driving him mad.

"What's bothering you, Daniel? Is it your head?"

Danny was ineptly trying to ask her essentially if she were a dream or some sort of ghost without coming off sounding like a fool. But just as he was fumbling to speak, the crowd grew hushed. They fell silent as Reverend Bliss broke into a solo rendition of "Silent Night."

The respectful crowd was reverencing the moment. Eva grasped Danny's arm and leaned against his side. "This is my favorite hymn," she quietly yet exuberantly whispered. "*Stille Nacht, Heilige Nacht.*" She told him in the original title. The two of them listened peaceably. It did not take long for Eva to start quietly singing and humming along under her breath with the tuneful reverend. Danny closed his eyes and took it all in.

The beautiful song was actually making his head feel somewhat better. *I hope this is not all just a dream*, he once again thought to himself. *This beautiful angel, leaning against me and singing so marvelously. This must be how Jenny Lind sounded. I wish... I hope this is all reality.*

As Eva was nearly singing Danny to sleep and the reverend had finished the song, the two of them were interrupted by a booming voice. "Miss Lindfors!" the voice rang out, startling Danny out of his stupor. "You remember Mr. Lundy, one of your father's old clients."

Eva exchanged greetings with him and introduced him to Danny. "Mr. Lundy, this is Mr. Daniel Dubenion. He is kindly accompanying me on my trip to meet Father in Ashtabula." Danny firmly shook Mr. Lundy's hand.

Mr. McCarthy chimed in. "Daniel, Mr. Lundy here really liked your suggestion on the new Bell Telephone Company. I told him all about it. We both agree that it sounds like a fantastic opportunity."

"I just have a hunch about it," Danny casually shrugged.

"That's how money is made, Daniel, my young man, on smart hunches like that," he bellowed as he rigorously patted Danny on the back. "Miss Lindfors, this young man should be working for your father." He gave Eva a smart wink. "I'm telling you, my dear, don't let this one get away," he added, boisterously laughing.

"Listen, Daniel," Mr. Lundy jumped in, "come join us and the guys a little later in the smoker car. "We'll play a few games of draw poker back there, have a few drinks, and talk a little Bell Telephone Company." Danny nodded and accepted his invitation, telling the two slightly inebriated businessmen that he would meet them back there a little later.

After the businessmen had scurried away, Eva filled Danny in on who Mr. Lundy was. He had invested money with her father in order to start up a distribution warehouse in Chicago a number of years ago. He operated the business fairly successfully. "Poor Mr. Lundy," Eva lamented. "He lost his entire business in that horrendous fire a few years back. Fortunately, with Father's help with the financial backing again, he was able to rebuild."

Danny listened as Eva told him about Cyrus McCormick also losing his business in the conflagration. But fortunately, he also was able to rebuild. "Do you know who else had his business devastated during that dreadful blaze?" she asked him. When Danny inquired as to who, she replied that her former fiancé's father suffered great loss and privation as a result of the ordeal. "Such a poor, poor man. Such a tragic fate he was compelled to endure. He lost his elder son out west while the other son brought on him such great shame. Then a couple of years later, the dreadful fire."

Danny expressed his sympathies, although he wasn't totally sure what she was altogether talking about.

After a few reflective moments, Eva leaned over to him and begged his forgiveness. "Daniel, I had been extremely unfair to you earlier by telling you that you reminded me of my former fiancé. I truly meant to suggest that only in his good qualities that he once possessed that you reminded me of him. You are far more trustworthy and kindhearted than he could ever be. I can truly tell that you are."

"Well, thank you; I try to be," he responded humbly, blushing.

"And," she added straightforwardly, "You are far more handsome than he." She leaned over and gave him a quick peck on the cheek, again causing his face to flush.

Eva paused, and then she opened up to him. "I guess it's only fair for me to explain what happened between my fiancé and me."

"Only if you feel that you have to"

"As I started to tell you back in Syracuse, in 1868, I was twenty; he was twenty-eight. He headed out west to help his brother and sister-in-law manage their claim. Now, Daniel, I know men … I understand they get lonesome. I can forgive if they visit and have a time with one of those … soiled doves out there. I know fully well that it is too strong of a temptation. Men get lonely, and there are too many of them available out there. But that was not the heartbreak." Eva was obviously heating up as she revisited this dark and demeaning episode in her life.

"You had asked me earlier if he were in an accident. Not him, but his brother was the one that had been befallen by a fatal accident. After or before his brother was stricken, my fiancé had run off with his sister-in-law." Eva began to hyperventilate. Danny held her tightly by the hand. She reached over and clutched his forearm with her other hand. "His brother's wife, Daniel! His own brother." Eva paused and fought back a tear. "He later wrote me about it. It took him some time to tell me. When the shocking news came to us that his brother had perished, I wrote to him and asked him whether he was with her … you know, Daniel, whether he was with her before or after his brother's demise. He never responded. I never heard from him again." She wiped a tear from her flushed, quivering cheek. "I wasn't sure if I could ever trust or love another man again." She gently sobbed. "When I was in New York this past week, my brother-in-law offered to properly introduce me to one of his associates. Sister understood why I was hesitant and why I begged to decline. She knew that I wasn't ready and didn't force the issue with me."

Danny held her in his arms. He felt so terribly for her. He didn't quite know exactly what to say to her. *After all these years*, Danny thought, *she is still pained. Still distressed about this.* She was sorely wounded. The harsh ordeal had left her bitter and untrusting—emotions and traits she was not fond of herself being or wanting to display. She was reticent to ever fall in love again. However, after eight long, lonely years, when she first saw Danny sitting in the day coach on the train outside of Albany, he must have projected some image of trustworthiness and kindness about him. This image of accessibility to him enabled her to approach him and maybe take a chance—a venture she hadn't dared to attempt in all that time.

Eva spun out of his sideways embrace and faced him. She looked squarely into his kind and gentle eyes. "Thank you, Daniel, *min söta.* You are so kind." She kissed his forehead and embraced him tightly, leaning securely against his breast. She rested against him for what seemed like a pleasant eternity. Again, Danny grieved that he wasn't sure if this was a dream or a vision or some ghostly realism.

After some time, Eva excused herself to go wash her face and lie down in her drawing room for a spell. She apologized to Danny for needing a little time to herself. Danny reassured her that he totally understood. He once again admonished her to be careful crossing the snowy gangway in between train cars. He offered to assist her along the way. She declined, assuring him that she would be careful and that she had much experience traversing cars being that she had ridden on many trains in the past. She again apologized for leaving him alone for a while. He let her know that he would be fine. He said that while she rested, he would visit Mr. McCarthy and Mr. Lundy in the smoker car for a little while and play a few games of cards with them. He insisted that he accompany her to her room, pleading his concern for her safety crossing the treacherous metal platforms. She consented, and so he walked her to her room and then headed to join the men for some gaming. He wasn't sure what the purpose was for him having this dream about playing poker, but his subconscious was deciding to let him have a little fun.

Danny found himself tossing in a few of his antique coins and a dollar bill or two for a game of high-stakes poker, 1876-style, with a couple of high-living Chicago businessmen and another fellow who happened to join in. Danny sipped a little whiskey and shared a few laughs as well as a few unsolicited stock tips as he dealt out a fresh hand of five-card draw poker to the table. Although Danny knew enough about history to bluff his way through the conversation and get by, he mostly kept quiet while listening to the other men speak.

Danny was enjoying himself immensely. It was a little past 11:00 a.m. By now, the train had skirted just south of Rochester and was on its way toward Batavia. The heavy snow that was pounding the Syracuse area had somewhat abated. He was rolling his way across scenic New York State, having the time of his life. Sitting in with the guys, dealing out poker hands, and getting caught up in the revelry of a classic old smoker car, it was just like in the old westerns that he always enjoyed watching.

Naturally, the conversation turned to everyone's opinion of some of the ladies who were on board. Their tone grew respectful whenever Miss Eva Lindfors's name came to the fore. The other men at the table, especially Mr. McCarthy, were quite surprised when they asked Danny how long he had been courting her, thinking perhaps the two of them were getting engaged, and he informed them that he had only met her earlier that morning. The dubious looks he subsequently received in response made him more than a little embarrassed and uncomfortable. He knew the men all respected her father and in turn Eva herself. Danny capably covered himself by explaining his noble and honorable intentions for her. This fast thinking but honest gesture allowed the game to continue. Danny was holding his own.

They were in the midst of another game. Danny was holding a pair of sevens. He sat back and imbibed a sip of his whiskey, threw down his unwanted cards, and requested three fresh ones from the dealer, Mr. Lundy. As Danny's eyes were trained on him, he thought of how Eva mentioned that he had lost his business in a great fire a few years back. He felt very badly for him. Mr. Lundy seemed like a very affable fellow. As Danny waited for him to furnish his three draw cards, it hit him like a ton of bricks. How did he not realize before what Eva was alluding to? She was describing the great Chicago fire.

All that Danny had ever known about it was that it happened in 1871 and something about Mrs. O'Leary's cow starting the blaze. The only reason he remembered the year was because he had once asked his Grandpa Ed when the tragedy had taken place.

Danny calmly picked up his three draw cards. He took a peek, showing no emotion. He contemplated another sip of whiskey but abstained. He had drawn the third seven, the winning hand. That's when he was struck with a thunderbolt, the winning idea. He would convincingly be able to differentiate whether he was merely in dreamland or involved in some sort of macabre manifestation of being in a strange voyage back to the past, back to December 29, 1876, on an old passenger train, traveling with Eva Lindfors to Ashtabula, Ohio, all the way down to the hellish base of the burning river gorge, underneath a collapsed, twisted, gnarled, and seared bridge, awaiting an unspeakable and indescribable death. Danny attempted to take that sip from his whiskey glass but was too shaky to do so.

Danny cashed in his winning hand and politely excused himself from the table amid the jeers of the other gentlemen. He sincerely begged their pardon and then made a hasty retreat back to his sleeper car berth, slowing only as he carefully went across the slippery gangways between the cars. He folded the bed down and eased into it. He sat and pondered. He wanted to be absolutely sure that the only two things he ever knew about the great Chicago fire was the year it occurred and the legend of the cow. At the right opportunity, when Eva was rested and calmed down from her retelling of her ordeal with her former fiancé, he would ask her to relate to him all the details she could remember of the great conflagration. Then, when he either woke up or this bizarre visitation ended and he was back home in 1985 Ashtabula, he would go to the library and check her detailed facts against any number of volumes there documenting the event. If what she would tell him in this so-called dream matched up with the historical accounts, along with the other astronomical long-shot coincidences that had been tied up with the whole matter, he would be absolutely convinced he was being somehow carried between 1876 and 1985—that this whole bizarre occurrence was not merely just part of his dreams.

Danny sat in his berth and contemplated the magnitude of the whole matter. He understood one simple but dynamic fact. As mysterious as all of this was, if he indeed was traveling back and forth in a fantastic vision to be a passenger on this horribly fated train ride on December 29, 1876, he had to do everything in his power to stop it from reaching the Ashtabula River Gorge. He needed to first talk to Eva about the Chicago fire in order to go back and prove his theory. Then, if it was proven to be more than a dream, his mission lay squarely in front of him.

Before he would be able to prove the theory, Danny would rest a lot easier if he could convince Eva to get off the train at the Buffalo stop before he returned to the present. What method he could use to accomplish that feat, he did not know. This way, when he returned to 1876 and Eva was safely off the train, his mind would be clear, and he would be free to work on the porter to help him convince the conductor to get the two engineers to stop the train before it met its awaited doom.

Danny came out of his berth and made his way over to the parlor car. Eva was seated all alone and quietly staring out of the window. The snow had begun picking up again. The train was now past Batavia and heading to Buffalo, less than thirty-five miles away. The closer it got to Buffalo, the more the snow intensified. Eva turned to Danny as he entered the car. She assured him that she would be all right.

"Eva, there is something I have to ask you about."

"Please wait, Daniel. I must retrieve something from my room. Please, I'll be right back." Eva excused herself and went to her drawing room. After a few short moments she returned to Danny's side. When she returned, he inquired as to where she had gone. "This is for you, my sweetheart Daniel, *min söta*." She held out a fine, lace, hand-embroidered, perfume-scented handkerchief with a finely embroidered letter *E* in Spencerian script on the face of it. "I have not felt this way about anyone for a long time."

"What's that for?" the puzzled Danny asked.

"This goes right here," she replied as she folded and tucked it inside his frock coat pocket. "*Mizpah*!" she uttered as she enthusiastically patted her hand against the pocket.

"*Mizpah*?" Danny questioned.

"Yes, Daniel, *mizpah*. It is from the book of Genesis. Do you know the book of Genesis?"

Again, Danny reacted with a blank expression.

"You know, Genesis – Adam and Eve… Noah with his ark," she persisted.

"I'm familiar with it." He nodded with a curious smile. "*Mizpah* is a Hebrew word."

She sighed. "From Genesis chapter 31 verse 49. It says, 'The Lord watch between me and thee, when we are absent one from another.'"

Danny nodded with interest.

"Mother always says that to me when I travel apart from her. In fact, she just said this to me before I departed for New York to visit my sister. When we get to Ashtabula and you go home, and Father and I finish our business there and return to Chicago, you will look upon my handkerchief that I have just given you. You will think of Miss Eva Lindfors. The tragic, lovelorn Miss Eva Lindfors. The Eva Lindfors who has fallen in love with you. And, by thinking of me, you will perhaps miss me and wish to marry me and be with me always. If so, if this is the case, I will be waiting for you there."

Danny reached his hand and felt her folded handkerchief in his coat pocket. Her token and her words had touched his heart. He was indeed falling in love with her, also. He would love to marry her and be with her always, but he wasn't sure if she were real or only still a sweet dream of his. And, if perchance she was a real vision, then what was this train they were on heading for if not disaster?

Danny gently but firmly put his hands on Eva's shoulders. "Eva, what day is today?" he asked her in an urgent tone.

"What day?" she replied, puzzled.

"The date. What is today's date?"

"It's the twenty-ninth," she responded.

"What year is it?" he hastened.

"Daniel, what is wrong with you? Where have you been? It is December 29, 1876, silly."

Danny turned pale. "Where are you headed?" he inquired, hoping she would tell him differently from before.

"Daniel, dear, I told you earlier that I'm stopping at Ashtabula to meet Father."

Danny grew frantic. "Is there any way you can get off the train before Ashtabula? Maybe get on another train tomorrow?"

"Dear Daniel, you're impossible. Your head must be really hurting you. Father will be waiting for me in the cold air. I can't leave him there waiting longer."

Danny kept trying to convince her. "Listen, Eva," Danny said desperately, "wouldn't it be nice to stop off at Buffalo and get off this cramped train and spend the night in a nice, comfortable hotel?"

"Daniel! We're not even married yet!" Eva recoiled sharply.

"We will have separate rooms, I mean," Danny defended. "I have money."

"Daniel, money is not the problem." She told him to wait as she ran to her drawing room again. She grabbed the telegram she had received on Christmas Day.

Eva raced back to where Danny was nervously seated. She thrust out the telegram and read it to him.

> MY DEAREST EVA (STOP) I HOPE YOU ARE HAVING A BLESSED CHRISTMAS (STOP) GIVE MY LOVE TO ANNAFRIDA (STOP) I HOPE YOU ARE ENJOYING NEW YORK CITY WITH HER (STOP) I WILL BE WAITING FOR YOU AT THE STATION IN

ASHTABULA, OH (STOP) THE TRAIN SCHEDULE SAYS IN THE EARLY EVENING, AROUND 5 O'CLOCK (STOP) I WILL SHOW YOU WHAT I HAVE INVESTED FOR YOU (STOP) CLEVELAND, YOUNGSTOWN, AND ASHTABULA RR (STOP) SEE YOU THEN (STOP) ALL MY LOVE, FATHER (STOP)

She reiterated to him that it was compulsory that she meet her father on time so as not to rudely make him wait. "I can't make Father tarry an extra day in the frigid cold all alone in town!"

"Wait a minute, Eva!" Danny exclaimed in an urgent tone. "Won't you at least reconsider? Tomorrow the weather will be so much better for traveling."

Eva smiled as she tenderly touched his bandaged brow. "Daniel, you are so thoughtful, but I just can't leave Father all by himself tonight. It'll be fine. Around 5:00, you will get to meet him. I can hardly wait."

10

Danny grew frantic. The situation was urgent. He needed Eva to relate the facts about the fire before he returned to 1985. "Eva, please," he said as he grabbed and gently squeezed her hands. "I desperately need to talk to you about something very important. Wait a second. Did you just say that your father is meeting you at 5:00?"

"Yes, Daniel, the train is scheduled for a 5:00 arrival at Ashtabula Station." For a brief shining moment, Danny had a glimmer of hope. His brain was racing. He might be grasping at straws, he thought, but he reasoned that the disaster occurred round 7:30. If they would arrive around 5:00, maybe it was a later train that was on the collapsing bridge. Maybe the purpose of him entering the scene that he was thrust into was to keep her from getting off the train and arriving safely at 5:00, after all.

Danny pondered for a moment. His glimmer of hope was fleeting, however, as he quickly recalled what the article in the *Tribune* stated as fact—that because of the heavy blizzard along Lake Erie, the train was nearly three hours behind its time. Plus, he morbidly realized, if she had indeed arrived at 5:00, her name would not be on the base of that monument. Danny was crestfallen at the realization.

"Daniel, I thought you said you had something important to tell me," Eva reminded him.

Danny was starting to panic. Eva was not being easily swayed to get off that train before meeting her father. By now, it was nearly 12:45. He understood quite well that this train they were on had a little more than six and a half hours before its fate and doom were forever sealed. He reminded himself that he was getting a little too far ahead of himself with worrying about everything. He would have to first ask Eva about the great Chicago fire's details and go back and see the proof of whether he was being caught up in a vision from the past or simply having a detailed recurring dream. Then and only then could he plot his next move.

He asked Eva some probing questions about the historical blaze. She described it in vivid detail. "Yes, Daniel, it was five years ago—October 1871. The weather was extremely dry—so dry I can actually still feel it. The O'Learys who live on DeKoven Street seemed to have all the blame thrust upon them. It was rumored that their cow started it. That has never been proven, though."

Danny concentrated. He attentively clung to every word that issued from her beautiful, wavy lips. "Total lawlessness ensued. Such mayhem, Daniel." She went on to inform him that many businesses were destroyed and that, remarkably, the rail and transportation system was miraculously left intact. "Which was a huge relief and blessing to Father and us," she reiterated with gratitude. "The next month, in November, Joseph Medill was elected as our mayor. He had promised everybody that he would have businesses erect better buildings in case of any more fires in the future. That's how he got elected. Father knew many gentlemen whose businesses were devastated by that horrible blaze." She reminded Danny about their conversation before in which she'd told him how Mr. Lundy's and Mr. McCormick's as well as her former fiancé's father's businesses suffered tremendous damage and loss. "Hundreds of lives lost. You can only imagine such a horrendous fire, Daniel."

Danny stared off in silence, thinking about the massive conflagration that very train would experience in just a matter of a few hours from then.

"Yes, my sweet Eva, I can only imagine."

"Our grand city revived, however, with great reconstruction efforts. Chicago is still recovering from it. Because of that fire, our White Stockings had to have a new baseball park built. The one on Twenty-Third Street."

Danny had all the details that Eva told him firmly locked in his brain—details he had never heard before. He would compare them at the library when he returned home.

It was coming up on 1:00 p.m. The train was nearing Buffalo. The snow, which had intensified dramatically, was fiercely pounding the entire area. For the first time since leaving New York City, the engineer was compelled to deploy the sand tubes. The sand tubes, which were lined up in accordance with the width of the track gauge at the bottom of the engine adjacent to the wheels, drew from a reservoir of warm, dry sand. The sand was located in a storage bin called the sand dome, on top of the boiler. The sand dome's proximity to the hot boiler assured that the warm, dry sand would flow freely through the tubes and onto the icy tracks. The primary reason for the injection of sand onto the tracks was to assist the iron wheels to gain a good bite of traction during an icy situation such as the one the train was facing at the time. Secondarily, being that the sand was very warm, it could be a factor in melting the ice as it was ground and pulverized into the track by the heavy iron wheels.

There would be a considerable delay in Buffalo, as the train would be switching lines. With Buffalo as the western terminus for the New York Central Railroad, the train would be switching out with two fresh and fully fueled locomotives. The newly switched engines would begin the western trek along the Lake Shore and Michigan Southern Railway. Along the way, the train would steam past Lackawanna, Athol Springs, Silver Creek, and Erie in Pennsylvania; Conneaut, Ohio, and to Ashtabula before continuing westward for Chicago and beyond.

Danny sat pensively staring out of the window at the hypnotic snowfall. Weighing on his heavy heart were the precious lives of those who were destined to fatally plunge into the inferno of the Ashtabula River Gorge. Why was he seeing this vision? Was there any way he could interfere with history and stop it from occurring, saving countless lives, such as those of the good Reverend Bliss and his wife, Mr. McCarthy, Mr. Lundy, and the wonderful family with the two active children? What about the kind physician, Dr. Penwalt, who thoughtfully bandaged him up, or the friendly porter and baggage man? Especially, what about the woman he was falling deeply in love with, Miss Eva Lindfors? Danny continued staring off into the muted drab grayness of the sky and the mesmerizing snow. After a while, it started to put him in a trancelike state.

Everything started to look blurry to him. His ears began ringing. Then suddenly, he awoke. He was in his bed, wearing his old period outfit. It was early morning. His hat had fallen and landed in front of the mirror, sitting there the whole time. He stumbled out of bed and reluctantly began his tedious daily regimen.

As much as he loved dreaming about Eva and wished he could go right back to sleep and be with her again in his reverie, there were rent and bills to pay, food to buy and important work to be done. The factory was burgeoning with new orders. With new orders came a lot of product testing for the quality control lab. Danny's talents at work would be sorely needed. He would soon find time to research the library for the facts concerning the great Chicago fire, but in the meantime, the real world was calling him. Danny was obliged to answer the call.

Danny had a lot on his agenda for the week, not only at work, which had him pulling some overtime, but also, he wanted to call the local historical society up there and make an appointment to talk to someone about joining. The marine museum, also. He really felt the need to get heavily involved with Ashtabula history, especially in the light of his fixation with the bridge disaster and a certain person whose name was on the base of the monument dedicated for its dead. He would have his steady diet of real-life chores to keep up on, such as laundry, taking care of the yard, an appointment to service the car, and more. On top of all that, Richie was hounding him to go fishing with him and take some time to unwind. Even his friends and former coworkers from Niles called him, hounding him to get together with them. Eventually, maybe by the end of the week, he would find the time for research at the library.

After work on Monday, Danny stopped for a quick bite at Garfield's, gassed up his car at the Flying Saucer, and then took the ten-mile drive to Jefferson to meet with Mrs. Lane at the Ashtabula County Historical Society. Mrs. Lane, a retired schoolteacher who was the society's director, was meeting him there to sign him up as a new member. Danny had talked on the phone to the former Ashtabula school history teacher, who herself was a distant relative of William Hubbard. William Hubbard was one of the city's early pioneers who came here in the late 1700s as part of the Connecticut Western Reserve land company's division of the lands in the Ohio Territory. He was a member of Ashtabula's antislavery society. Together with his brothers, he helped to found the *Ashtabula Sentinel*, an abolitionist newspaper. He was also heavily involved in the Underground Railroad that helped runaway slaves escape to Canada, a fact that Mrs. Lane told Danny on the phone and that she was extremely proud of.

Mrs. Lane cordially greeted Danny when he arrived at the society's building in Jefferson. She was familiar with both of the historical societies in Niles that Danny had belonged to and was impressed with him for all his involvement in them. When he told her about the public reception they had in March, she expressed her willingness to try to have something like that up there someday. "We meet once a month here, Mr. Dubenion," she informed him. "We sponsor and help preserve various historical sites here in the county." She went on to list projects they discussed and got involved in, like the Underground Railroad houses of the Hubbard and Blakeslee families. The Blakeslee family, like the Hubbard family, were also avidly involved in the Underground Railroad movement in Ashtabula. They also sponsored and helped maintain the Great Lakes Marine and Coast Guard Memorial Museum, the Civil War monument, and the annual Harbor Days Festival on Bridge Street. "We also get involved with restoration projects for the county's many scenic, old, covered bridges," she told him. "A couple of times a year we meet at one of the local eateries and take a field trip to one of the bridges. We all just talk and fellowship and have a good time."

Danny asked her if they ever studied or discussed the great Ashtabula Bridge Disaster. "Oh, yes, that's always a subject of conversation around here … especially among the men," she replied. "Mr. Kirkpatrick, one of our longest-standing members, is always bringing it up. Are you familiar with Mr. Kirkpatrick?" Danny replied that he wasn't. "He owns the Harbor Antique Emporium in Ashtabula. He's lived here his whole life."

"Ah, yes, I do know him," Danny replied excitedly. "In fact, I have purchased a few really fine items from him since I moved up here in October. I didn't even know his name until you mentioned it right now. He told me before that his grandfather was a little boy when the disaster occurred. He said he used to tell him stories about the horror."

Danny was very interested in joining. He was already eager to get involved, but now that he knew Mr. Kirkpatrick was a member, he was really excited about it. He also just wanted to contribute his efforts to support and preserve historical landmarks and institutions like he had done in Niles. Obviously, the prospect of discussing and picking the brains of other people who also felt very strongly about the disaster such as he did was a huge factor in him wanting to join, as well, but it certainly was not the only reason. Danny registered with Mrs. Lane to join right then and there. He paid the fifteen-dollar annual fee to her right on the spot, as well.

She filled him in on some of the other projects and local tours, as well. "One of the more exciting events we host – usually once, maybe twice a year – is a local author who has published something with local interest to come in and give a little talk and have a discussion on what he or she has written. It is usually accompanied by a book signing."

"That sounds really interesting," Danny responded. "Who have you had here recently?"

"We actually had a local man here a few years ago who wrote a documentary on the bridge disaster," she answered. "Also, someone who wrote a book on the Underground Railroad up here, as well as someone who wrote on our country's local impact on the Civil War and the world wars."

"My Grandpa Ed was in World War I… at Meuse-Argonne in 1918."

"The author mentioned that battle," Mrs. Lane said with great admiration." It's always a treat to have one of our local writers come her to speak," she added. "It is nice for our members; they really enjoy and take pride in people chronicling our rich local history. In fact, Mr. Dubenion, next month we will be hosting a local man who researches and writes articles about the local railroad history."

That really caught Danny's attention. "That sounds great," he affirmed. "I love railroad history. I will definitely be here for that, I guarantee you."

Before he left, Mrs. Lane gave Danny a quick tour of the place. Danny listened intently as she showed him pictures of such area landmarks as the Blakeslee log cabin, the area's oldest church buildings and covered bridges, and historical barns. She showed him pictures of the harbor and lift bridge from many decades past, during the port's heyday. She showed him around the grounds outside. Danny was impressed. He thanked her for her time and told her he looked forward to attending the meetings and functions, and that he was eager to get involved in cultivating his growing appreciation for Ashtabula County history. Danny drove off toward town, where he had some errands to take care of. Afterward, he drove around and down into the harbor and then down the road to the lake. He got out for a few moments and took a short stroll on the shore. He just wanted a quick taste of the early summer lakefront air. He was still thinking about Eva and his ever-growing suspicion that all of it wasn't just a dream. He planned on going to the library on Saturday to do his research. It was only Monday. It would be a long five-day wait. He was a little unnerved about finding out the chilling possibility that he could be traveling back, experiencing a trancelike vision from 1876. Living on another level of existence isn't something you ever expect to do, to put it mildly. The thought of it alone was very petrifying. As much as he wanted Eva to be real and for him to forever be with her, the specter of it all was very frightening. Danny got back into his car and took off for home. If the weather held up, he would go bass fishing after work the next day with Richie off the rocks in Conneaut to enjoy a little time with his friend. Hopefully it would help him relax.

*

"Come on, Wildcat!" Richie yelled to Danny the next day as the workday was ending. "Let's go get a couple of beers and catch a few bass and make up some urban legends."

"Let me go home for a couple of minutes and wash up, and I'll meet you at the "Six" around four o'clock," Danny fired back. He drove home quickly and took a shower, got dressed, and met Richie at four o'clock. They had a quick beer and a small bite to eat at the Six before driving to Conneaut.

When they arrived at the lake, they went out on the rocks and quickly got their gear set up to start fishing.

"Ah, a nice relaxing afternoon catching us some bass," Richie reveled.

Danny nodded in agreement as he sat quietly on the rocks and slowly reeled his line back in. After a couple of minutes, he broke his silence. "Hey, Richie, I joined the Ashtabula Historical Society yesterday."

"Okay… that's exciting. What, are you still fighting the Civil War?" Richie mocked him sarcastically.

"No, man. I'm just really starting to get into Ashtabula's history, that's all," Danny said defensively.

Richie was quiet while he cast out a new line into the water. After a few moments, it hit him. "Oh, come off it, man!" He shrieked. "It's this bridge thing, isn't it? Man, you're really letting this disaster eat you away."

"You know, I had that dream again a couple of nights ago," Danny said, not sure if he should have mentioned it.

"What, that girl on the train again? …Come off it, man."

"I don't know, Richie. There's a lot of uncanny coincidences."

"You are pathetic, Danny. Do you know that? …Pathetic."

Danny didn't answer back. He knew he shouldn't have brought it up.

"You know what I'm going to do?" Richie asked. "I'm going to go out and find you a woman. Would you like that? But not the kind of woman that you go for in those dreams. I'm going to find you a real flesh-and-blood female."

"I knew I was in trouble even mentioning it to you. You have to admit, what are the odds of dreaming all those accuracies without ever hearing about it first? Millions to one. I think… maybe it's more than just a dream… maybe it's some sort of vision from beyond."

"You are pathetic. I thought we settled this already, man You've had to already have heard all that before or read about it somewhere. You just can't remember. It's that simple," Richie charged.

"I'm telling you, Richie, I never have. I'm positive." Danny almost told him of how he was going to prove his theory about Eva's telling him of the Chicago fire and him checking the details at the library on Saturday, but he stopped himself from doing it.

"You are Mr. Pathetic. That's your new name—Mr. Pathetic," Richie snarled. "No woman is ever going to want to marry you because who wants to be known as Mrs. Pathetic? Am I right?" Richie chided, not totally joking.

Danny ignored him and minded his line, staring off into the blue summer sky.

"I take you out to go fishing so we can have a fun, relaxing time, and you just keep talking of that girl you've dreamed about on the monument …Pathetic!"

After a couple of strikes Danny and Richie decided to call it quits. They agreed to head back to Ashtabula for a beer and some good bar food back at the Six. As they were getting ready to leave their fishing spot on the breakwater rocks, Danny stood up too fast and got a headache and became dizzy. Richie asked him what was wrong. After a moment of trepidation, Danny started to feel okay.

"It was like that time at the cemetery a while back!" he exclaimed. "When I went up the stone steps up to the ridge too fast. I got that same feeling just now. I'll be all right in a minute." Danny soon shook it off.

The two of them wrapped everything up, got everything in the car and headed off toward the Six.

*

For the next couple of days, Wednesday and Thursday, Danny worked overtime a couple of hours to help get the lab caught up on its sample testing. For Danny, it did him some good to stay over at work a little bit. The company of his coworkers helped keep his mind off his dream. Not that he wanted to forget about the dream, especially Eva, but again, the fact that it might be real, and he might be caught up in some kind of time warp astral plane was making him more than just apprehensive. After work on Thursday, before getting something to eat, he drove down to the Harbor Antique Emporium to pay Mr. Kirkpatrick a friendly visit.

Danny entered the antique shop to find Mr. Kirkpatrick occupied with a customer. Danny shuffled around to see if there were any newly dropped off items that were for sale. He browsed about until Mr. Kirkpatrick was free.

"Hello, Danny. I have a whole stack of old *Life* magazines someone brought in the other day. Most of them are from the 1940s. Do you collect any of them?"

"Oh, hello, Mr. Kirkpatrick … actually, I do have a pretty sizable old magazine collection. Actually, Mr. Kirkpatrick, it's funny. I just found out what your name is. Mrs. Lane told me."

"Mrs. Lane?" he questioned as he pointed in a southerly direction.

"Yes, Mrs. Lane from the historical society down in Jefferson. I just became a new member."

"Oh, how exciting. That's great, Danny. I think you will really fit in well. A lot of good folks there. Welcome aboard." He informed Danny that the society was really big on studying and discussing the Underground Railroad movement and the Civil War. He repeated what Mrs. Lane had told him the other day about some of the local authors coming there and giving talks on their writings and published works. With the bridge disaster constantly on his mind, Danny brought up the fact that at next month's July meeting, a local writer who had articles published on the area's railroad history would be there doing a program. Danny asked him if he thought that the writer would discuss the tragedy.

"Oh, for certain he will," he affirmed. "I have read this gentleman's articles before. He will most definitely discuss it. Feel free to bring the subject up to him. He is always willing to educate people on the bridge disaster." Mr. Kirkpatrick informed him that he himself, along with a few other fellow members, were always having a discourse on that subject. Danny told him that he was looking forward to hearing and speaking with the writer, and he said he was also anxious to attend the meetings with him, as well. Danny excused himself, shook Mr. Kirkpatrick's hand, and took off for home to make something to eat.

*

Saturday morning had finally and painstakingly arrived. Danny packed the backseat of his car with a couple of baskets of dirty laundry. He figured he would hit the Laundromat on West Avenue after he researched the library downtown. Of course, since he was headed downtown, he would stop off at Garfield's on the way before all of that for a nice, hearty breakfast. It was a beautiful late morning in the middle of June. Danny wanted to drive with the top down on his car, but with all the laundry in the backseat, he couldn't. His convertible was a big hit at the diner every time he brought it there. All the regulars there would be disappointed when they got a look of the classic ragtop pulling in with the top up.

Danny had a nice omelet and some coffee along with some good chatting with the familiar folks there. He couldn't stay too long, though, he insisted. He had some very real soul searching—and quite possibly some spirit world searching—to attend to.

Danny strode into the library with a singleness of purpose. A quick hello and a harried "You gotta help me" comprised his short-but-to-the-point greeting to the reference desk clerk. She took him to where a trove of information was located about the Great Chicago Fire of 1871. Danny sat at the table and sifted through a cache of material that had been documented on the tragedy. The volume was a laborious collection of articles, references, and photographs from various Chicago and other surrounding cities' newspapers. Danny couldn't make heads or tails out of all the pages of information. He spent about a half an hour trying to locate something that fit Eva's detailed description about the fire. Then the gracious reference desk clerk came up to him with a little box in her hand.

"Here, sir," she said to him, extending the flat box to him. "Maybe this will be of some help to you."

She handed him the box. Inside, it contained a reel of microfilm from the library's national history section. She helped him load the film into the viewer and explained to him how to operate it. Danny thanked her and began to scan the microfilm, which contained a treasure chest of historical data about the fire. After reading awhile, Danny was astounded. Right in front of his eyes were the words *Patrick and Catherine O'Leary from 137 DeKoven Street*, just as Eva had told him. Danny knew with all his heart that he had never known or heard of that piece of information before Eva told it to him in his dream—a dream that Danny was increasingly doubting was just a dream. His theory gained momentum a few minutes later when he read about Joseph Madill, the newly elected mayor of Chicago a month after the fire. It referenced his campaign promise immediately after the blaze to impose stricter building and fire codes as he helped to institute a great rebuilding of the city. Another article echoed Eva's words about the railroad and transportation industry going virtually unscathed, thus allowing shipments of aid and material to flow in freely from across the country. There was even a reference to how extremely dry the air was that day. Danny felt like her words were literally jumping off the microfilm pages and into his heart. He could still hear her telling him, "The weather was extremely dry—so dry I can actually still feel it."

The word *uncanny* didn't even begin to describe the situation. Danny now pegged the probability at upward of a billion to one that all the details that he had dreamed about without ever before hearing of them that were able to come to pass as being dead-on accurate, starting with seeing Eva's name on the monument. The Albany train split off, the details of her conversations with him, especially now with what she described about the Great Chicago Fire. He marveled at how he would be able to simply dream about somebody telling him about a couple who lived on DeKoven Street, where the fire started. Dreaming about someone telling you about a Main Street or a Maple Street, maybe, but DeKoven Street, which he had never even remotely heard of before? He cautiously scanned with his ballooned eyes to see if a ghostly vision of Eva would materialize from behind the multitude of bookshelves that lined the rooms there. He began to get an eerie and unsettling feeling again. He started to sense that he was hovering—or better yet, wafting—between the physical world and the realm of apparition. He was experiencing a quite literal chill running up and down his spine. As Danny finished poring over the voluminous pieces of information, his hands, which were connected to his goosebump-riddled arms, worked the knob to rewind the reel of microfilm and unload it from the viewer to put back in the box, which he returned to the clerk along with a hearty thank you. Danny was all but definitely assured that his three realistically defined night visions were actually instances of him being mystically transported back in time in a wraithlike existence to being a passenger on the ill-fated train heading to Ashtabula. But as to why, he still did not know.

Before he was about to leave the library and head for the West Avenue Laundromat, he was seized upon with one more notion. *This will be the clincher*, he told himself. He went to the desk clerk and asked her where he could find a book or encyclopedia about the complete history of major-league baseball. Within minutes, Danny found himself back at the table, perusing one of the most authoritative volumes on major-league baseball history. Naturally, he started right at the beginning of the book, being that he was seeking out details from the very first year of the first major league of baseball. The founding of the National League, 1876. Right there on the early pages, it was again as if he could hear Eva talking about her father bringing her to the park to attend the National League games.

Before reading those pages at that present time, the only thing he knew about baseball in 1876 was that it was the year the National League was founded. He didn't even know who any of the original teams were, let alone who any of the players were. But there it was emblazoned in black and white in the historical index. The Chicago White Stockings were the league's inaugural champions. They beat out such teams as the Saint Louis Brown Stockings and the Hartford Dark Blues, as well as the New York Mutuals and Boston Red Caps, just like

Eva had said they did. It was all too astounding to be anything but a real vision. He asked himself how in the world would he even have known all those teams' quirky names, let alone match them with their corresponding cities. If Danny were not already convinced, the book also noted that William Hulbert was the team's owner, as well as the league's founder. Mr. Hulbert fielded a winning team of Albert Spalding, Cap Anson, Cal McVey, Deacon White, and Ross Barnes. For the decisive clincher, the text even mentioned their ballpark at the Twenty-Third Street grounds, which was built to replace their former ballpark, which was destroyed in the Great Chicago Fire of 1871. Danny was now more than convinced. The inordinate and astronomical odds of probability were by far too innumerable to be coincidental.

Danny meandered out of the library in a near stupor. As he drove to the Laundromat, he was gravely troubled inside. As much as he was in love with Eva, he was deeply disturbed about existing on two planes, two dimensions. It was wrong. It wasn't natural. He was never the one to believe in the supernatural, but for some unknown reason, he was being pulled into it by an irresistible force. The matter was immensely vexing for him. He was floored.

While there, waiting for his clothes to finish, he was reading the articles he had brought along that he had made copies of at the library when he'd gone there before with Richie. As he was in the middle of the *Chicago Tribune* story, he was greeted by a female patron. She was a fairly attractive woman in her early sixties. When she asked him why she had never seen him there before, Danny informed her that he had only been going there since May. He introduced himself to her and told her that he was still relatively new in town, having moved there the previous October. The amicable lady introduced herself and asked him how he liked Ashtabula thus far. Danny responded positively to her question about the city and his job and the people that he had met up there since he'd been in town. He told her where he was working, and that his parents had just moved to Florida recently, that it was just him living all alone in Ohio. She told Danny that she had lived in Ashtabula her entire life. Her grandfather had come there from Finland as a young man to work at the docks in the harbor. She sympathized with Danny when he informed her that his grandfather had passed away only a few months prior.

The two had a very nice chat. She shared with Danny some places to see and things to do in the city. They both agreed favorably on the Swedish Pastry Shop when she asked him if he had ever been there and tried any of the delicious desserts. When she eventually pried it out of him about his being single, the affable woman offered to introduce him to her daughter, Collette, who was about his age. She said Collette, who was named after her own mother, was a registered nurse at the nearby hospital. She bragged that Collette was a pretty girl and had simple pleasures.

"She loves going on picnics and spending the day at the lake," she informed him. "She is a very sweet girl, too, very easy to please." She encouraged him to stick around for a bit and meet her, since she would be back soon to pick her up. "She stopped at the clothing store down the road in the plaza. She should be back in about a half hour to pick me up," she said in a tone that seemed to suggest that he wait around to meet her. She told Danny that he seemed like a fine gentleman and assured him that he and her daughter would go well together. Danny thanked her and, somewhat red faced, accepted her tacit invitation to wait around to meet her.

Danny was in the middle of having a conversation with her about his new membership in the area's historical society.

"I have friends who go there," she exuberantly said. "They have a lot of photographs of the railroad and dockworkers from way back. I think my grandfather is in a couple of them."

Just then, in walked a tall, slender, long-legged woman about thirty or so years old. She was slightly tanned, with long, light brown hair, attractive high cheekbones, and the clearest blue eyes Danny could ever remember seeing on a woman. It was Collette. Although it was unbeknownst to Danny at that time, Collette possessed the classic Finnish looks of her female forebears. He just realized that they were classy looks.

"Collette, honey … this is Danny," the woman said to her as she neared the two of them. "I'm having a nice talk with him. He's pretty new in town."

Collette smiled at Danny, who was, as Eva previously pointed out to him, a very handsome young man. Danny returned the smile as he gently shook her petite hand.

“I told you she was pretty,” her mother said, winking at him and causing some embarrassment to Collette.

“She sure is… I mean, you sure are. Such a beautiful name, as well, Collette.”

“It’s Finnish. It was my Grandma’s name, as well.”

Danny hung around for a few moments, as the two of them hit it off very well. They seemed to take well to each other right on the spot. The two ladies seemed to be in a hurry to go to their next appointment, so Danny politely excused himself. Before departing, Collette asked him if he had any favorite nightspots in town that he frequented. He replied that he really hadn’t. She told him that she and her friends from work usually hung out at a place called Sardi’s at the end of the plaza down the road.

“It’s right here on West Avenue. It’s a nice place. It’s a good place to hang out and have a few drinks, maybe go dancing,” she enticed. “We’ll be there tonight around ten. Please feel free to join us. It’s a nice time.”

Danny accepted the invitation. “Only if you’ll have a dance with me,” he joked.

“You got it, Danny!” she exclaimed with a beautiful smile accompanied by her typically wavy Scandinavian lips, her clear blue eyes never being more persuasive.

“Then I guess I’ll see you at Sardi’s around ten,” he affirmed.

Danny raced home from the Laundromat with a newfound enthusiasm in his heart. A very attractive girl was interested in him. She had invited him to hang out and have a couple of drinks and go dancing with her.

While home, he called his parents in Florida. He had been meaning to do so but had been so busy he kept mindlessly putting it off. They had a nice talk. They hounded him to take some time off work and come down there to visit them. Danny assured them that he would but couldn't tell them when for sure. He promised to call them back and talk to them about it soon. Afterward, he called Richie on the phone and talked him into meeting him at the Six for a beer and some billiards. Richie told him that he would meet him there in an hour.

While shooting pool, Danny told Richie about his meeting Collette at the Laundromat. He told her how gorgeous she was and that he was going to meet her at Sardi's that night.

"Well, it's about time, old Wildcat!" Richie exclaimed. "I can't believe it… a real, live, physical girl."

Danny asked him if he had ever been to Sardi's before. Richie told him he had been there once or twice.

"It's nice for a place to meet a woman or bring one. It's not like here, where you just hang out with the guys from work," he told him.

"Well, I'm not planning on hanging out with you chumps from work. I'm meeting a woman. A beautiful woman. I hope it's a classy place."

"Yeah, and it's about time. It's a nice place. Enjoy yourself, Danny boy."

They finished shooting pool and had one more beer together. As they were drinking their beers, Richie asked Danny what the girl's name was that he was going to be meeting that night.

"Collette. Isn't that a sweet name? She is Finnish," he replied.

"Well, let's drink this one for Collette," Richie proposed.

Danny hoisted his bottle and rejoined. "This one's for Collette and the Kaiser."

His toast receiving a hearty chuckle from Richie.

*

Later that night, Danny was getting dressed to go out to Sardi's to meet Collette. He wanted to look nice but casual. He showered and shaved. As he was combing his hair and getting dressed in front of the mirror, a strange thought hit him. He began to think of Eva. He started to feel guilty to be going out to meet another young lady. It was as if he were going out behind her back to go see Collette. Eva's words began to play in his mind from when she was telling him of her former fiancé, how she told him that she knew men and understood that they got lonesome. He brought to mind how Eva wiped a tear from her eye when she recalled how her fiancé had double-crossed her and broke her heart with another woman, his own sister-in-law. He remembered with fondness how he'd held her in his arms and comforted her, how she gently kissed him, how he was falling in love with her and she with him. But Danny was lonely. He was a lonesome young man in Ashtabula. Eva was an image, an apparition, a vision from 1876. Perhaps very real and lifelike, but yet a phantom vision. This was 1985. This was the physical world. Collette was real; she was flesh and blood. She was here for him in the here and now. Maybe she would be the one he had been looking for all this time. He finished getting ready and took off in his car to Sardi's on West Avenue.

He got inside and ambled around for a minute. It was somewhat crowded inside. Danny assumed that it must be a popular nightspot. The place was not too large, however, and it didn't take him long to spot Collette sitting at a table with two other girls. She also spotted him and gestured for him to come join them.

"Danny, come over here!" she yelled as he approached them. "Danny, this is Jackie and Tanya. I work with them at the hospital. Girls, this is Danny, who I met today at the Laundromat."

They all invited him to sit down. Tanya elbowed Collette and told her, "Maybe I should start hanging out at the Laundromat with you."

Danny quickly endeared himself to the girls by buying them a round of drinks. He sat patiently at the table, out of the loop for a while as the three nurses vented about their stressful week at work.

"I had a patient in ICU today that crashed," Jackie groaned. "I had to hang a lidocaine drip to keep him out of V-TACH. His wife was out there in the hall, yelling and screaming at everybody."

"You think that's bad," Tanya chimed in with a one-upping tone, "this morning we had to take care of fifteen admissions … without enough staff, as usual. They floated one of our girls to another floor, and we were short. Yesterday, one of my patients had PVCs. We had to transfer him to ICU."

"Yeah, thanks a lot," Collette weighed in. "I was working up there then. You couldn't handle that one on your monitor floor?"

This went on for a few more minutes as Danny patiently waited them out. After a while, though, after a few more rounds, Danny loosened up with the girls and soon held their attention. As the night went on, he had them in stitches with his funny and charming personality. Later, as some good music was playing in the nightclub, Danny and Collette danced a few songs together. Later, as Danny was about to get back home, Collette jotted down her phone number on one of the bar counter napkins and gave it to him, exhorting him to give her a call that coming week and they could talk. Danny elatedly strolled out to his car as if walking on air. He could have flown home, he was so smitten, his convertible in tow, merely going along for the ride.

When he arrived home at around 2:00 in the morning, he went to his spare bedroom and turned on the light. He stood in front of the mirror, clutching Collette's phone number in his hand. The mirror appeared different to him. It was the same mirror; it just seemed to lack its usual brilliance. It didn't have the same sparkle as it normally seemed to have in the light as it regally towered like a giant among his antique furniture in the corner. Maybe he was just imagining it. Danny went to bed and lay there staring in the mirror's direction. It was a cloudy night. Thunder was rumbling in the background. There was no glint of moonlight to give the mirror its usual vivaciousness. It stood there lifeless. He drifted off to sleep. Soon, he was awakened by a loud cracking of thunder. He sat up and again stared toward the mirror's glass. Soon, a sharp flash of lightning emanated from the darkness and illuminated the sky, penetrating Danny's bedroom, causing the mirror to emit an ominous, phantomlike glow. Danny was startled. He got that same spine-chilling feeling that he received earlier at the library. He remembered looking around the library for Eva's ghost. He started scanning around his bedroom for the same. Was she angry about him meeting Collette?

11

Mid-June 1985

The following Monday morning, Danny glided into work with a sense of purpose and a new outlook on life. For the first time in quite a while, a few years, he had met a girl that he felt he could have a really special relationship with. She was very attractive, with a nice and easygoing personality. She also seemed very fun to be around. He could hardly wait to see Richie that morning to tell him all about the other night.

"How did it go Saturday night?" Richie jumped him, beating him to the punch.

"It was really nice. The place was a bit crowded, but all in all, Sardi's is a nice place," he answered, holding back on him.

"I don't mean the place, you moron. How was the meeting with Collette?"

"Oh, Collette," Danny mused. "We had a really great time. She's a lot of fun. We had a few drinks and a lot of good laughs. We even danced a little."

"He's back, man!! Wildcat Danny is back in business," Ritchie boisterously announced to the other lab workers. "I'm so happy you are dating real women again, my friend," he concluded.

Danny returned a sarcastic laugh. He reminded Richie and everyone that he and Collette were not actually dating yet, but he was planning on calling her that evening to talk with her and maybe ask her out. Needless to say, Danny was floating on air for the rest of the workday.

Danny and Richie worked over for about an hour to catch up on the busy workload. Danny agreed to go to the Six afterward for a quick beer and some billiards. He made sure his buddy knew that he couldn't stay too long, as he was anxious to call Collette around 6:00. "Don't worry, Danny boy," Richie chided. "I won't interfere with you two lovebirds. Sheesh, I wish you'd go back to falling in love with girls in your dreams."

"I can guarantee you, my friend, she is a dream girl. I can tell you that for sure," Danny straightly informed him.

Richie sighed dramatically. "I guess you still are pathetic, my man. You still are pathetic."

The two played a game of pool and had a quick beer. Within an hour, Danny was heading home to make his much-anticipated phone call.

Danny talked with Collette for about an hour. For someone who didn't really care to be on the phone hardly at all, that was some sort of record for him. Danny reiterated how nice of a time he'd had with her Saturday night. Collette responded in kind. They chatted some about where each of them worked. She told Danny that she knew a couple of girls that worked in the offices where he worked. When she described her workday at the hospital from Sunday afternoon, Danny had to jokingly ask her to speak in plain English. Collette giggled when he explained how confused he was as he patiently sat at their table Saturday night as she and her friends vented in hospital lingo about everyone's stressful jobs.

The two of them talked on for a while. She had a wonderful voice. Danny admired it. It was soft but distinctly incisive. Danny was fully enjoying the whole conversation. Like her mother boasted, she definitely seemed like a sweet girl. As they talked and compared their daily existences with each other, it was obvious that they were both searching for somebody special in their lives. Danny quipped that if the world were a box of crayons, he felt as though he would be burnt sienna.

"Burnt sienna? What is that?" she giggled.

"You know, the one in the box that people look at kind of funny. They really can't find any use for it. It kind of gets ignored," he cracked, causing her to laugh.

"You are so silly," she chuckled. "I have a hard time believing that."

After chatting for a little bit longer, Danny told Collette that he would love to take her out to dinner one day that week. "Your mother told me at the Laundromat before you walked in that you love to spend time at the lake. Maybe we could hang out at the beach after we eat sometime."

Collette mentioned that she worked afternoon shift at the hospital that week but said she would love to go out on Saturday with him. When he asked her what she liked, she told him that there was a nice seafood restaurant at the top of Bridge Street in the harbor.

"It's just a couple of blocks from Walnut Beach. We can hang out there afterward," she said.

Danny told her he had driven past the place several times but had never eaten there. He told her he would really be looking forward to Saturday and said he would call her around midweek and confirm it. The two of them hung up. Danny was elated.

The next day at work, Danny couldn't stop telling Richie and the other guys about his pending date with Collette. Richie sarcastically bemoaned the fact that Dany would be on a leash from now on and wouldn't be allowed to hang out with him or the others anymore. Lucky and Wild Bill joined Richie in the razzing and wouldn't let up on him the whole day.

"Just to prove to you three idiots that I'm still as free as a bird, I'll meet you at the Six after work today," Danny countered.

"What's the catch?" they demanded, "Is she out of town today or something?"

"No," Danny fired back jokingly, "she works evenings today and tomorrow."

"Ooh, lucky us. Aren't we the lucky ones? We get to hang out with pathetic Danny Dubenion. Don't get any sap all over us, lover boy."

They all laughed, including Danny. Richie asked him if that meant he would be able to go fishing with him the next day after work. Danny concurred.

"I would be delighted to join you, Mr. Kelleher, in the fine art of angling. Will you please teach me all your secrets for letting the big one slip away?"

*

Danny joined his buddy for some bass fishing again on the breakwater rocks of Conneaut's Lake Erie shore. Danny had a new purpose in life indeed. They laughed and joked and made up a few new urban legends. Danny didn't even mind that he couldn't catch a single fish. Richie didn't fare much better. After they wrapped up the whole venture, they headed for their usual spot, the East Sixth Street Café, their beloved Six. They enjoyed a couple of beers and more than a couple of laughs, as Danny and Collette were the subject of most of Richie and the regular patrons' friendly harassment. They actually stayed long enough to shoot a few extra games of pool. Danny was loose. Richie commented that he had not seen Danny this way since he had met him at work back in October.

The rest of the workweek went smoothly. Danny was starry eyed. He worked a little more overtime in the lab on Thursday and then rushed home to call Collette on the phone to confirm their date for Saturday. Everything was a go. Collette told him that she was really looking forward to it. She expressed hope that the weather would be nice so they would be able to enjoy a nice walk on Walnut Beach. Danny agreed but assured her that regardless of the weather, they would have a nice time together. After talking to Collette, Danny washed up and took the 1965 Wildcat, top down, to Garfield's for a nice, well-deserved dinner.

*

Finally, Saturday arrived. Danny had some running around to do in the morning. He, of course, went to his favorite haunt for breakfast, Garfield's. He needed to mail some bills downtown. He went back to Columbus Avenue to the barbershop and got himself a nice trim. Afterward, he drove down to the car wash and gave the old Wildcat a good shining. Later, since the early afternoon air was so nice, after he drove home, he went for a nice stroll down Columbus Avenue and down East Sixth Street to the harbor. All the while, he was thinking about Collette and what he would talk to her about. When he got back home, he took a nice shower and got ready to go and pick her up. The weather was turning out to be near perfect. The sky was almost cloudless, and the temperature would be hovering around eighty degrees. He drove back around through the harbor and onto Lake Avenue, then onto West Thirteenth Street to her rented place on Myrtle Avenue.

Danny arrived at her front door and was greeted cheerfully. She invited him in for a couple of minutes to show him around her place.

"I know it's an older house," she told him, "but it's really close to work." She pointed in the direction of the general hospital.

"Mine is a lot older than this. You have a nice place," he replied. She didn't live too far from the top of Bridge Street either, and they were there in minutes. Collette ordered her favorite fish dinner, Icelandic scrod. Danny got the haddock.

The two of them were making small talk and enjoying a drink before the food arrived. As a sign that she was attracted to Danny, as they were chatting, she was tensely clutching her napkin under the table in her left hand while nervously picking at it and shredding it with her right hand. They were enjoying each other's company, however, and both felt at ease enough to mention that one day they would love to have a couple of children, in spite of the fact that he was already just about thirty-five and she was thirty-three. The meals came, and they had a great time throughout their early dinner. Danny was full of his good charm, frequently making the slightly nervous Collette giggle.

When they had finished eating, they motored up Lake Avenue to West First Street for the quick jaunt to Walnut Beach.

"I love your car. What year is it?" Collette commented as Danny drove into the beach parking lot.

"It's a 1965," he answered.

"I love the color. What kind of blue is that?"

"It's Astro blue," Danny replied. "I had it repainted in the original color."

They got out and started to walk around the beach. She remarked how her older brother, Randy, her only sibling, once had a 1963 Impala. He had purchased it right out of high school in 1966.

"He's ended up having to go to Vietnam," she lamented. "He seemed okay when he returned home, but some years later, he got really sick. He had cancer and died about seven years ago."

Danny felt very badly for her. He figured that it must have been from the effects of Agent Orange exposure, but he didn't want to put her through him even mentioning it. He simply expressed his sympathy to her.

"My father passed away about three years ago. Now it's just me and Mom. I try to help her out whenever I can."

"By the time that I got out of college, the war was winding down. Fortunately for me, I missed out on 'Nam," Danny said softly, expressing his empathy for those who had to go there.

As they continued to walk down the shoreline, Danny told her about his parents moving to Florida and his Grandpa Ed passing away a few months back.

"It's only me up here now," he sighed.

"Well, I'm glad you're here, anyway," she said as she playfully punched his arm.

He talked about his job and how he moved up there from Niles back in October. He told her about him getting involved with the local historical society. He admitted that he hadn't dated anyone in a long while, not since well before he moved from Niles.

"I just don't get a chance to really meet anybody nice anymore," he acknowledged.

She explained to him that she went to nursing school right in town at the Kent State Ashtabula campus. She had been so busy with school and now with working at the hospital a lot, she really hadn't had the time to meet someone nice, as well.

"Well," Danny playfully sighed. "I guess we'll just have to be stuck with each other."

That remark caused Collette to smile broadly and say, "Well, Danny boy, we'll just have to see about that."

They took off their shoes and ran ankle deep along the refreshing waters of the shoreline. Danny stooped down to pick up some smooth flat stones to skim across the lake's calm surface. They got into an impromptu contest to see who could cause a stone to make the most number of skips through the water. Danny remarked that with no wind and the smooth waters, it made the stones move easier atop the water. Danny also collected a handful of driftwood that had made its way near their feet.

"Did you ever collect beach glass?" she asked him as she treaded carefully near the soft shoreline near the lake's edge, looking down as if searching for something.

"No, I've never even heard of beach glass," he responded.

"They're broken pieces of glass that have been lost in the Great Lakes and other bodies of water, mostly broken or discarded bottles. Over time, they make their way to the shore.

Lake Erie has tons of it hidden just under the surface of the sand, almost right on top."

They searched the sand together and plucked out smoothed shards of colored glass that had been ground down through a lot of exposure to the rolling and churning action of the waves. After a little effort, they claimed a handful of brightly colored gem-like pieces. Some were red, orange, yellow, and deep blue.

"Maybe we'll find some Astro blue ones, Danny," she joked, eliciting a laugh from him.

Danny was having such a time. *Collette is a wonderful girl*, he thought. It made him forget those phantom apparitions he had been visiting in his night visions.

"Come on, slowpoke!" she challenged, "I'll race you to the lighthouse." To put it simply, it was a great first date. Danny wouldn't have to wait long for a second date, either. When he asked Collette if she would be interested in taking a ride the next day to Geneva and maybe to Fairport Harbor and then find a place to eat, she didn't hesitate to accept.

*

It was a pleasant Sunday drive heading along the Lake Erie coast as Danny and Collette motored west of Ashtabula toward Geneva-on-the-Lake. Along the way, they passed by the college she'd attended for nursing school. She laughed as she told Danny about some of the weird professors that she'd encountered on her way to her nursing degree.

"The psychology professor tried to cram all of that '70s junk down into our heads," she told him. The two of them talked and laughed the whole fifteen-mile trip. Collette was definitely an '80s girl—the music she liked, the movies, the lingo. She was an absolute contemporary female. Danny, of course, was her antithesis. He loved his old-time music from the 1950s and '60s. He appreciated all the old-time classic movies, television shows, the whole culture. He did not enjoy the contemporary scene at all. He'd even noticed when he'd picked her up the day before and she'd showed him around her place that she did not possess even one piece of antique furniture, and she didn't appear to own any antiques at all. It did not matter to him, though. In their case, opposites were definitely attracting. Besides, he couldn't resist her good looks and her acute sense of humor.

While in Geneva, they enjoyed a game of miniature golf, walking around finding a good ice cream cone, and just plain making each other laugh.

"I love how you make me laugh, Danny," she confessed. "Working at the hospital, especially the ICU, is very stressful. It can drag you way down. You cheer me up."

"My pleasure. I enjoy making you laugh. You've brought me a lot of cheer yourself," he echoed.

They continued their walk until they reached the beach. Again, Collette took off her sandals and walked ankle deep in the cool, wavy water.

"This feels great, Danny. Come join me."

Danny took his shoes off as well and cuffed his blue jeans so they wouldn't get wet.

"Why don't you wear short pants? It's over eighty degrees out here," she prodded.

"I just like my blue jeans," he answered simply.

"Come on, Danny, I want to see those legs. Don't you want me to see your sexy legs?" she teased him, laughing.

They walked around for a while and then proceeded westward for another twenty miles to Fairport Harbor. Along the way, they talked more about life and work. Both agreed that someday they would like to be doing something else instead of the jobs they currently had. They just didn't know what. She reiterated that hospital work was very stressful, but she had invested so much money and effort going to college and ten years at the hospital that it would be a waste to try to start some new profession.

Danny was thoroughly enjoying the wind in his hair as they cruised along the roadway. He was content to listen to Collette do most of the talking. He heard about all her friends at work and again about her deceased brother, Randy, and about her family.

"You know that Fairport Harbor, just like Ashtabula, has a large Finnish American population," she informed him.

Danny told her that her mother mentioned that she was Finnish and that her grandfather came here from Finland.

"My father's grandfather came here from Finland, as well," she told him. "He was a Swedish Finn."

When Dany asked her what a Swedish Finn was, she remarked that they were folks from Finland who many generations ago went to Sweden for a generation or so and then came to America.

"I've heard of Swedish fish, but never Swedish Finns," Danny joked, making her giggle.

While at Fairport Harbor, the two of them found a little diner and had something to eat. They walked around the shoreline and went to the two lighthouses that the town was noted for—the West Breakwater Lighthouse and the scenic Fairport Harbor Lighthouse. As they were strolling along the water's edge, Collette grabbed Danny's hand and held it firmly all the way back to the car. Her smile was charming, her clear blue eyes enchanting. Danny was captivated. He had been looking for a girl like this for a very long time. As they drove back to Ashtabula, they seemed all talked out. Collette just leaned on his shoulder and quietly listened to the music playing on the car radio. Danny was in seventh heaven.

They got back to town and hung out together for a while. He asked to see her again. She said that she had to work the evening shift for the next three days but would love to do something on Thursday. Danny asked what other kind of food she enjoyed, and she proposed the Bali H'ai Chinese and Polynesian restaurant across town on Route 20. The third date was set.

*

The following day after work, it was gray and rainy. Collette was working the evening shift. Richie had an appointment after work, so Danny couldn't hang out with him at the Six. He decided to satisfy his craving for local history by taking the short drive through the harbor and up around the Walnut Beach area to patronize three of the area's showcases of Ashtabula Harbor's rich past. He visited the Hubbard House, the marine and maritime museum, and the Harbor-Topky Memorial Library. He was treated to an array of old photos with captions and write-ups of turn-of-the-century Bridge Street, as well as the Pinney Docks and the New York Central docks and railyard from the 1950s and '60s. There was a phot of the coal conveyor under construction in 1967. He examined some much older photos and artifacts from the Ashtabula River and harbor from its early beginnings around 1870. There were photographic displays of the old "strawberry box" coal unloading machines, which came into use starting in 1894. On display were also several models of train engines and machines from different periods of motive power operated throughout the past century in what was once one of the world's busiest ports.

Danny was enjoying all the material the three institutions had to offer. It was just the right stuff for such a railroad aficionado as he. He marveled at the fact that as much as he was impressed with the current volume of commerce and hustle and bustle of activity in the harbor at that present time in 1985, what he was witnessing was nothing by comparison to the area during its glorious heyday thirty years, fifty years, or even nearly a century prior. All the pictures and displays depicted a hub of activity during an era when Ashtabula was, according to the curator of the museum, at one time second only to Singapore in volume of reciprocal shipment activity. Danny was taking it all in. Just being near Walnut Beach reminded him of what a nice time he had there with Collette the other day. He was enjoying patronizing the memories of Lake Erie's legendary past, while making new memories there in the present.

Next, he came upon a display commemorating the Ashtabula Bridge Disaster. His fond memory of the last couple of joyous days with Collette were turned into bitterness as he once again visited the absolute horror of that ill-fated day that had occurred literally right down the road. His heart sank to his feet as he thought about all those poor souls that suffered and perished. He again began to think about Eva. He began to realize how much he missed her. The one outstanding problem, to put it mildly, was that, as sweet and lovely as Eva was, she was still just an apparition. She was a paranormal, preternatural essence—albeit a very lifelike and loving essence, yet still, one who resided in another dimension. By huge contrast, Collette was real, living, breathing, flesh and bone. Attractive flesh and bone, at that, with a great and fun personality. Was there really any other choice?

*

On Wednesday, Danny and Richie worked over an hour or so again and decided to make a quick stop at the café for a beer and a game of pool to help wind down. Danny was really missing being with Collette. Of course, the guys at the bar, including Richie, razzed him about her. Danny was unfazed. He told everyone there that he was really starting to like her, and maybe something was starting to become of it.

When he got home, Danny went to take a nice shower. While in the shower, he got the idea to go Garfield's and pick up a little something to eat for the two of them and surprise Collette at the hospital for her dinner break. After he left Garfield's with the food, he had an additional thought. He remembered when he'd met her mother that day at the Laundromat, she told him how much they loved the Swedish Pastry Shop. He decided to stop on the way to the hospital and pick up a couple of their famous coconut bars for Collette and her mother.

Collette was very pleasantly surprised indeed to find Danny waiting on her floor with a bag of hot sandwiches in one hand and a pastry bag in the other. She thanked him vociferously, while letting out her well-known giggle at the same time. Then she gave him a healthy squeeze.

"I just couldn't wait until tomorrow to see you," he told her.

"Ahh, aren't you a sweetheart. Hey, you brought me something from the Swedish Pastry Shop?" she excitedly squealed. "I love that place. Don't you just love their funny sign?" She introduced him to her coworkers, who all took to him on the spot.

"You're all she talks about," proclaimed one of her fellow nurses. "It's Danny this and Danny that." She winked at Danny, making Collette blush.

"Don't listen to her. She exaggerates," Collette joked, accompanied by the giggle.

They went down to the cafeteria and had a quick visit while eating. Before leaving, Danny confirmed their dinner-and-movie date for the next evening.

*

Danny left his house a little early to pick up Collette for their date the next evening. He first wanted to stop down at the harbor to go to the flower shop and pick her up some red roses. He decided to include a stuffed teddy bear for good measure. He also wanted to quickly peek in on Mr. Kirkpatrick and confirm the date and time for the upcoming historical society meeting. He was looking forward to hearing the speaker talk about the area's railroad history.

Mr. Kirkpatrick would go on to tell him that the speaker was set to discuss the other, lesser known, Ashtabula train–streetcar wreck that happened in town in December of 1912. He encouraged Danny to feel free to ask the speaker any questions pertaining to the bridge disaster when he got finished talking about the other wreck. He said the man would talk to Danny about it all night if he would let him. Danny told him that he was really looking forward to it and hoped to get a lot of nagging questions answered.

He got to Collette's place around 5:30. She was very touched with the roses and gushed fondly when he handed her the teddy bear.

"Hmm," she exuberantly pondered out loud, "What do you think I should call him? How about Danny, so I can cuddle with him every night so I'm not lonely?"

They went out to eat at the Bali H'ai and then went to see a movie. They had a very enjoyable time together.

*

In the ensuing days, a romantic relationship began to blossom. It began when she invited him over to her place a few days after their dinner-and-movie date. Danny was falling hard for her. One day after work, he drove east, past Lake Shore Park a couple of miles. He parked his car off the road near a secluded section of the beach. As he leisurely walked on the warm sand, skimming stones across the water, he began to think about the day way back in October when he'd first moved to Ashtabula. He recalled when he was looking around and surveying the beach and scanning the water and the surrounding docks, wondering if he would ever find that special girl for his life, someone sweet and caring to share it with. He considered if perhaps Collette was that one remarkable woman that he had been long searching for, the one he had been pining for. She was very beautiful, indeed, he thought. She was very special. He picked up a smooth, flat stone and let it fly above the top of the water, giving it to the insatiable waves that were gently curling into the shore.

"Yes, very beautiful," he whispered to himself. "Everything about her. Maybe she's the one."

That night, in the middle of the night as he slept, Danny experienced another perplexing nightmare. He found himself at the bottom of an empty old railroad hopper car in the middle of the harbor's massive railyard. The train that he was on was methodically moving forward toward the spot where the huge crane bucket from an immense ore bridge was unloading tons of iron ore from a ship's hold and transferring it to the empty hopper cars, filling them to the top. His car was nearing the loading point. He struggled to get out of the car but wasn't able. He fell back down to the bottom of the hollow, cavernous hopper. He looked up from his deep pit and saw nothing but a clear, blue sky. What appeared more strangely was that the ore bridge had no base or platform for which to stand upon and anchor it to the ground. It just sort of seemed to hover over the east side of the railroad docks, floating, in spite of its ponderous load. He was moments away from being crumbled into nothingness by tons of the taconite iron ore pellets that were about to engulf his hopper car. He tried to scream, but not a sound would come out of his mouth.

Danny tossed in his sleep but didn't wake. The grim dream continued. The next thing he knew, he was on top of the ridge at Chestnut Grove Cemetery. It was warm up there, yet for some reason, he was shaking as if it were freezing cold. He felt compelled to walk to where the monument stood. It took him quite some time to reach it. When he arrived at the site, he was shocked to find two monuments side by side. They were identical to each other in design. There were no words or names upon either of them, except for Eva's. Her name was inscribed all around the front of one of the edifices, maybe fifty or more times. There was nothing on the front of the other one. On the back side of each monument were eyes, numerous eyes, all around. The eyes were not in pairs, like on a human face, but were all singular. They were all staring at him. Then it began to feel very cold and windy.

Danny peered down and viewed the uneven stone walkway. The parking lot below was buried in snow. The snow appeared to be at least ten feet high, maybe deeper. It seemed to get deeper and deeper as he stood there. He began to wonder out loud how he was ever going to get down from there. Suddenly, the snow melted and became a turbulent river, a torrent flowing from the cemetery and raging toward town. Within seconds, the river stopped. The river ceased its flowing and became stagnant and malodorous. He began to hear sobbing again, just like the last time he had this nightmare. Then he heard laughing. It was not a joyous laughter but was very lurid and uninviting. He began to hear footsteps as if he were being chased. Danny tried to run, but he stumbled and fell off the ridge toward the marshy, fetid water. He didn't land but kept falling and falling. There seemed to be no end. That's when he suddenly woke up. His heart was pounding. He was in a cold sweat. He got up to get a nice cold glass of water. It was just after three in the morning. He sat down at the kitchen table, wiping his perspiring, clammy forehead, contemplating the meaning of it all. What he didn't realize was that there was a conflict taking place in his heart, way down deep in the recesses of his psyche.

*

The following weekend brought with it the annual Harbor Days Festival on Bridge Street. Danny drove to Collette's place, and together they walked from there down to the harbor to enjoy the food and music, the sidewalk art, and—especially for Danny—the many classic cars lined all the way up Bridge Street for the annual car show. Collette jokingly scolded him for not entering his Wildcat in the show, telling him that it would have looked great alongside of all the others. While they were strolling around listening to the live music, Danny told her about the strange dream he'd had about being in the cemetery earlier in the week. She sarcastically told him that it probably meant that he needed to learn to relax more.

"You need to come over to my place more often," she said with a wink.

She grabbed his hand, and together they paraded up and down Bridge Street hand in hand. They both bumped into a few people from their workplaces and made some quick small talk. After a while, they got something there to eat and walked back to Collette's place, where the romance continued.

Before Danny drove back home, Collette invited him to come back later that night for a get-together with Tanya and Jackie from work. At first, he didn't want to interfere with her girls'-only night, but she insisted.

"Come on. I've been telling them all bout you since that night we all met at Sardi's. They want to get together with you."

After a bit of cajoling, he promised to stop by later that night. “All right,” he finally agreed, “but I’d rather come back and just be here alone with you.”

“Oh, there will be more time for that,” she chuckled.

Danny told her that, in the meantime, he might as well meet Richie at the East Sixth Street Café. The guys were having a little billiards tournament going on down there. He kissed her goodbye and said he would see her later.

Later that night, around 10:00, Dany drove back to Collette’s place. She greeted him at the door. The 1980s music was playing loudly, much to his irritation.

“The girls are in the kitchen,” she told him with a devious wink. “Come join us.”

Danny ambled over to the kitchen, where Collette was leading him. To his utter shock and heart-dropping dismay, there were a couple of scruffy guys in there with them. The three girls were snorting lines of cocaine with them from the top of the kitchen table. They invited Danny over to join them. His face grew pale. He refused.

“Come on, Danny. Don’t be a prude!” Jackie goaded.

“Ah, that’s okay. I really don’t.” Danny squirmed.

“Come on, sweetie. Don’t worry. We just do it now and then to escape a little bit,” Collette retorted, feeling somewhat guilty.

“We have stressful jobs,” Tanya shot back, trying to justify the whole matter. “This just helps us to unwind.”

Collette was more than a little embarrassed. Danny couldn't help noticing that one of the disheveled punks couldn't stop ogling Collette. She took Danny by the hand an led him to the living room couch.

"I'm sorry, Danny. I didn't think they were going to bring those guys over here. I didn't know that they would bring any of that over. Please, sit down and relax. I'll be back out in a little bit. I'm sorry, Danny."

Collette slipped back into the kitchen, which had now grown hushed. Danny sat there in a stupor with what seemed to be a mild case of shock. The giddy laughter that had emanated from there, which greeted him at his arrival, had ceased. There was enough embarrassment to around for the six of them.

Moments later, Collette came back out to placate Danny, who seemed a little upset about the whole thing. "Don't be upset, Danny," she entreated. "I just use it a little… just once in a while to take the edge off. You can understand."

Ashamed, Collette retreated back to the kitchen. Danny sat alone on the couch for a few minutes and tolerated the loud music. He again began to think of Eva. She was a vastly more innocent young lady from a more innocent time. He still really liked Collette. He reasoned that maybe she did only experiment with cocaine, and maybe he would be able to tolerate that flaw in her. Maybe he could convince her to just stop doing it. After a few more awkward minutes, he excused himself and drove back home.

By Monday morning at work, Danny was still stunned. Although he was the only one at Collette's place the other night who had not done the cocaine, it was he who felt benumbed by it. He was quiet all day at work. It was obvious to everybody that something was eating at him. They all could have guessed that it had something to do with Collette. Richie tried to pry it out of him all day, but to no avail. He told him that he and Collette were still seeing each other, and he would talk to him about it privately at the Six after work. Needless to say, the entire workday seemed like an eternity to him.

Later on at the Six, Danny tried to rationalize the problem. "I really like this girl. I don't know, man. Maybe she just does use it a little. Maybe I can help her to quit doing it."

Richie was less sympathetic. "You can't help people like that, dude!" he roared. "She did you wrong, man. She should have told you she took that junk before you two started getting serious."

"I know, man. But I still really like her."

"Come one, man. You like her looks. She's trouble. You can get girls. There are better ones out there."

"Well, I really want this one, all right?"

"Well, I'm going to shoot some pool. You can stay at the bar and cry in your beer," Richie said coarsely as he arose and walked away from the counter.

Danny sat quietly and gazed at the television set on the shelf that was broadcasting a midafternoon baseball game. Oddly enough, the Cleveland Indians were in Chicago, playing the White Sox. Danny stared blankly up at screen, daydreaming about how Eva was warmly telling him how her father had taken her to the Twenty-Third Street grounds to watch her beloved White Stockings play in their National League games.

*

In the ensuing days, Danny called Collette and tried to talk to her about what had happened. She was standoffish, maybe more than just embarrassed. Strangely, she acted more disappointed with him than he was with her. In the days ahead, she put him off more and more, insisting that he was too square and uptight for her. Soon after, she broke it off. Danny was crushed. In spite of her weakness, he still really liked her very much. He was willing to overlook that character flaw and maintain a special relationship with her. Whether it was her friends' urging or her own feelings, she was the one who wasn't willing to abide with him.

Again, Danny found himself at the Six with Richie. He was more figuratively than literally crying in his beer.

"I was really falling for her," he lamented into Richie's sympathetic ear, while quaffing his beer.

"I know, man. Like I said before, you can find another girl, and you will—a good girl," he encouraged.

"I thought I had found her," he stewed.

"Come on, buddy!" Richie patted him on the back and stood up from the bar stool. "The table is open. Let's shoot us a game of pool."

Danny reluctantly joined his pal at the billiard table. His heart was obviously not in it. He listlessly shot the cue ball without really taking his time to aim. The usually competitive Richie patiently tolerated Danny's lack of concentration. Danny suffered through the game until Richie beat him. Then he sidled back over to the bar to polish off a couple more bottles of beer.

Danny decided to get back home. He just felt that he had to be alone.

"Are you gonna be okay, man?" his buddy dejectedly asked.

"Yeah, I guess I'll be fine." He sighed, trying to force a happy expression for him.

"You call me if you need to talk, buddy. All right?" Richie offered.

"Thanks, man. I'll be okay. See you tomorrow," he replied.

Danny moped out to the parking lot and drove back home. He walked in, tossed his keys on the kitchen table, and then went to his room and slumped down on his bed in a flurry of mental exhaustion.

He lay down on his bed for a little more than an hour, trying to get some rest. He got very little. He got up and trudged over to the spare bedroom and gazed into the mirror. He looked like hell. He felt even worse. He got undressed and took a long, hot shower. He was sorely wounded. He was surely stinging from it. He finished his shower, dried off, and contemplated what to eat. He plodded over to the closet to find some clothes. While in the closet, he fumbled around for a nice, clean shirt to put on. While sifting through his wardrobe, he accidently knocked his period suit off of its hanger, and it fell on the floor. He bent over to pick it back up and grabbed his frock coat by the breast pocket. It felt as though something were inside of it, something soft. He carried the coat over to the bed and reached inside.

He pulled out what looked like a handkerchief that was folded up and stuffed inside of it. He unfurled it curiously. What he amazingly found was a fine lace, hand-embroidered handkerchief with an embroidered Spencerian scripted *E* on the face of it. It was Eva's. The one she had folded up and put in his coat pocket when she used the word *mizpah.* The wonder of it all was that it was still fairly new looking, just like when she had given it to him. He held it up to his nose with wondrous expectation. He could smell the beautiful fragrance of her perfume.

"Eva is real!" he gasped audibly. "She is real, physically, bodily. She is not just an apparition or a phantom from another dimension. She is real. I was physically with her on that train. I was on the Pacific Express, physically among all those people!"

His heart raced. He was shaking. His nervous excitement caused him to fumble the handkerchief to the floor. It wafted in the air and then slid on the floor, halting in front of the antique mirror. He stooped down to pick it up and caught a glimpse of himself. To his utmost astonishment, he looked and beheld an open and uncovered cut upon the brow of his forehead.

12

Danny put his hand on his brow and gently felt where it was cut.

"It feels the same!" he exclaimed. "It's the same cut that I received on the train when I fell in the express car. It's exactly the same. It hurts the same, also." Danny was bewildered. He gazed long and deep into the mirror. "Eva?" he called out. "Are you there?" There was no reply. Danny was perplexed, to say the least. "This is unbelievable!" he cried. He held his one hand on his forehead while stooping down to retrieve her handkerchief with the other. He stood back up and slowly raised the handkerchief back to his nose, taking in the sweet savor of her aroma. "Eva is real. I was really there. I wat to go back. I want to be with her forever. I want to save her and all those poor people from that horrible disaster." Danny planned on going back that night. He finally figured it out. It was always at night and when he was dressed in his suit from Eva's time period that he was able to go back. He would go back that night, he thought, and do whatever he could to alter her fate and everyone else's on that train.

Danny was so enthusiastic he was almost hysterical. The thought of Eva being a real flesh-and-blood person and the fact that he could travel back in time to be with her had him near delirium he was so joyful. Danny neatly put his suit back together on the hanger and set it on the doorknob of his closet. It would be all set to put on that night to travel back to Eva. He took another long, slow draw from her handkerchief, delighting his senses. He folded it up and tucked it back into his coat pocket. It was around 7:00. He decided to fix himself something to eat. He poured some water in a pot and put it on the stove to cook some spaghetti. He went into the bathroom to wash his hands and tend to the cut above his brow. He turned on the faucet and then looked in the mirror. What he saw next was staggering.

He did a quick double take as he stared into the bathroom mirror. Suddenly, his cut above his brow was no more. It was totally healed up. He touched the skin where it had been, and it was totally like new. It felt fine, also. Danny was flabbergasted. He shook it off, however, and went back to the kitchen to tend to his supper. When he finished making his food, he brought it into his living room and ate while watching his favorite old television shows.

After a couple of hours, Danny decided to get ready for bed. He went to the spare bedroom and turned on the light. He headed for the closet door to take his suit from off the doorknob. He picked it up and began putting it on. He gazed out of the window. It was a dark and cloudy night. It was breezy. Rain was looming on the horizon. Danny was in great anticipation as he put on his trousers and shirt. This would be the first time he would see Eva since making the startling discovery that she was real, and he had actually been time traveling back to the past to physically be with her. As amazing as those past visits with her were, knowing that it was all actually taking place in the corporeal realm, tangibly, would only make it exponentially more amazing to be with her again.

Danny was almost finished getting dressed. Soon he would be in bed falling asleep, and then the process of transmutation would begin. Soon he would find himself in the loving arms of the beautiful and warmhearted Miss Eva Lindfors. He grabbed his cravat and headed for his antique mirror to tie it on in front of it. He looked up into it and again he was shocked to see that the cut over his brow had reappeared. He felt it, and it was still sore. He was amazed. It wasn't a throbbing pain but enough to be bothersome and disturb his sleep. He finished tying on the cravat and then ambled over to the bathroom to get something from the medicine cabinet to dull and deaden the pain. Again, his reflection in the bathroom mirror showed no blemish at all upon his forehead. He came back to his spare bedroom to put on the finishing touches of his outfit. He walked over to his dresser and seized his John Bull top hat from off the top of it. He gazed again into the antique mirror. Again, his cut had mysteriously reappeared.

"There is definitely something insane about this mirror!" he acknowledged nervously. Then he turned out the light and excitedly jumped in bed, clutching his hat firmly against his chest, and tried his hardest to fall asleep.

Falling asleep right away of course proved to be a difficult task. Not only was he very eager to see her, which made it almost impossible to fall asleep, but suddenly he was gripped by a sense of deep brooding. It had just dawned on him that Eva might be very angry or deeply hurt over his being with Collette. He could never forget the heartbreak she expressed when telling him about what her former fiancé did to her, how it crushed and devastated her. It took her all those years for another man to gain her trust again, and it was he himself!

"She trusted me," he said to himself regretfully, "so much so that she was willing to marry me, if I was willing."

Danny knew with all his heart and soul that if he had known before what he just found out now, that this all was a reality and no dream, no mere vision, he would never have sought love and affection from somebody else. *Perhaps Eva will understand and be able to comprehend that, he thought. I will have to be honest and up front with her about it and confront the issue. I hope she will be able to acknowledge that it is only her that I love and desire.*

Danny eventually drifted off to sleep. Before he could know it, his alarm clock wet off and woke him up. Nothing had occurred that night. He never left his bed. There was no traveling back in time or to anywhere for that matter. He never even woke up to travel to the bathroom or kitchen to get a drink of water. His disappointment could only be described on a grand scale. He ruefully got up and got ready for work. Strangely again, as he was combing his hair in the bathroom mirror, his forehead was clear, completely devoid of any cut or blemish whatsoever. On the car ride to work, he gazed into the rearview mirror to back out of the driveway. Again, nothing but smooth flesh above his brow. The soreness was gone, as well. Danny was completely baffled. He had not explanation for it.

At work, Richie and everyone else pretty much left him alone. They figured he was still smarting from his breakup with

Collette. If they only knew who or what was really going on in his mind. The day couldn't go fast enough for Danny. He was hoping beyond hope that he would be able to journey back to Eva that night. The only thing that Richie really spoke to him about was why he kept checking out his forehead in the mirror all that morning. Danny replied by telling him that he just had a headache.

That night at home Danny performed the same routine in front of the antique mirror. He finished getting dressed, sauntered over to the open-shaded window, and looked out into the night sky. This night was different from the previous cloud-covered night. The night was clear and bright, with a nearly full moon glowing in all its nocturnal glory. Danny hopped into his bed clad in his full 1870s regalia, again firmly clasping his top hat against his expectantly fast-beating heart. What Danny hadn't yet realized was that the gleaming moon up above was about to provide the final ingredient in order for his retro transportation to be set in motion.

As he lay on his bed, drifting in an out of sleep, the moon beamed into the ornate mirror's glass face. It cast an unearthly luminescent glimmer, shimmering against the wall. It appeared as the sunset glistering upon rippling waters. The bemused Danny shot from his bed like he was just fired from a cannon. He gaped into the mirror as though he were an expectant father peeking into the delivery room, awaiting news from the doctor. He placed his hat upon his head and held it down fast. He was careful not to aggravate the cut above his brow that, strangely enough was only visible in the antique mirror.

*

Danny found himself in the middle of an old cafe, seated next to Eva. He was joyously happy to be with her again but was a little worried about how she felt toward him, being that he was with Collette before.

"It's a good thing we found this nice eatery down the road from the station house!" Eva exclaimed. She appeared to be in mid-conversation with him as though he had never left her side. "Mr. Lundy just told me that because of the heavy snow and the delay from the line switch, we are going to be late arriving in Ashtabula. Maybe 5:30, perhaps 5:45. This gives us a chance to have some decent food to hold us over. We probably won't be eating at Father's hotel until a little later now."

Danny sat and stared at her. What a beautiful woman she truly was. He hadn't realized how much he had truly missed her. He wanted to be up front with her and confess to her about being with Collette. He hoped to assure her that the only reason he had even looked at another woman was that he wasn't sure until now that she was actually real, flesh and blood, and not merely an abstract manifestation. Now he was absolutely positive. And he was absolutely in love with her.

Danny wasn't quite sure how to even begin to tell her about everything he knew. He wanted to tell her that he was fully aware that she was real and alive. He was in a straight as to how he would even start to explain everything to her. His biggest concern, first and foremost, was of course how to convince her and everybody else to get off the train and then try to persuade the conductor to get the engineer to halt the train before it left Buffalo and went any farther. He was fumbling around to find the right words to speak when she chimed in.

"And where is your bandage, Daniel?"

"I don't know. It must have fallen off."

"We'll have to get the kind Dr. Penwalt to redress it for you," she said, being concerned for him. "So anyway, Daniel, tell me, what do you think of Mother's present?"

"Her present?" he muttered.

"Daniel, Mother's present, in the crate. I just showed it to you moments ago."

"Uhh, I don't…"

"Well, I can't show it to you again until we unload at Ashtabula. I think the porter and baggage man are starting to get a little perturbed about letting us into the express car."

"I'm sorry, Eva. I can't seem to remember."

"Oh, Daniel, poor dear. Your head must be making you feel awful."

"Eva, are you angry with me?"

"Daniel, of course not," she said as she gently took his hand. "Why would I be angry with you? You are such a sweet soul. Why would you ask if I'm angry at you?"

"Ahh… no reason. I just thought… maybe because I…"

"My sweetheart, you haven't left my side this whole trip, other than to get some sleep, since we met early this morning. On the contrary. I'm very happy to be with you. You have been so kind to me."

Danny felt the top of his head and then he put his palm on his forehead and looked about the café and around the floor.

"Daniel, what is the matter? Are you all right? Is it your forehead?" Eva asked with growing concern.

"Oh, yeah, I'm okay. It's just… I had my top hat on two minutes ago when I… when we walked in."

"No, you didn't, Daniel. You probably left it in your sleeper berth still." Eva was growing alarmed with Danny's seemingly increasing lack of memory. "You shouldn't even be putting on and taking your hat off anyway," she mildly scolded. "That's probably how you knocked your bandage off."

"It's not how it… I mean, I just wish I had my hat on me again. I just wish that one time I could tip my top hat to a pretty lady, that's all."

"You're incorrigible, Daniel. Hopeless, I say," she kiddingly reprimanded him. "But I just can't help but to love you."

Danny smiled, but his joy quickly turned grim. In his blissful enthusiasm at returning to Eva's side, he had almost forgotten what his prime mission at hand was. If he could not prevail upon her to stay off the train, they would have no future together. He wished to convince everybody on board to get off before it proceeded any farther down the snowbound tracks.

"Eva," he whispered cautiously, "have you given it any more thought to staying behind here in Buffalo until tomorrow morning? The snowstorm is worsening."

Eva stared at him with her lips creased and a tense expression. "Daniel, how many times—" she sternly began to say but couldn't stay upset with him. "Listen, my dear," she chuckled, "I am boarding this train. The only time that I'm going to get off it is if you need to get a spot of fresh air when we make a brief stop in Erie to pick up and let people off. Father is waiting for me in this atrocious weather, and I will not keep him waiting a minute longer than I have to. We are already going to be almost an hour late as it is."

Danny stared at her impassively for a moment, not knowing how to react. "We are stopping in Erie?" he asked, slightly perking up, knowing he would have more chances to persuade her.

"Yes, Daniel, we are stopping in Erie. Union Station is very large. There are probably a lot of travelers heading to Chicago."

Danny managed a labored smile. The two of them talked for a couple of minutes. It was bittersweet for him. He was in love with her to no end, but he couldn't bask in her love until he prevented her from reaching Ashtabula—if not now, then hopefully in Erie or the next stop, wherever that was.

Just then, Mr. McCarthy arrived at their table along with Mr. Lundy.

"There you two are," Mr. McCarthy blared. "The train is going to be boarding soon. We should be getting back to the station house. The snow is really coming down heavily out there," he informed them.

Danny, frustrated with Eva's refusal to listen to his logic and stay behind until the next day, invited Mr. McCarthy and Mr. Lundy to join the two of them for a few minutes before they had to get back on the train.

"Gentlemen," Danny posed as the two of them sat down by them. "You two are very fine and astute men of business. The lovely Miss Lindfors here is also about to be a woman of business and investments. Allow me to ask you a few pertinent questions related to finance and commerce," Danny proffered as an idea was hatching in his brain.

"Sure. Anything, Mr… what did you say your name was?"

"Daniel Dubenion, he replied.

"Mr. Dubenion, what is it that you would like to ask?"

Danny put forward some business questions for them to give him a learned response to. He asked them about asset management and risk taking. Eva was impressed with Danny's knowledge and use of terminology. The two gentlemen spoke frankly and gave Danny sound and upfront advice related to their prior experience with high finance.

Eva sat by and proudly listened to Danny ask them about risk mitigation and futures contracts. The men were greatly impressed, as well. Little did the other three know, but Danny had a sizable advantage with market history, entering their world from the future.

"I told you, Miss Lindfors," Mr. McCarthy roared merrily, "don't let this one get away. He's going to make a lot of money in the future. I still think your father ought to take a look at him as a partner."

"Why, thank you, Mr. McCarthy. I do know a little about business. It seems that my specialty lies in the principles of risk mitigation," Danny boasted.

"How so?" Mr. Lundy chimed in.

"Well, Mr. Lundy," Danny held forth. "As a businessman, you want to take steps to reduce any adverse effects of your investments." The three of them leaned in to hear what Danny was proposing. "Just like in the futures market in Chicago that you are all familiar with," he continued as they nodded their heads in agreement, "you want to benefit in the future… from carefully made and perhaps cautious decisions you make today."

Danny continued the conversation by offering an analogy. "Just like in business investments, just like Eva's father is doing for her today, you need to know the right time to get in. Mr. Lindfors is surely getting Eva invested in Ashtabula transportation at the absolute right time."

Eva smiled broadly as the two gentlemen again nodded in agreement.

"However," Danny cautioned, "one has to, without question, now when to immediately get out before a horrible downturn occurs. One needs to know when to get on board… and one needs to know when to jump off."

Eva started to get a little suspicious as to where she perceived Danny was trying to lead them.

"Take, for instance, this train we are about to reboard." Danny looked over at Eva and saw a scowl growing across her tightening face. He sheepishly continued. "It's an absolute blizzard out there… very dangerous. Wouldn't it be beneficial to our future lives to invest the time and stay off—?"

"Daniel!" Eva shrieked. "You are starting to cause me to get cross with you!" she glowered. "Why are you weighing these two fine gentlemen down with this burdensome, skylarking buffoonery? These two men have very important business to see to in Chicago. They both have families to go home to who are waiting for them. They can't linger around here while their transportation home rides away from them, leaving them stranded in the grips of this abysmal snowstorm. Please, Mr. McCarthy, Mr. Lundy, I'm very sorry. Daniel has not been feeling well all day since he has injured his head."

As everybody stood up to head to the station and board the train, Eva took Danny firmly by his hand and assured him she would ask the porter to summon the physician to the parlor car to tend to him once they got aboard and sat down. Danny was remorseful as he trudged back to the station's platform—not so much about getting Eva upset and her losing patience with him as he was about missing an opportunity to convince the two gentlemen to stay back and not board the train. As he neared the train, the words of the grisly article from the *Chicago Tribune* echoed in his head. Eva followed closely behind him, keeping her extended arm upon his shoulder, all the way into the parlor car.

When the two of them sat down, Eva leaned over to him and gently said, "Daniel, I'm sorry for scolding you and embarrassing you like I did. You mustn't carry on like that about the train in this weather. Everything will be just fine. We are in this nice and warm parlor car, enjoying each other's company. Now, you need to relax. You are acting like what father would call a *lura*."

"What's a *lura*?" Danny asked, a little chagrined.

"It means 'fool' in Swedish. Father would call someone that if he perceived that that person was making an unwise business decision." She laughed, causing Danny to produce a pained grin.

"Well, Eva, I guess I'm just a *lura* when it comes to being in love with you," he admitted.

"My sweetheart, I'm so in love with you, too," she acknowledged with a delightful smile. "Now, I have to call on the porter to bring Dr. Penwalt to you."

"Eva, just be careful wh—"

"I know, Daniel. I'll be careful when I step out and cross the gangway," she said with a smile.

Eva got up and went across the parlor car and into the day coach in search of the physician. Danny stared at the cast-iron heater. He felt the heat radiating from its midst. His heart sank at the thought of the gruesome image portrayed in the newspaper articles of the horrendous fires that were started because of them and the toppled kerosene lamps. He knew how many people would suffer and die in the unimaginable conflagration. He looked around the room and wondered who among the crowd would perish and who would survive. There had to be a way to urge people to get off the train before it neared Ashtabula. He thought hard on the subject while waiting for Eva to come back with the doctor. Then it hit him. *The doctor!* He thought. *Everyone respects a doctor's opinion. Maybe I can urge him to warn everybody of the impending disaster, to warn the conductor and recommend that they stop the train.*

A few minutes went by, and finally Eva was walking back to where Danny was seated, the doctor following behind. Danny was busy trying to think of a way to convince him of the risk to everybody's health and lives if the train was to be allowed to continue on in the brutal snowstorm.

"Daniel, Miss Lindfors tells me your head wound needs re-dressed, the doctor said upon arriving to Danny's side. "How is it feeling? You took quite a fall back in Albany."

Danny told him that it was a little sore and throbbing somewhat, so the doctor took him aside to the other side of the parlor car where there was room to work on his forehead.

After he was finished fixing up his wound, the doctor asked him if he wanted to receive anything to ease the pain. "I can give you a little morphine. It will deaden the pain and help you get some sleep."

Danny refused any medication.

"You know, morphine is named for Morpheus, the Greek god of dreams?" Dr. Penwalt enlightened him.

"Ah, no, thanks, Doc. I've had enough with dreams for a while."

"Well, I can give you some laudanum to relieve the pain. It will allay any irritation you have with the cut, as well. It will also help you sleep."

Danny assured him that he would be just fine without them. He said he would just go back and rest up with Eva.

Before going back, Danny sidled up next to the doctor and posed a serious question at him. "Let me ask you something, Dr. Penwalt. You are dedicated to saving lives, correct?

"Of course I am, young man. That is my dedicated profession, my calling."

"You are sworn to keeping people alive and not dead, to see that people remain whole and not broken, for them to be healthy and not ill and suffering."

"Of course, Daniel."

"Doctor, this horrible snowstorm outside, it has the potential to be really disastrous for the fate of this train and all the precious passengers."

"What are you suggesting, Daniel?"

"Something very horrible is going to come from this brutal storm we are experiencing. Everyone on this train is at great risk for disaster. You are part of a profession that has a great influence. Wouldn't it be incumbent upon you to go to the porter, summon the conductor, and voice your concern by warning him of this looming tragedy?"

"Daniel, there is nothing for us to worry about. These engineers are the finest in their profession. They will be careful to use all proper caution and all manner of skill that they are endowed and exercised with. If the snow does not abate, they will slow the train down accordingly as not to jeopardize any lives on board. We will all be nice and warm and secure inside our cars."

"But, Doctor, the disaster… the bridge—"

"Now, Daniel, let's get you over to Miss Lindfors, and she will see to it that you get some proper rest. Are you absolutely sure you don't need any morphine?"

The doctor accompanied Danny over to where Eva was seated. She beheld his freshly dressed brow and thanked him warmly.

"Please, Miss Lindfors, see to it that he gets some proper rest."

"I won't leave his side. Thank you again, Dr. Penwalt." Eva put her arm around Danny's shoulder and pulled him close to her so he could rest his head on her. Danny was soon able to doze off for a little while, supported contently on Eva's feminine yet sturdy shoulder.

In the meantime, the train had rolled past West Seneca, going onward toward the town of Angola. The snow was relentlessly coming down, inundating the region with a thick, heavy blanket. The engineer was now repeatedly engaging the sand tubes to assist in gaining traction. After a few more moments of perfume-scented slumber next to Eva's delicate neck, Danny woke up. He rubbed his eyes and slowly gained focus in time to see the Reverend Bliss approaching where the two of the sat.

"Are you Daniel, young man?" he asked as he held out his reassuring hand, offering Danny a firm handshake.

The two of them invited the reverend to sit down and join them.

"I don't mean to impose on the two of you," he implored, "but I just wanted to stop by and see how Daniel was feeling. The good doctor just spoke to me about his condition."

"You are so kind and considerate, good Reverend. Daniel fell and cut his forehead in the express car back in Albany. He has been resting fine here with me."

"Yes, thank you, Reverend," Danny echoed. "My head does hurt some, but I think it will be just fine."

"Well, actually, your physical condition is not what seems to be presently concerning me," he said pointedly.

"What do you mean, Reverend?" Eva asked alarmingly.

Reverend Bliss explained to her how the doctor expressed concern over Danny's psychological state. "Daniel here has told the doctor frantically about being fearful of himself and everyone perishing aboard this train and that the doctor should impose his influence upon the conductor to halt the train immediately."

"Daniel, not the good doctor, as well," she berated. "He was kind enough to carefully tend to your wound, and you lay this hideous burden at his feet, also."

Danny sat there squirming. He didn't know how to answer them.

Reverend Bliss placed his hand sympathetically on Danny's shoulder. "Son, you don't have to fear. You simply need to have faith. Faith is the antithesis of fear. You need not worry about yourself and the others here about dying.

"Daniel," Eva jumped in, "you have been fretting about this dreadful fear of needing to get off this train since this morning, first to me earlier on the train and then near the Buffalo station. Then you tried to frighten Mr. McCarthy and Mr. Lundy. Now the doctor."

Danny remained tongue tied. He felt as though he were an impish child who had just been caught doing a most heinous act of lewdness. He just sat there frozen, pondering the frightful carnage that lay ahead on the treacherous, icy Ashtabula River Bridge and the abysmal gorge below it.

"All of this dire talk of death and horror, my son … there is no need to travel in such trepidation." In an attempt to allay Danny's fears and give him some degree of peace, the Reverend quoted for him from Psalm 23. "'Though I walk through the valley of the shadow of death, I shall fear no evil.' See, Daniel? With the good Lord's hand upon you, there is no need to fear, not matter how unfavorable it appears outside." He quoted a couple of more related scriptures to help ease Danny's troubled heart. Eva thanked him dearly as he excused himself so Danny could continue resting.

Eva urged him to go to his berth so he could lie down for a while and be more comfortable. She offered her hand to assist him back there. He convinced her to stay in the parlor car, promising her that he was capable of making it on his own. He emphasized to her his unwillingness to parade her through the smoker car with all its relentless cacophony of shouting and foul language, not to mention the occasional catcalls from the baser men whenever a female dared to wander in and through the car, whether she was accompanied or not. That was all on top of the smoke-filled haze she would be forced to navigate through. Danny also wanted to go back to his berth by himself, in hopes of chancing upon the porter. This way he could make another heartfelt plea for halting the train without Eva's well-intentioned but misplaced interference.

"I can get the porter to help me across the icy gangways to my berth if I need it," he said, scheming.

Danny sifted through the smoker car and through the hallway of one of the sleeper cars, and after a few minutes found the porter. Before Danny had a chance to speak, the porter asked him about his cut. He informed him quickly that he was fine, almost dismissing the question. Danny expounded to the porter in a more desperate tone than he did to the others about the compulsory need to speak to the conductor about halting the train once it reached Erie. All the dire talk made the ambushed porter take a step backward. Danny's rant about gruesome death and harrowing suffering at the bottom of the Ashtabula River Gorge had cut the poor, unsuspecting attendant to the quick.

"Now, slow down, Daniel," he condescended. "There is no need to be so alarming. I know the storm is very dreadful outside, but you must remain calm. We have plenty of confidence in our engineers and railroad to deliver you to your destination safely."

Danny did not remain calm. He was very graphic as he described the horror in detail and kept on insisting that certain peril awaited the crew and passengers if the train was to be allowed to continue on.

Knowing that Danny's head injury was affecting him more than he was letting on, the porter insisted that he go to his berth and lie down for some much-needed rest. He was worried that

Danny, who was starting to be overheard by some of the passengers, might be on the verge of causing a panic. He offered to get the physician to look in on him, but Danny declined. The porter agreed not to get the doctor only if Danny would go in and rest for a while. Danny consented. The porter was temporarily relieved that, for the time being, he had averted a panic among the passengers.

Danny tossed and turned in his sleeper compartment for about an hour while he agonized about how he would ever be able to convince the right people of the impending disaster. By now, the early afternoon was beginning to wear on. The train had progressed along the "water level" route of Lake Erie beyond the small burg of Silver Creek and was advancing toward Fredonia. The tormenting blizzard continued to plague the journey of the number 5 Pacific Express train as Danny wrestled in the grip of sheer frustration from the doom that awaited. He was already missing Eva and did not want to leave her sitting by herself any longer. Besides, he was growing impatient with his inaction and snuck out of his berth in hopes that the porter was appeased with his period of rest.

He strode back to the parlor car, only to find that the conductor was standing by where Eva was seated. He was involved in a discussion with her when he ambled up to them. Much to Danny's consternation, Eva bore a gravely concerned countenance. The conductor didn't exactly look all that happy, as well. Eva begged the conductor's pardon and asked if she could do the speaking. He obliged.

"Daniel, this is Mr. Perryman, our conductor. He knows and understands that your head injury is affecting you adversely, but he insists that you be careful to cease at once this babbling about this train nearing such a calamitous disaster. The passengers are beginning to be affrighted and are beginning to inquire in panic concerning it. I happen to agree with Mr. Perryman," she said sternly but lovingly.

Danny respectfully shook Mr. Perryman's hand. Mr. Perryman proceeded to echo Eva's straightforward admonition. Danny apologized to him. However, Danny dared not let the issue die. He remembered from the article in the *Chicago Tribune* that the conductor survived the ordeal with his life, being maimed. He began to rationalize and justify his ominous warnings of the train's impending doom. Just as he did with the porter, he spared no gruesome detail in his prescient description of what lay ahead for everyone on that train if it wasn't stopped. Although Danny had quieted to a whisper so no one else but the two of them could hear, Mr. Perryman grew hotly disturbed with him.

Eva quickly intervened and begged the conductor's assurance that she would tend to Dany and that he would not mention this "extremely burdensome prattle" to anyone else for the rest of the journey. Eva's wise and timely intervention sufficed Mr. Perryman and assuaged his wrath for the time being.

"Out of my utmost respect for Miss Lindfors here, I am willing to proceed no further on this matter." To show them that he was a man who was not without compassion, he attempted to lessen Danny's grief by assuring him, "No matter how snowy and blusterous the storm gets out there, old Socrates and Columbia, our most dependable locomotives, will pull us forward to our destination safely." Danny tried to manage a strained smile for him, but his heart sank fast at the hearing of the names of the locomotives he had so painfully read about at the library. Eva thanked Mr. Perryman for his understanding and held Danny by his hand and led him to sit down by the window, next to her. Mr. Perryman nodded cautiously and went about his business.

As Danny sat quietly ashamed, Eva glared icily at him.

"Not one more word about this, Daniel. Do you understand? Not to me, not to Mr. McCarthy, Mr. Lundy, Doctor Penwalt, the porter, Reverend Bliss.... not to anyone."

Danny remained motionless, exhaling a long deep, frustrated sigh.

"I don't understand why you are doing this. I know your head is hurting you, but I can't continue on the rest of the journey making excuses on your behalf."

Danny continued to stare straight ahead at nothing.

"Do you understand what they can do to you if you continue to induce a panic on this train? When we arrive in Erie, they can have you removed from this train and have you taken into town to be apprehended. Mr. Perryman has hinted to me as much."

There was a long, painful silence between them. Danny remained motionless. His mind was in full motion, however, as he contemplated the absolute death and destruction that lay on the horizon that nobody believed was coming.

Eva picked up where she had left off chiding him, breaking the long silence. "You get me to fall in love with you with your kindness and goodhearted and gentlemanly charm, then you decide to separate yourself from your good senses and ramble on with your gloom and despair and cause everyone to gawk at you as if you were a raving madman. You are making me look like the *lura* … the fool. Not one more word about this dreadful picture you are painting for everyone. Do you understand me, Daniel?"

Danny was speechless. He could only gape out of the window at the near-blinding snowfall. Finally, after what seemed like an eternity, he spoke up. "Eva, sweetheart, I do love you. I do. But there is something that I must absolutely tell you. You can be angry with me when I tell you. Afterward, you can walk away and never see me or speak to me again."

Eva sat up stiffly, with her arms folded, wondering what type of lunacy to expect next.

"This is 1876. You, me… this whole train, the Pacific Express… are in December 29, 1876."

Eva sat silently, continuing to glower at him, otherwise emotionless.

"I… I am not from 1876. I have come from the future… from 1985—109 years into the future. I fully know the ill fate that awaits this train."

Eva turned her head away, looking to the other side of the car. Danny knew and understood why she wasn't buying it. Who on earth would?

"I'm not from this time period." He attempted to phrase it one more desperately unsuccessful time. After another moment of brutal silence, Eva whirled her head back around to face him.

"Daniel, I don't know whether to laugh or to cry. Are you perversely jesting with me or trying to make an excuse to chase me away from you and break my heart? What are you trying to tell me? That you do not exist here? That … that you are absurdly suggesting that you are merely a dream that I am experiencing of you … so you can walk away and be done with me?" Eva had a tear in her eye.

Danny could only close his eyes and strain to further explain himself. "I'm just trying to say, Eva, that I know about this train. I know what's going to happen to—"

Suddenly, Eva stood up. She was no longer willing to abide with his perceived lunacy. "Well, Mr. Dubenion!" she said matter-of-factly. "If you are just a dream that I am having, maybe I need to wake up." Eva turned around and stormed away weeping, hurrying off toward her drawing room.

Danny turned his head toward the window. He had a tear in his eye as well. He was sorrowful for causing Eva so much grief but also for the fate of the people on board. He was upset with himself most of all for not being able to convincingly communicate to everyone the utter necessity to stop the train when it arrived in Erie. Danny continued staring hypnotically out into the frozen wilderness. The entire landscape was being continuously bombarded with a blinding snowfall. The train was slowing a bit. By now, the sand tubes were not as effective as they were earlier, due to the worsening conditions. Danny was mesmerized by the white methodical snowfall. He was drifting in and out of sleep. The Pacific Express train had eventually steamed past Westfield and by Ripley, near the Pennsylvania border, twenty-five miles outside of Erie. Danny, slumped over in his seat, soon was fast asleep.

*

Danny tossed and turned in his sleep, surreal visions of people crying out for help, grappling and wrestling in his tortured mind. Not only did he fail to make any progress at getting the right people to safely stop the train from its pursuant path, but he had gone backward. Instead of inspiring the most influential people on board to action, passengers and crew alike, he had become a loathsome execration to them, denounced as a lunatic by the very people he was desperately trying to save, Eva included. His mind was churning. The number 5 Pacific Express train was headed for the unimaginable.

Danny's grief-stricken slumber was seized upon by a loud ringing. It was his alarm clock. Danny was back in Ashtabula. Back in 1985.

He ruefully slid out of bed and turned off the alarm. He was still clad in his 1870s period suit. He stumbled over to go to his closet and nearly tripped on his top hat that had been lying on the floor in front of his antique mirror. He was puzzled at how it always wound up there. He bent over to pick it up, and he looked into the mirror. His forehead wound was still there.

13

July 1985

Danny's psyche was shaken, and his heart was storm tossed, but he was still steadfast and determined. Danny drove down Route 11, heading for Jefferson. This was the awaited initial historical society meeting with him as a new member. He was very anxious to hear the guest speaker, the writer who published articles about the history of the area's railroads. He was hoping to get a chance to pick the author's brain about certain aspects of the bridge disaster after he was finished speaking about his planned curriculum.

Danny, who was avid about returning to 1876 as soon as possible, wanted to find out if the Pacific Express train had made any other stops beyond the one it had made in Erie. He knew there had been, and still was, a large depot in Conneaut, Ohio. He figured that if nobody got off at the upcoming Erie station, he would have another shot at convincing everyone to avert disaster by stopping the train and getting off at the Conneaut station, a mere fifteen miles from Ashtabula.

Danny arrived for the meeting a little early. Mrs. Lane and Mr. Kirkpatrick introduced him to all the members around the room. Everybody enjoyed a cup of coffee served by the congenial Mrs. Lane before the speaker got started. He focused on two aspects from his latest publications. First, he described the vital importance of Ashtabula's bustling reciprocal rail activity to the massive steel industry decades prior to the Pittsburgh, Youngstown, and Wheeling areas. Secondly, he revisited a lesser known but deadly Ashtabula train wreck. It was a frightening railroad accident that occurred in town between Center and Prospect Streets in 1912, when a Lake Shore and Michigan Southern coal train hit a trolley car on another cold and snowy December day. Both topics held Danny's enthusiastic interest, as well as all the others.

After the program, Mrs. Lane invited everyone to stick around for a while and enjoy some refreshments, compliments of the women of the group. This would also be an opportune time to have a chance to converse with the speaker. Danny, Mr. Kirkpatrick, and some of the other men in the group brought up the subject of the bridge disaster to him. They discussed it in length. Danny picked an opportune time to ask the question about there being any stops after the one in Erie.

"No, Erie was the last stop," he answered Danny without hesitation.

"Erie was the last stop?" Danny asked ruefully.

"Yes, Erie was the last stop before it was supposed to stop at the Ashtabula station," he reiterated.

"I was hoping… I mean, I thought that maybe it had a scheduled stop in Conneaut."

"Actually, it was stuck in Erie for an extra hour or so," the speaker informed them. "Because of the massive accumulation of snow, they had to summon the help of four pusher locomotives to get the train moving on its way."

Danny reacted in amazement. "Four pusher locomotives… that's a lot of power!"

"That was a lot of snow," the speaker remarked.

The speaker informed everyone that the Pacific Express passed the Lake Shore and Michigan Southern depot in Conneaut. The Conneaut telegraph operator alerted the Ashtabula telegraph office at 6:52 p.m. that the train was on its way there. "And if you want to hear something crazy," the speaker added, "at 7:24, the westbound Pacific Express passed an eastbound freight train just outside of Ashtabula."

"Wow," Mr. Kirkpatrick remarked. "I wonder if the crew on that freight train could ever imagine the fate of the train they were passing."

"They were the last ones to see the Pacific Express before it attempted to go over the bridge," the speaker said lamentingly.

"So, Erie was their last chance," Danny murmured out loud.

Danny was aghast. He now knew that he had but one shot left—that was if the train had not already reached Erie and departed before he could have a chance to get back. If this were the case, it would be too late for everyone. Danny was fraught with confusion. Then it dawned on him. If he were to arrive back on the train after it would have departed Erie, his life would be in jeopardy, as well. He would have missed the final safe stop, as well, to his own peril. He would also be going over the bridge along with everybody else and plummeting into the deep, dark, snowy gorge, ready to be crushed and engulfed in flames.

On the drive home from the meeting that evening, Danny did a lot of heavy and deep soul searching. By the time he arrived in his driveway, he had made up his mind. He loved Eva immensely. He was fully resolved to go back and imperil himself to save her life and everyone else's. His life would be worthless without her, he concluded. He would go back as soon as possible in an attempt to save her, even to his own death, if necessary.

Danny had finally figured out that it took three components to be transported back in time and make this frenzied fairy tale come true. It had to be nighttime. He had to be wearing his 1870s suit. Also, the night had to have plenty of moonlight visible so the moonbeam could reflect off the mirror and, in some inexplicable way, convey him back to 1876. He didn't comprehend the wherefores and the whys, or even why it was always December 29, 1876 when he arrived, but he now fully understood the proper mode of transportation.

Later that night, he donned his suit before slipping into bed. It was a cloudy, overcast night sky, however, thus his grand entrance would be curtailed for at least one more night. He wore his suit to bed anyway, just in case the murky sky cleared up in the middle of the night so he could be on his way. It was to no avail. He woke up in the morning, having never left his bed. He got up and disappointingly had breakfast and a shower. He had taken the day off work on what might have possibly been the last day of his life. He would try to go back again that next night.

In the meantime, now that it was morning, while he was waiting for his chance to make his nocturnal conveyance and return to 1876, he decided to take a trip down memory lane. Just in case he wouldn't ever have the chance again.

Not knowing if he would ever return again to the present once he again went back to 1876, Danny decided after his quick breakfast to take the hour-long drive to Niles and take a good look around. He had not been back down there since before the tornado hit on May 31. The first thing he wanted to see was the old house that he grew up in and that his parents still lived in until their recent move to Florida. He took a slow, sentimental drive through his old neighborhood, replaying all the fond memories of all the great times he had as a young boy. He wondered if this would be the last time he would ever see it. He drove around to his old high school. He was stunned to find a lot of the tornado damage to the area so near to his old neighborhood. His parents' old house came a little too close for comfort.

Danny drove to his company's Niles facility, where he used to work before transferring, and showed the guard his company identification card. He went inside to pay a visit to his former coworkers and acquaintances, and they shared a few fond laughs and memories. They tried to nail him down on a promise to come back some night to go out on the town with everyone. Danny halfheartedly said he would but knew most definitely he wouldn't ever see any of those people again. He walked around a little bit and took one last look around, and then he told everyone that he had to be going. He had a few more stops to make before heading back to Ashtabula.

Two of the stops were at both of the historical societies that he had belonged to and was a committee member for. He wanted to catch up with both of the directors of each respective place and thank them for all the great experiences he had with them. He apologized to both for leaving them. He insisted to them that he had wanted to keep his membership, but the distance from Ashtabula was getting to be a problem for him. He complimented the one director on the success of the public reception back in March and told him of the enjoyable time he'd had.

"This may sound very strange to you," Danny mentioned to him, "but in a remarkable way, dressing for that reception changed my whole life." The director managed a smile but knew nothing of what Danny was alluding to.

After leaving the historical societies, Danny headed for the cemetery. He was truly amazed at all the trees that had been wiped out by the twister. He wound his way around to the veterans' section and got out to say goodbye to his grandparents. Danny's brown eyes grew misty as he talked to his Grandpa Ed. He thanked him for being so brave and courageous during his nightmarish experience in World War I. He thanked him again for being such a great friend and mentor to him when he was alive. He repeated how much he looked up to him and what an inspiration he was to him. He told him that he wished he could have met Eva and how much he would have loved her. Danny stood motionless for a few moments and pondered. He reflected on Eva and all the other wonderful and unsuspecting passengers on the Pacific Express train. He knew full well what his Grandpa Ed would do if he were in his shoes. Even if it meant risking his own life, he would go back and give it all he had to save her and all those folks from destruction. He stared at his grandfather's veteran's plaque. His resolve was steeled. He knew beyond any doubt what he must do. Danny said one last tearful goodbye. What he didn't even realize was, that if he did go back and stay in 1876, he would end up never even knowing his grandfather, and would never end up being his grandson.

Danny left the cemetery and drove toward the northbound highway, bidding his old former town goodbye.

About an hour later, he arrived in Ashtabula. He began to get hungry, so he zipped over to Garfield's for what might be one last time. He went all out and got his favorite burger meal to eat. It felt kind of strange. It was a beautiful early afternoon summer day. Hardly any of the regulars were there. No one to ask him to put the top down on his Wildcat, and there was no one to laugh or make small talk with. Maybe it was appropriate. Now that he was becoming more unattached to the present, it was probably for the better that he didn't see many of them. He would miss them. Not really sure if he would have a need to gas his car up again, Danny still went over to the Flying Saucer gas station to buy a little gas for old time's sake. What a unique gas station it indeed was. However, he thought, there would be need of gas stations in 1876.

Next, he took a drive down to the harbor. He wanted to visit Mr. Kirkpatrick at the antique shop one last time also, just in case he never returned. He wanted to thank him for everything he did for him, especially for selling him the antique mirror. He would thank him, in spite of him not being able to know the full measure of Danny's gratitude or not fully understanding what he would mean by it.

Danny stopped in and had a warm chat with him. He mentioned to Mr. Kirkpatrick what a nice time he'd had at the meeting the evening before. Naturally, the talk turned to the bridge disaster as Mr. Kirkpatrick related to Danny some of the stories that his own grandfather had told him about it from his youth. Danny praised him for being such a wonderful man and thanked him for all the great memories and inspirations his merchandise had provided him. Mr. Kirkpatrick in turn lauded him for being his favorite client and told him that he looked forward to seeing him again. Danny had to hurry and walk out, not wanting the kindly old man to see him well up with emotion.

Next, Danny drove through the harbor and then along East Sixth Street and headed for Lake Shore Park. He got out and took a walk along the beach. It was a clear, picture-perfect summer day. Danny strolled up to the breakwater and walked out into the lake on the big rocks. He looked about at the greenish-blue water. It was calm, with a light breeze. Around the corner, he caught a glimpse of the busy activity of the east end of the harbor docks. He heard the clinking and clattering of machinery as iron ore was being moved from one vessel into another. He stood there, again bringing to remembrance the

October day when he stood in the same spot and wondered if he would ever find that special woman that he could spend the rest of his life with. It was not that long ago he thought that woman would be Collette. Now he was absolutely positive about whom he'd been wondering about all those months ago. He ambled about for a few more minutes, thinking of the beautiful Eva Lindfors. He got back in his car and headed for home.

When Danny got into his house, he immediately made two phone calls. First, he called his parents. He told them how much he missed them and loved them. He admitted that he wasn't sure when he would be able to see them again. He told them that he drove to Niles and went by the old house. They discussed a lot of fond memories about it for a while. They tried to make him promise to come down and visit. He echoed that he wasn't sure when he could. Then he gave Richie a call on the phone at work. When Richie expressed his concern about Danny not being at work that day, Danny told him that he had taken a couple of vacation days off. Danny asked him to meet him at the Six for a couple of beers and some billiards later. Richie said he would be there after work.

Danny took a quick shower and got dressed. Before he left to go meet Richie, he grabbed an extra house key to take with him. He took off and got there a few minutes ahead of his friend. When Richie came in, Danny was already having a beer.

"I bought you one," Danny greeted him, handing him a cold bottle of brew. Richie thanked his buddy and suggested a friendly game of pool.

As they were in the middle of the game, Danny brought up the time back in October when it was the first day of his new job there and Richie showed him around his new work environment and invited him to come there and have a beer and shoot pool. Danny thanked him for being such a good friend.

"Oh, come on, man. Quit getting all schmaltzy with me," Richie thundered. "I was just trying to be a friend, man."

"Well, you are a good friend," he echoed. Danny held out his spare house key.

"What the heck is that?" Richie asked, bewildered.

"I want you to have my spare house key… in case something happens to me and you have to get in."

"Man, you're getting all goofy, Wildcat!" he exclaimed.

Richie held out his hand and swiped the key out of Danny's hand. They shot around for a while longer when Danny asked him if he wanted another beer. Richie jokingly asked him why he was being so generously out of character. Danny replied that he just had a lot to celebrate. Richie boisterously asked him what he had so much to celebrate for.

Danny answered, "You were right about something."

"What was that?" he asked, confused.

"You said that I would find another girl. You were right… I did."

Richie held up the game to hear the details of this girlfriend.

"Now, is this one real, as well, or is she just a dream?" he jested.

"No, she is real. She is a dream come true, but she is a real woman."

"What do you mean, a dream come true? You guys just met."

"Well, I'm in love with her."

"What? It wasn't that long ago when you were saying that about what's her name. Collie dog?"

"Her name is Collette," Danny smirked.

"Well, what about this new girl?" Richie asked.

"Well," Danny began, "she is beautiful. She is intelligent. She's fun. She's great to be around. She is very special."

"All admirable qualities," Richie affirmed.

"She is very complex. I don't know how to explain it. Being with her… she's like no other woman I have ever known. I tell you; I am smack-dab in love with her."

"I don't know about you, man," Richie chuckled. "Well, I tell you what. If this girl is as special as you say she is, you'd better not let her get away." Richie continued the game and took a shot that missed the target and caromed off the eight ball. "Dang it all. Your shot, Wildcat."

Danny stood there frozen, in deep thought. Then he beamed, "Don't worry, Richie. I'm not going to let this one get away. I'm going to try my very best to never let her get away."

14

That night, Danny was getting ready for bed. He anxiously got dressed in his period suit once more. The clear skies that prevailed all that day held sway into the night, providing the lustrous moon with a straight shot at his antique mirror. He knew time was growing short. His chances at rescuing Eva and the others from their horrible fate were at a scarce premium. By every other instance when he went back in time to Eva, he always showed up pretty much where he'd left off, even if it had been months in between his time-traveled visits. There should be a little extra time, considering all the delays the train experienced at the Erie depot that he had read about. However, there was always that chance that he could show up late and the train could already have left Erie when he entered the past and be wheeling toward sheer destruction at Ashtabula. It was a chance he was willing to take for the woman he had fallen madly in love with, as well as all those wonderful, precious passengers.

It also dawned on him that he had two major obstacles. He realized that before he could take on the gargantuan task of trying to convince her and everybody else to get off the train, he had to first prove that he was not a hysterical lunatic. That, in and of itself, would be no easy task, as everyone with whom he had talked to about it on the train was convinced he was going mad. Eva seemed sure that all his dire warnings were aimless, as a result of his head injury. He wrestled with the agonizing weight of how he would be able to pull that off. He thought hard on it for some time. Then suddenly, an idea jumped into his mind. If he could bring something along with him that was modern and unique to his current time and show it to her, she would have to stand up and take note, along with everyone else—especially if he could produce for her something with a modern date inscribed on it. The choice for such evidence was an easy and obvious one. He would bring his driver's license with him to show her. It would have his name and picture on it. It would be a color photo, with his birth date of 1950, and an expiration date of 1987 clearly displayed on it. Also, for good measure, he would grab a couple of quarters from his change drawer. One was dated 1982, and the other was 1979. He would take Eva's handkerchief from his frock coat pocket and place the evidence in it and fold it up nice and snugly around them. When she beheld them, he figured she would have no other choice than to accept the fact that he was from the future. Thus, it would only follow suit that she would realize that he would positively know the fate of the Pacific Express and its passengers. Then, in realizing such, she would have no other recourse than to get off the train with him and help him to persuade the others to follow along.

Danny once again put on the finishing touches with his suit. He went into his dresser drawers and got the quarters and got his license from his wallet and wrapped them neatly into her folded-up handkerchief. He gently kissed her Spencerian scripted initial and steadfastly secured it into his pocket. He confidently patted his hand on the pocket and smiled. He also drew a deep, uneasy breath and then blew it out slowly. His thinking, if not his dire hope, was that she would have to believe him. He also went and got out all his antique money, bills, and coins and stashed them in his trouser pockets. He figured he would surely need it on the other side. As he placed the money in his pockets, another wonderful idea rose in his head. He figured if he took along one of the articles he had photocopied at the library about the disaster, that would be the proof-positive clincher. Everyone would have to believe him when he presented that as evidence of the impending fate of the train and passengers, and there would be no other choice other than for the complete halting of the train at the Erie depot. He went to his desk and pulled out the copy of the *Chicago Tribune's* account and folded it up and inserted it inside Eva's handkerchief along with the modern coins and driver's license.

Lastly, as was the norm, he grabbed his top hat and, just like the other times, cinched it down tightly on his head. His cut above his brow remained visible and exposed, but again, it appeared only in this particular mirror. He keenly hopped in bed and lay down, hoping to be able to fall asleep. Once again, he lay there firmly pinning his hat with his hands upon his chest.

After about only a half an hour, the moonlight struck the mirror at an acute angle, redirecting a splendid shaft of phosphorescence, shimmering and dancing against the opposite wall. Danny, a lot hastier than the other times before, sprang out of his bed and leaped front and center at the mirror. The glass face began throwing off a scintillating array of sparkling flashes. It once again started to ripple like agitated waters. Danny began to be reacquainted with vertigo. The room started spinning. He backed up and fell upon his bed.

*

Danny found himself in the middle of Union Depot in Erie, Pennsylvania. The crowded, noisy, ornate Romanesque revival-style building was burgeoning with a mass of frustrated and irritated travelers who were growing increasingly impatient with all the delays associated with the massive snowstorm. Many people had been stuck there waiting for their eastbound family members, who were now past due for hours, to finally arrive. The unabated blizzard has slowed travel to a near standstill all along the Lake Erie shore, from Toledo to Buffalo. Westbound travelers were hogtied as well, waiting for their snowbound train to get moving. The original forecast of the 5:00 arrival into Ashtabula, which had already been re-estimated for 6:00, was now in peril of being pushed back even further because of the prodigious accumulation. The heavy amount of formidable snow that was continually pounding away was about to prevent their train from having the ability to even get rolling again on time. Of every person in the packed, stuffy train station, only Danny knew the exact time the Pacific Express would be approaching Ashtabula. His repeated poring over of the articles about the disaster had the time of 7:28 p.m. seared indelibly into his conscience. That was the precise minute it would be on that bridge, a mere hundred yards or so away from the safe haven of the train depot on the other side of the river.

After pushing and jostling his way around the densely packed station house searching for a sight of Eva, he finally caught a glimpse of Mr. McCarthy sitting down on a bench, talking with Mr. Lundy. He struggled his way to reach them an asked if either of the two of them knew where he could find Eva. They informed him that the last they had seen of her, she was in the parlor car, sitting quietly by herself. Danny wanted to immediately make his way back to the train to see her, but he took a few minutes to stay and try once more to talk the two men into waiting in Erie for the night and starting out for Chicago in the morning. This time, he could talk to them unencumbered from Eva's well-intentioned but ill-timed interference. He described to them the total congestion of rail travel from there to Toledo and beyond. He tried to warn them of the danger and peril that they could encounter. The two men, however, shrugged it off. They told him that they had done so much rail travel on business through fair weather and foul, and they assured Danny that everything would turn out fine.

"We might get there a little late, young man, but we'll get there," Mr. Lundy uttered confidently.

With the two stubborn businessmen in staunch denial, Danny wasted no further time with them. He onerously wended his way through the masses to the other side of the station and back outside into the brutal winter maelstrom and then back onto the train. He hastened to the parlor car and immediately spotted the lovely but forlorn Eva, seated unassumingly by herself, gazing down at the floor. He reached for his top hat but realized that it was again missing from his head. He couldn't understand why it kept failing to cross through the time warp with him, why it always wound up sitting on the floor in front of the mirror when he returned. Danny unabashedly walked up to her.

"Eva, are you all right?" he cautiously asked her.

"Daniel," she said, surprised. "Yes, I'm fine, I think. Please come here and sit with me."

Danny rushed to her side and vehemently apologized for unintentionally making her feel so badly. "Eva, I can't even begin to describe how I feel about you." He reached in his coat pocket. "here. This will finally prove to you that I am not a lunatic. That I have indeed come here to you from many years into the future."

He handed her the folded-up handkerchief.

"Why are you giving this back to me?" she asked him with a hushed tone in her voice.

"Just unfold it and you will see. You will see that I'm not a raving lunatic."

Eva opened up the folded handkerchief. She stared down and let out a muted sigh. "It's empty, Daniel. Is that how your feelings toward me have become? Empty?"

"No, my sweetheart. What? It's empty!" Danny howled in stunned disbelief. He couldn't fathom why the items he had brought back as proof had vanished.

"Have you come here to make a mockery of me, Daniel? Are you returning this to me, my token to you of my earnest promise that I would wait for you once I got back home to Chicago, to marry me?"

"No, Eva, listen to me. That was supposed to have something in it to prove to you—"

"Have what in it, Daniel?"

"Please listen to me, my dear sweetheart. I love you; I swear it. I want to marry you so badly and always be with you."

"Then if that is so, my love, sit quietly here with me and hold me in your arms. Accompany me to Ashtabula, and we will talk to Father about our impending marriage … and no more preposterous, foreboding ranting about death and awful destruction on this train. It is downright frightening me."

Danny emphatically attempted to backpedal. He was flummoxed to his core. After some moments of incoherent stammering, he finally blurted out the only prescient utterance he could think of.

"Listen very carefully to me, Eva. There are going to be four pusher locomotives brought in to get this train unstuck in a little while so it can get moving again."

"Why are you doing this to me, Daniel? You don't want to accompany me to Father and ask him for my hand in marriage? So, they are bringing four locomotives to push us free from the snow. Did somebody tell you this? Mr. Perryman, perhaps?"

"No, nobody told it to me. Not anybody here, anyway. I'm just telling you; I know what's going to happen here next. When you see the pushers lining up behind the train, then you'll know that I have heard about and read about this from the future."

"Daniel, please stop doing this to me. I beg you."

"Eva, I'm dead serious. Look at me. Look into my eyes! Look at my lips. When you see them lining up to push this train out of the deep snow, four of them, and this train prepares to get rolling again, you won't have much longer to make a decision to get off this train and stay off."

Danny fervently excused himself from her. He told her that he had to run down the road and take care of a couple of things. "Don't worry, I'll be back. I still have an ample amount of time."

"My darling, stay here with me. It's dreadful out there. Where are you going?"

"Later on, it will be more dreadful to stay in here," he warned her. Then he turned around to head out of the room but stopped and turned back to her. "Eva, I promise you. Get off the train and stay here in Erie tonight with me. I will without fail accompany you to Ashtabula and visit and talk to your father… tomorrow."

Eva drew a deep breath and stared up at the ceiling. "Daniel, why must you worry? We mustn't keep Father waiting any longer than he has to. He's already going to be sitting all alone in that station until well after 6:00 as it is now."

Danny took a long, pensive look at her. "I'll be back shortly. I love you, Miss Eva Lindfors. You just think long and hard when you see them get those four locomotives ready."

Danny exited the train and headed back out into the cold, harsh winter storm. He entered the station house, where he inched his way across the throngs of people and exited out from the other end. The station was located in front of Peach Street, in between Fourteenth and Fifteenth Streets. The back of it was adjacent to Turnpike Street, where a number of hotels were located prudently near the major rail hub, which was the only Pennsylvania stop on that Lake Shore and Southern Michigan route. Danny trudged through the deepening snow and fought through the menacing wind and made his way one block behind the station house to where the hotels were located. This was basically what he'd had in mind when he'd stuffed his pockets back home with all his antique money collection. The monetary value for this rare collection in 1985 was very lofty. The sentimental value was even steeper to someone like Danny, who'd spent much of his life pursuing the endless hobby of searching out shops and sellers to buy and trade with.

Now his grand collection would prove invaluable as the only way to purchase anything of necessity in 1876—in this case, two warm and dry hotel rooms. He was still the consummate gentleman and would see to it that Eva would get her own room. Even though this would be considered an emergency and Danny would behave around her, he still did not want this wonderful lady to feel uncomfortable sharing a room with him while they were not yet married. He stopped into the first hotel he encountered and sought to rent two rooms on the first floor. There was only one room left on the first floor, so he rented one for himself on the second floor. He wisely figured if he was able to coax Eva from the train and get her to spend the night there, then it would be the smart thing not to lug her heavy crate up to the second floor.

Danny's old money collection went further than he had expected. For what it cost to rent two rooms in 1876 dollars, he didn't even scratch the surface of his archaic treasury. He would have plenty left over to treat Eva to a nice romantic meal at the hotel's restaurant and be able to run back to the station to wire her father at the Ashtabula depot that they would meet him in town the next day. Even still, after all that, he would have plenty of his money left over. The most difficult part of all this planning, of course, was being able to pull off talking the adamantly stubborn Miss Lindfors into going along with his scheme. He also figured he'd better save some money to buy a train ticket for himself; he counted it as pure good fortune that the conductor of this train hadn't already checked to see if he had one on him, especially in light of him incurring his wrath a short while back on the train. He decided he would purchase one the next morning for the short twenty-five-mile hop from the station there in Erie to the one in Conneaut. He ascertained that if he failed in his attempt to get the train to stop before it headed toward Ashtabula that evening, they would have to stop off in Conneaut tomorrow and proceed no farther. He and Eva would have to take another conveyance to where her father was waiting, being that the bridge leading to the station house there would be destroyed. Now all he had to do was fulfill the tall order of talking her into all of this.

Danny rented the two rooms and headed outside again. Before exiting the hotel, he stared out into the blustering scene outdoors. He felt poorly about the way Eva had reacted when he'd handed her what he didn't realize was her empty handkerchief. He managed a small smile when he pictured in his mind when she gave it to him as a promise to wait in Chicago for him to come and marry her. His smile disappeared at the thought of the sadness he'd brought upon her when she thought he was returning it, thus spurning her in the process. He turned back to the hotel clerk and asked him if there was any place nearby where he would be able to purchase something nice as a gift or a token for a beautiful woman that he loved. The clerk walked over to the door and pointed to a shop a few doors down from where they were. A jewelry store called B.F. Sieger's. He assured Danny that, without fail, he would be able to find something nice for a special lady there, at any manner of cost. Danny thanked the clerk and started to walk out. As he did, the man inquired as to what had happened to him to receive the cut on his forehead. Danny reached up and softly touched it, almost forgetting it was there. He explained that he had bumped it on something. Then he thanked him again and headed off for the jewelry store.

Danny reached Sieger's store with his hair all tousled and his face beet red from the furious gale-force winds. He walked up to where an elderly man was tending the display counter, preparing to close up shop. They introduced themselves. The man was B.F. Sieger himself. Mr. Sieger immediately inquired of Danny's cut forehead, as well. Again, just like he had with the hotel clerk, he brushed it off as just a little mishap.

"Well, that looks quite painful, young man," Mr. Sieger cautioned. Danny told him it was nothing. Mr. Sieger asked Danny if he could help him find anything for him in the store.

"I'm looking for something special for a very special young lady who I am in love with." He beamed as the elderly owner raised his eyebrows and grinned. "I just want to show her a token of the deep admiration and affection that I have for her."

Mr. Sieger showed him around the display cases and told him to take his time. He wasn't in that much of a hurry to close up and go out into the snowstorm. It was starting to get a little too late for Danny to linger around for too much longer. Pretty soon it would start to be dusk, and he knew they would be starting to gin up the pusher locomotives soon. He needed to find something nice for her but do it soon. He wanted to convey something to her that spoke to her of his promise to marry her.

Danny hastily scanned around the shop. He knew at the time, without his 1985 funds available to him, that he couldn't afford an engagement type of ring or diamond. He just needed some kind of token, some type of symbolic gesture, like she had given to him with her handkerchief. He came upon a case full of cameo brooches. He inquired about them. Mr. Sieger explained to him that they were very popular among the ladies.

"They wear them pinned on their collars. It's very fashionable," he told him.

They were oval-shaped pendants. Some had portraits in profile on them; others had various carvings embossed on them, made out of shell, coral, or ivory. Some were gold filled or framed in gold. Danny knew he would be able to afford them with the cash he had on hand. As an antique collector, he knew how pricey they would be at an antique shop in 1985.

"These are all very nice!" he exclaimed. "So many. I don't quite know which one to get her."

"Well, young man, what does this lady look like? What are her features?"

Danny closed his eyes as if he were in dreamland. He waxed poetic as he described her beautiful bluish-gray, almond shaped eyes; her dark brown, shoulder-length hair; her wavy lips; and her attractive and full, youthful cheeks.

Mr. Sieger chuckled. "My, you are in love with this girl. These are all very exquisite but let me show you this one. This one will go splendidly with the features you described to me." He reached into the case and pulled out an ivory cameo brooch with a bouquet of flowers that were designed in raised relief, encircled in a gold frame, with a background of sage green. "I think the young lady will be impressed by this one, sir," he confidently crowed to Danny.

"You're the expert, Mr. Sieger. I'll take it." Danny paid him the money.

Mr. Sieger offered to wrap it in paper for him. Danny thanked him for his tremendous help and scurried on his way.

Danny hustled back to the station house. Dusk was beginning to descend. He wanted to reach Eva as quickly as possible. Along the way, however, he bumped into Reverend Bliss and Mrs. Bliss having a small bite to eat inside the still-crammed depot. Danny took a brief moment to attempt to persuade them to stay in town that evening and head out with him tomorrow morning. Citing the dangers the storm posed to their lives, Danny recommended to them the vast array of hotel rooms still available on Turnpike Street. Still, Reverend Bliss refused to capitulate to Danny's fears. He again tried to encourage him not to fear, much to Danny's heartbreak. Again, he headed off for the train, and just before he reached the door, he ran into the family with the two rambunctious children. Danny pined for them to be rescued and pleaded with the parents to keep their children's well-being in their minds and stay behind in Erie that night as well. Again, his prophetic warning was ignored.

Danny raced outside to the platform and boarded the train. He scrambled to the parlor car, but Eva was not there. He momentarily panicked. The clock was ticking. He wandered around until he saw the porter, who told him Eva was around and probably would be back momentarily. Danny returned to the parlor car and nervously sat down where Eva had been seated earlier. He fidgeted for a bit but perked up when, out of the corner of his eye, he saw her coming. He stood up and greeted her anew. She had somewhat of an astonished and cautioned look about her.

"What is it, Eva?" Danny inquired.

She stared at him and hesitated a second. "I just finished talking with Mr. Perryman," she said in a faint undertone. "He just informed me that they are readying the four locomotives to try to push our train through the heavy snow."

"All right," Danny sighed. "We still have a little bit of time."

Danny approached her and took her by the hand. He asked if she would give him her handkerchief back. As she was handing it back to him, she questioned him once again about his open cut that was again undressed and exposed. He replied that there was not time to worry about it and that he would have the doctor attend to it later. He turned around and stealthily tucked her new cameo brooch inside the handkerchief, neatly folding it over. He turned around and handed it to her.

"What's this now?" she chuckled hesitantly.

"This is for you. It's just a little something. It's my token pledge to you that I will accompany you back and meet your father and ask him for your hand in marriage."

Eva felt it and knew this time it wasn't empty. She slowly unwound it from the handkerchief and loosened the paper wrapping. She beheld it in her open palm. She closed her eyes silently as Danny waited for her response. She was practically in tears.

"Daniel, how beautiful. I don't know what to say. Such a beautiful token." She embraced him tightly.

Danny reiterated that it just a small token, meant to represent his love for her and as an earnest promise to forever be with her. Eva started to weep for joy.

"It's just lovely," she muttered with her tear-shaken voice. "I will keep it pinned on my neck collar. Thank you, my love… *min söta*."

Danny received the handkerchief back from her and neatly folded it up and tucked it back into his coat pocket. The two kissed and remained in a long embrace. She whispered in his ear how her father and mother would undoubtedly love him and how she could scarcely wait until he met them.

"Annafrida will absolutely adore you, as well," she said, beaming and laughing through her joyful tears.

Danny was lost in her warm embrace but was suddenly jolted back to the pertinent reality at hand. He pulled back from her and looked her square in the eyes. He agreed that he was looking forward to joining her whole family. He reaffirmed that he truly was in love with her and that they would be married. He insisted to her that with all that, he had only a singular request. It was more like a demand.

"All that I ask of you, Eva, is that you take into deep consideration what I knew about this train needing four locomotives behind it to get it push started. I knew it as fact… before anyone else here said a word about it."

"What should I take into consideration, Daniel? That you knew all of this because you came here from the next century? That's inconceivable."

"Eva, you have to trust me. I am not a lunatic. I know what this train is destined for. What is there to lose from just taking this precaution? I already have booked the hotel rooms. You have a room on the first floor; I'm on the second floor. We'll stay the night in Erie. If I am wrong, I will never cease to apologize to you and your father for this inconvenience. But if I'm right, Eva, there is no going back if you go on to Ashtabula."

Danny returned to her tight embrace. Eva was touched by his weighty concern, but she was still balking, not knowing how to receive his dire warnings.

"But, Daniel, Father is waiting. He will be frightfully worried when he finds us not to be on the train when it arrives."

Danny tried his best to settle it in her mind that her father would be forever grieving when the train never arrived and found out she was on it. He again bitterly described the disaster to her, insisting that time was slipping fast. She again hesitated and let out an enormous sigh, signaling that she was totally confused at what to believe.

"We can wire your father from the station house," he reminded her. "I know he's been waiting there past the scheduled time in the cold and snow, but don't you think he would be very relieved and comforted knowing that his daughter is safe and warm in her own hotel room, out of the nasty elements of this blizzard?"

The porter let them know that the pushers were being coupled into place and that it would not be much longer until they would be moving once again. Danny grew pale. He grimly warned her one last time. He told her he would run to see the porter and the baggage man and get their help unloading her bags and her mother's crate from the express car. He told her that the hotel was just one block away and he would pay somebody to help him carry it to her hotel room. Then he would pay to send a telegraph wire to her father at the Ashtabula depot. She was still not sold on the whole idea.

"Daniel, I told you that I have money. I can pay for my things. It's just that … I don't know about all of this. It is still inconceivable to me that you can be from the fut—"

"Eva, I can only insist to you one more time. We and everyone else who wants to survive had better not be on this train when it departs! Please, Eva, meet me out on the platform before it leaves. If not, I give you one more bit of prophetic insight. When you are approaching Ashtabula from the east—around 7:24 this evening—you'll be passed by a freight train approaching from the west. When you are, remember me and what I've told you, but it will be too late. You will have just four more minutes on this earth." Danny turned around and fled to catch hold of the porter. Everyone who had assembled in the parlor car had overheard what he had said to Eva, causing a minor stir.

Danny found the porter and begged him and the baggage man to assist him in unloading Eva's mother's crate as well as her baggage. He told him that they were going to get off and spend the night there in Erie. He asked him also to help Eva out to the platform, where he would meet her in a few minutes. He advised him that she might make a fuss but to please see that she got safely out of the train. Soon, the call to board the train heading for Ashtabula was given. Danny jumped outside to go the station house to wire Mr. Lindfors about Eva's delay. From the platform, he could hear the pistons hissing from the roaring locomotives. It was about 5:15. The train would be rolling out in about fifteen minutes or so. He knew he had to act quickly. He hoped to be back out from the station house soon, where he would be expecting to find Eva by the platform waiting for him to escort her and her cargo over to the hotel. He sifted his way across the loading platform, trying to frantically warn people not to get on board. Dirty looks and shaking heads were all he garnered.

Danny entered the station house to find a scene of pure chaos. People were trying to get out and board the train. Others were trying to get inside. Everyone was shouting, bumping, and jostling one another. Snow and wind were blowing inside the structure. Danny was trying to muscle his way to the telegraph office when it dawned on him. Why was he trying to convince people individually to stay off the train? He wondered to himself. It had only caused a stir and had everyone thinking he was a raving lunatic. He would wend his way to the telegraph office, but instead of wiring Eva's father, he would have the operator send a telegraph to the Conneaut depot.

I only need to convince this one man. With one well-aimed telegraph, he thought. If he could coax him, maybe with a little extra cash, he would have the operator wire ahead to the Conneaut station constabulary and inform them of urgent comments some eastbound passengers at the Erie depot were making about hearing loud cracking noises when they were traveling over the Ashtabula River Bridge. He would request of them the urgent need to hold the train up there until an inspection could be made of said bridge. He figured the odds were long, but he was desperate.

When he arrived in the rear of the station, Danny found the telegraph office in total disarray. There was a long line of very irate, long-detained passengers trying to send wires back home. There was no way in the world he would have time to wait his turn before the train started to leave, not knowing Eva's whereabouts, not knowing if she complied with his pleadings or not. The only thing left for him to do was make an attempt to strong-arm his way to the front and plead for his pressing appeal. This only got him into fierce disfavor with the rest of the tired and weary people who had been impatiently waiting in line, and a wild cacophony of accusations and base expletives filled the stale, fetid station house air.

This riotous scene served only to draw the attention of the station constable, who took hold of Danny and promptly escorted him back out to the loading platform, threatening to remove him "headlong into a heaping, icy pile of snow" if he dared return inside the station house. Danny was frustrated and totally spent. He wandered around the loading platform with his head down, feeling somewhat dizzy. He though he heard someone calling for him. It was hard to hear with all the wind blowing and locomotives roaring. It was Eva. She was at the other end of the platform, standing near the train. Her hands were folded. She had the now-familiar scowl that she wore on her face whenever Danny was in hot water with her.

"Was this all necessary, Daniel, to have the porter fetch me off the warm train and into the bitter cold, to have him and the baggage man attempt to remove my things? Am I not capable of making my own decisions, my own rational decisions?"

"Where is all your baggage and your mother's crate?" he gasped, not bothering to answer her rhetoric.

"I had them put everything back in the express car," she answered crossly just as the final call to board the train boomed out.

Danny stood there stupefied. He was powerless to stop the hand of fate.

She turned around and started to reboard he train.

"Eva, listen to me, please," he begged. "Th snow is horrendous. My head is pounding. I feel dizzy. The constable and all the people are about to throw me out of here. Come with me into the station. We'll wire your father. I will purchase two tickets to Conneaut for us. I promise to get you to him tomorrow morning. Please."

Eva stood there frozen, including her dubious scowl. The whistle blared. Hot steam belched furiously from the piston valves, as Socrates and Columbia roared to life.

Eva scurried back into the train. Danny went in after her. On the way in he bumped into the porter. Danny feverishly begged his help in unloading Eva's belongings once again. The porter balked at first, citing the urgency to get the train moving.

"I don't think she wants to leave," the porter cautioned. "She was quite cross with me for trying to lead her out a few minutes ago."

Seconds later, however, seeing and sensing the absolute desperation in Danny's voice and demeanor, he relented and agreed to help him out. Danny went in and pleaded with her. He gave one last desperate plea. The conductor, Mr. Perryman, hustled up to the scene.

"Miss Lindfors," he charged her, although he was looking Danny square in the eyes, "either get this man to stay here and keep absolutely quiet and still, or I will be forced to remove him with the utmost rigor and have the constable run him into town and lock him up for inciting a riotous panic!"

Just then, the porter came to them and told Danny that Eva's belongings were ready to be unloaded and were resting with the baggage man in the express car. This caused her quite a bit of aggravation. When Mr. Perryman overheard her display of agitation, he wheeled back and had Danny escorted outside to the platform. Danny stood outside in the bitter winter fusillade. His head was now pounding. He held his hand over the cut, sheltering it from the hard-stinging snow. Just then, Eva appeared from inside the doorway. The locomotives were screaming, the seething boiler ready to unleash its powerful and forceful thrust. Eva was saying something to him, but it was impossible to hear her above the noisome din. He could see her beautiful wavy lips moving for perhaps the very last time, but he could not make out what she was saying. Danny stood there motionless; his hand clasped to his bleeding brow. The engine's piston rods shot forward and back to the crosshead axles, engaging the coupling rods to the driving wheels. The leaf springs and the axle boxes shook mightily. Escaping steam inundated Danny with a misty ferocity. He staggered to the ground. He was crying out her name. "Eva! Eva!"

15

Danny was tossing back and forth upon his bed. He was softly but despondently murmuring Eva's name over and over again. He woke up in a jolt and lay motionless, distraught upon his bed. He despised himself for being unable to halt this horrific tragedy. Moreover, he had failed miserably to save Eva from such a disastrous fate. The woman he had come to love so deeply. The woman he wanted to marry. The woman who loved him. His thoughts were swirling, churning in his confused head. He knew she was on that Pacific Express train, heading for Ashtabula, and that she had perished in the tragedy. He bewailed the horrible fact that he could not save her. He could not persuade her to get off the train. He could not save anyone on the train. He agonized painfully again about Mr. McCarthy, Mr. Lundy, Doctor Penwalt, the porter, and the baggage man. He pictured the Reverend Bliss and his wife in his mind. He sadly remembered the Christmas hymns he joyously sang to everyone on board. It saddened him to think of the fate of the parents with the two rambunctious children. Even the combative conductor, Mr. Perryman, who, according to the newspaper account, would survive but be maimed. He was only doing his rightful duty concerning him. He had miserably failed them all. He loathed himself. He had miserably failed Eva and them all.

He slowly got out of bed and, with great sorrow and misery, began to take off the old period suit. He wandered across the floor, only to once again find his old top hat lying on the floor in front of the mirror. To his bewilderment, he could not figure out why that old hat couldn't pass over with him. As he was hanging up his coat, he felt something in the pocket. He reached in and pulled out Eva's handkerchief. What was wrapped up in it startled him. It was his driver's license and the two quarters, along with the news article copy he had put in there to prove to her that he was from the future. It didn't take him long to figure out that, since those items did not exist back in 1876, they couldn't transport back in time from 1985. However, since her handkerchief did in fact exist from back in 1876, it could also exist in 1985. He took his license and the quarters out of the handkerchief and set them on his dresser. He unfolded the photocopy and sadly stared at it. He slowly raised the handkerchief to his nose and delighted his sense with Eva's delicate fragrance. He clutched it in his hand and held it against his heart. It was all he had left to remember her by.

He needed to clear his embattled conscience. He desperately needed to find closure, to say one last goodbye. He showered and got dressed. Without further hesitation, he got in his Wildcat and zipped to the west side of town to the cemetery. He knew he had to speak to her, whether to apologize to her and somehow beg her forgiveness or just talk to her gently. He knew either way he had to see her grave one more time. To look upon her name and bid her one last fond farewell. He got out of his car and drew a long, nervous breath. He slowly stepped across the gravel parking lot to the bottom of the old, uneven stone steps, and then slowly and apprehensively trudged his way to the top.

Danny made his way to the monument. Once there, he closed his eyes and looked down. He opened his eyes again and stared at the base, facing the side that was dedicated to the unrecognized victims. Again, the faces of the people that he met on the train flashed in his tortured mind. He was consumed by the darkly menacing idea that if only he had done all that he could, there would have been no need for this monument to be erected in the first place. Those poor unfortunate souls would not have been buried in the mass grave right underneath his feet. They would have gone on to live full lives. He strained for the right words to say to them all, as well as to Eva, at their graveside. He gazed skyward as if to request divine assistance in the matter.

He slowly inched his way around to the other side of the base to where the list of names known to be among the unrecognized dead were engraved. At first, he couldn't muster the courage and confidence to look upon the engraving of her name. He tried to summon the words to console her with. His thoughts were storm tossed and scattered. He wanted to tell her how much he loved her and how longed to be with her, how sorry he was for failing her, for failing everyone. Danny stepped away for a few moments and walked a few paces as he let out an exasperated and doleful sigh.

Danny stepped back to the base of the monument with a regained sense of purpose. He knew what he would say to Eva. He scanned the list on the memorial's engraving for her name. Danny scanned slowly and carefully. He remembered from before that the names were not listed alphabetically. He methodically sifted through the nearly thirty names that were memorialized. However, when he had finished reading, he could not find her name on it. Danny carefully re-read the engraving, figuring he had somehow missed Eva's name. Again, when he was finished, he did not see her name upon it. At first, Danny was overcome with frustration and disbelief.

Did she ever really exist? He asked himself. *Of course she did. Her handkerchief is proof of it.* But he knew that her name was upon the monument when Richie had gone with him there to show him the somber memorial not too long ago.

Suddenly, his frustration was supplanted by a sense of gripping fear, just like he'd felt as if he had seen a ghost when he'd first viewed the monument with Richie and seen her name emblazoned on it. Now the same eerie feeling had seized him again, now that her name had somehow mysteriously vanished. Perhaps this place was haunted, he thought. Again, he slowly read the names. Again, to no avail. For a moment, he thought perhaps he was going crazy. He figured there was only one way to find out. He would dash home and call Richie and ask him to confirm that they both had seen Eva's name on the engraving when they both had visited the site earlier in the spring. Either way, Danny figured this whole thing was not sitting well. If her name was never on there, then maybe this whole experience was turning him into a raving lunatic. If, however, her name was on the memorial and suddenly was now no longer upon it, then he felt this place definitely was haunted. Needless to say, Danny bolted to his car, uneven stone steps notwithstanding, ad hightailed it out of the macabre establishment. He dashed home and, without hesitation, called Richie on the phone at work.

On the phone, Richie confirmed that Eva's name was on the monument when they had gone there.

"Are you positive you remember?" Danny asked him in near hysteria.

"How can I not be positive? You pointed to it a thousand times and shouted her name," Richie gushed half-jokingly. Richie was unprepared for what Danny was about to tell him. At first, he totally doubted Danny's bizarre claim. At Danny's fervent insistence, Richie was forced to take him seriously. He tried to reason that maybe they both really didn't see the name in the first place or perhaps it was on there and he missed seeing it.

"I read it three times!" Danny protested heatedly. "There are only about thirty names on it. I carefully read it three times!"

"All right, listen," Richie said, trying to calm Danny down. "We'll go up to the cemetery tomorrow and check it out. Maybe you missed something. Maybe you were looking on the wrong side or something."

Danny was a mixture of frustration and puzzlement. After he hung up with Richie, he went over to his antique floor mirror and decided to grab his bottle of brass polish. He figured that he would at least try to solve one mystery: whose name was on the plaque on the mirror's backing. Danny applied the polish vigorously, perhaps taking out his perplexity and anxiety on the nameplate. After a few moments, the outline of another letter or two appeared. He went to the kitchen drawer and grabbed his trusty magnifying glass and peered at the brass plate. Now he could see *TO… MO*. Moments later, his vigorous rubbing had brought more letters to the surface on the second line. *LO.* He continued to vehemently apply the compound and his elbow grease to it.

Danny was still rubbing away forcefully when a few minutes later his phone rang. It was Richie calling him back.

"Listen, Danny, I have an idea," he voiced confidently. He went on to suggest to Danny that if there was really a person named Eva Lindfors from Chicago on the ill-fated train, then it would behoove him to go to the library and look in the local history section. He reminded Danny that since it was such an epic disaster in the city, there should be plenty of information about the people involved in it there. He offered that a list of passengers, whether the dead from the wreck or the survivors, should be listed somewhere in there. "Not only that," he added, "if her father, Gustav—whatever you said his name was—became a big investor in the local shipping and railroads, his name should be listed in something at the library."

Danny agreed that it was a great idea and thanked Richie for it. "I just need to clear my head first. I'm feeling a little spooked. It's very overwhelming. This is a lot to try to digest for one day. Besides, my head is killing me right now. I'm starting to get a little dizzy as well. I think I need to stay put. Anyway, I have another mystery here to unravel. I'll make sure to go to the library the first thing after work tomorrow," Danny affirmed enthusiastically. "I just hope I can sleep tonight!" "Well sweet dreams my friend." Richie said sarcastically. "Are you for sure coming back to work tomorrow?"

"Yeah, I'll be back tomorrow."

"Well, then, I'll see you then."

Danny went back into the room to polish the brass plate. To his surprise, his vigorous rubbing before the phone rang had proved fruitful. More of the engraving had been brought to the surface. He was now able to read with the magnifier *TO... MOT.* On the line below, it read *LOV.* At the end of the second line, the number *6* was legible. Excited, Danny continued to rigorously apply the compound.

Later that night, as expected, the jittery Danny had trouble sleeping. He went to the refrigerator and had a couple of bottles of cold beer. Still, he couldn't fall asleep. The mystery surrounding Eva, as well as his curiosity with the brass plate on the back of the mirror, had him tied up in knots. He got out of bed and paced in the darkness. He even tried rubbing the brass plate some more in order to tire him out enough to fall asleep. He sat in the near darkness, toiling away with the compound, the moonlight through his window offering the only minor glint of light. Finally, after quite some time steadily polishing, he managed to doze off for a few hours of restful sleep.

*

The next day at work, time seemed to creep by interminably. Danny stared at the clock all morning while he performed his tedious tensile strength and sonic tests. Why was Eva's name not on that monument when he knew it had been there before? That incessant question plagued his mind the whole time. On top of that, he had meetings to attend and had to be mentally attendant. He would suffer through those, all the while fixated on Eva. Plus, he had to put up with Richie's badgering, albeit friendly, all day about her. He questioned Danny a dozen times if he was certain he had read all the names on the monument or if he indeed was positive that he was at the right one to begin with.

"You had only been there once before, you know," he told him. "Are you sure you were in the right spot?"

Finally, and painstakingly, the workday wound down. When 3:30 did finally arrive, Danny was obviously irked when he had to stay over a little while to perform a couple of retests on some samples that failed the specs. By four o'clock, however, Danny was pulling out of the parking lot and heading downtown toward the library. Every red light he had to wait out seemed like an eternity. He even got stuck at a railroad crossing for a while. Normally, Danny, who appreciated the rich railroad history of Ashtabula, would not have minded the delay. This time, however, was obviously very different.

When he finally arrived, he sprinted out of his car and into the grand eighty-year-old structure. After asking the attendant for some information, Danny was searching the index for Eva's name. He was perplexed at his failure to find anything on Eva Lindfors. However, after some astute digging, he was able to find some info on Gustav Lindfors. Much to Danny's excitement, he read that Gustav was indeed a wealthy investment banker from Chicago, heavily involved with multiple railroads there, and who most certainly had made local shipping and railroad investments in Ashtabula. Danny was astonished, to say the least, as the general time period for said investments was true to what Eva had told him. Chills ran down Danny's spine. He had a deep pit in his stomach. If Chestnut Grove Cemetery did indeed house a ghost, as folklore suggested, Danny pondered, then that ghoul's twin brother was definitely abiding in the library.

Danny read a little further about Gustav Lindfors and then tried again, unsuccessfully, to find anything on Eva. He researched old articles about the bridge disaster, even finding a roster of known people who had perished. Her name was nowhere on that list. Other than what he had read about Gustav, Danny concluded that he had struck out. He retreated from the library and drove the short distance to Garfield's, where he enjoyed a conciliatory Greek-style cheeseburger. His sense of taste was in heaven while his other senses were out in foggy left field.

After his meal, he dejectedly went home. When he arrived, he took a nice relaxing shower. Then he wrote out a few checks to pay some bills that he'd neglected to do the day before. He tried to watch a little television but was too distracted to pay attention. He ambled into his room to try to accomplish more on deciphering the tarnished engraving on the plate in back of the mirror. Danny pivoted the mirror around to face the back side. He noticed that much more of the outline had appeared on the surface. He ambled to the kitchen and fetched his magnifying glass once more. He held the glass in his left hand and the bottle of compound in his right. Suddenly, upon reading the plate, Danny gasped. All the intense buffing from the previous night's insomnia had dispelled the mystery.

"No way!" the astounded antique collector shrieked. As he backed up a few paces, he dropped his bottle of rubbing compound on the wooden floor, spilling the liquid all over. He now knew he had just seen an eerie specter. He cautiously inched back toward the mirror and gazed again at the plate. Through the magnifying glass, he read it plainly, *TO MOTHER... LOVE, EVA, 1876*.

Danny's forehead began to perspire. He began to feel dizzy as his ears started to ring. He had to sit down a moment but suddenly was compelled to get up and read it again.

"Could this be Eva?" he mused out loud. "My Eva!" He jogged to the kitchen to get some water as his heart fluttered. He repeatedly wondered as to what the odds were that this was the actual mirror that she had purchased in New York for her mother's anniversary all those years ago. Could her mother's gift be the same mirror as the one that he purchased at the Harbor Antique Emporium back in October? He stood motionless for a moment and stared at the priceless antique. Then it hit him like a ton of bricks! A broad smile beamed across his flushed, astonished face.

He retreated a few steps and then gushed out loud, "If this is the same mirror that Eva had," he surmised, "then that means she got off in Erie!" He couldn't contain his sheer glee. It dawned on him that if Eva had continued on the train beyond Erie and headed to meet her father at the Ashtabula depot and into the deep, dark, icy gorge, then the mirror would have been smashed to pieces and burned in the conflagration. The paper said that the express car was crushed and splintered. This proved to him beyond any doubt that she had gotten off at the Erie depot, about forty miles east of Ashtabula. The only thing that still puzzled him was why he couldn't find anything about her at the library. He had found something on her father, why not her? He checked the time. It was too late. The library closed at six. He would have to endure another seemingly endless day at work before he could go back and dig deeper.

*

To say that the next day dragged slowly would be a gross understatement. When Richie observed to Danny that it looked like he had seen a ghost, Danny replied in the affirmative. He enthusiastically explained to the unbelieving Richie as to his discovery on the brass plate of the mirror's backing. Danny spent that day at work together fruitlessly trying to convince his buddy of the truthfulness of the whole matter. Richie started to doubt his coworker's sanity. Danny invited him to come over later after he got back from the library in order for him to prove his claim. By the dubious look on his face, Danny wasn't so sure that he was convincing his friend.

After work, Danny again hastened to the doors of the library. This time he at least knew where to locate information on Gustav Lindfors, which he promptly did. He picked up where he had left off from the previous day. He made sure that this time he would take his time and delve deeper into Gustav's bibliography. Danny researched and read. He was there for quite some time. Then it happened. Danny had previously heard that not only was Chestnut Grove Cemetery haunted, but also someone had mentioned in passing that so was the library. If Danny had thought he'd come in contact with one mere specter the day before there, he had just been introduced to a whole roster of them.

As Danny was reading one particular write-up of Gustav's career, it mentioned his two successful daughters. The older sister from New York, Annafrida, and then Eva. Danny turned absolutely pale as the entire mystery came marvelously and wonderfully dispelled. He glowed in total disbelief as he read about Eva. It also became obviously clear, much to his absolute joy, why he didn't find anything about Eva the day before. He hadn't been looking up the correct last name. His flurried heart raced as the article read, "Gustav Lindfors, along with his younger daughter, Eva Lindfors Dubenion, had many successful endeavors in the fledgling Pittsburgh, Youngstown, and Ashtabula Railroad." Danny looked on, flabbergasted, as he continued to read in the local publication of how her father had started her in a series of timely and important business investments at the local port.

Now it dawned on him to research the name Eva Lindfors Dubenion. *This all has to be a dream,* Danny thought. It could not be real. He searched for a bit, and there it was: an article from the local newspaper that could only have been written in a fairy tale. Danny's heart pounded as he read, "Daniel Dubenion and his wife, Eva Lindfors Dubenion, Ashtabula's millionaire couple who had successfully invested in the up-and-coming Ashtabula Harbor shipping ventures around 1880, also helped provide investment capital in the early 1890s to help the start-up of the 'strawberry box' coal unloading machine for the local docks here in Ashtabula Harbor." The article, an honorarium to one of the county's wealthiest couples back in the day, went on to explain the success of the coal unloading machines by 1894.

If that article were not enough, explaining the impressive wealth he and Eva garnered, another article went on to express immense gratitude to the local couple for their generous philanthropic endeavors for the area. One article went on to praise them for proving the funds through the Ladies Railroad Auxiliary to start up the Emergency Railroaders Hospital; built in 1882. Danny continued reading with pure pleasure as the writing mentioned further still about their contribution in starting up the Swedish Lutheran Capernaum Church located on Bridge Street in 1885. Then came mention of the generous donation they made in 1901 to help fund the construction of the Ashtabula General Hospital, finished in 1904. It went on to mention their continued support afterward for the maintenance of the hospital. Danny was grinning from ear to ear. His joy was filled to excess, however, as he read another article about themselves.

The article mentioned that he and Eva lived a long and healthy life together and that in 1952, their four children, assisted by their many grandchildren, helped to dedicate the new Ashtabula General Hospital, which was partially funded through the auspices of the Daniel and Eva Lindfors Dubenion Memorial Philanthropic endowment Foundation.

Danny was nearly in tears when he finished reading the articles about Eva and himself, as well as their offspring. The fear and trepidation had now gone. No more eerie feeling gripping him any longer. All that remained was a welling up of tears of joy and elation. He placed his reading materials promptly back where he had found them and then ran hastily from the library before anyone had the chance to see him crying. He was able to hold back his tears until he reached his car. He hurried home. He didn't even stop at his beloved Garfield's for a bite to eat as he had the previous day. He wanted to return home without delay. He wanted to be in front of his precious antique mirror, where he could summon Eva and return to her side and be with her forever.

Danny arrived home and sprinted for the mirror. "Eva, dear!" he shouted. "Eva! Are you here?" He talked directly into the mirror as he spoke aloud to her. "Eva, we are going to have a long, beautiful life together… our children… grandchildren." He pleaded with her to speak, to answer him. He told her of all the great things they would do together. He spoke to her of all the good they would do for the community, how together they would have a tremendous life and make a great life for their children and how well the people of Ashtabula County would fare because of the great work the two of them would do together. He waited in silence, with bated breath, his anxious heart fluttering.

Danny was kept waiting. There was no reply. He tried to have a bite to eat, but his nervous, churning stomach wouldn't allow him. He waited a little longer. He could no longer sit still. He decided to go for a nice long walk in the summer air so he could collect his thoughts. It was now almost seven o'clock. He would have plenty of daylight left to enjoy a long stroll. He left the house and took a right and walked along Fields Brook. He hung a left onto Harbor Avenue next to Strong Creek, his thoughts racing, focusing only on Eva and how he could return to her. As he continued down Harbor Avenue, he assured himself that going back to her forever would absolutely be the best thing for him to do. His parents were now a thousand miles away. He would scarcely ever see them again, anyway. His job had become boring and repetitive. He was growing lonelier and lonelier here in 1985. Hanging out at Garfield's and the Six after work was also becoming tiresome. Lately, that was all he'd seemed to be doing. Eva, even just thinking about her, had now become his entire existence.

Danny hiked nine blocks to East Twenty-Fourth Street all the while joyfully straining his mind on how to explain everything to Eva. He took a sharp right to continue on East Twenty-Fourth toward the river. Much to his delight, off in the short distance, the Ashtabula County Medical Center came into full view. He beamed as he beheld the structure, recalling the article he had just read about his and Eva's memorial foundation helping to make it all possible. He decided to go inside the lobby to just look around. It wouldn't even bother him if he bumped into Collette inside.

When Danny got inside, he found it to be a busy, stirring place. He decided to just sit in the lobby so as to not get in anyone's way. He sat and pondered the fact that it was absolutely compulsory that he go back and be with Eva and how a great many lives, generations of people, would benefit from their union and how his life and hers would also greatly benefit. He thought of their children and grandchildren carrying on a tremendous legacy. Their names and the names of their offspring would go on in high esteem throughout the county for decades and decades to come.

As Danny sat and mused on these things, he gazed up across the lobby to the main desk. There it was. A polished brass plaque, fastened to the wall just to the right of the main desk. Its dimensions were a couple of feet square. He rose up slowly and walked up to the plaque. There it was, in bold letters: DEDICATED THROUGH THE GENEROUS DONATIONS OF THE DANIEL AND EVA LINDFORS DUBENION MEMORIAL PHILANTHROPIC ENDOWMENT FOUNDATION. The names of their children and grandchildren were gloriously emblazoned on the bottom half of the immaculate plaque. Danny couldn't contain his joy. He was so proud of his offspring, whom he had yet to meet. But most importantly, this was absolute confirmation that he and Eva would be reunited. It was now after eight o'clock. Danny ran outside and headed back up toward Harbor Avenue and headed for home.

On his way back, he began to realize that he was so deliriously overjoyed, he had forgotten something while trying to contact Eva in front of the mirror earlier. Every single time he had been transported back to her he was always dressed in the period suit he'd worn for the historical society reception. It of course had to be nighttime, as well. He couldn't forget about the lustrous moonlight that was so much a requisite ingredient of his ability to journey back to her. The fortunate thing about that was that the sky was absolutely clear that late evening. The forecast spoke of rain for the rest of the week. If he were going to go and be with Eva, this was the night to do it.

As soon as he got in the house, he took a nice shower. He even killed some time getting something to eat. By around 9:30, he began putting on his antiquated attire, everything buttoned down and tucked in neatly and gentlemanly. When he was done dressing so carefully, he reached in his trouser pocket and pulled out what was left of his antique money collection. He counted it and secured the bills into the old money clip that was in his drawer and slipped it back into his pocket.

"Eva, dear, it is I, Daniel Dubenion, your loving husband. Are you there?" he playfully joked out loud to himself. He reached back into the cabinet and sifted through the remainder of his antique coins and stuffed them in his pants pocket, as well.

He stood motionless and waited. Finally, he reached over on his dresser and grabbed the keys to his cherished '65 Wildcat. He threw them on the kitchen table. He figured when Richie came to the house looking for him, he may as well keep and enjoy the classic car for himself. He took out a piece of paper and jotted down a note. It read:

Dear Richie,
The Wildcat is all yours. Please take care of it and enjoy it. Thanks for being a great friend. I'm off to join my beloved southern Swedish girl... the girl of my dreams.
Sincerely,
Danny

The keys sat on top of a photocopy of a picture from the library of Eva and him with their names on it that he had taken from the newspaper. It was beginning to grow late. It was growing dark outside.

After some time, as he was staring into the mirror, Danny caught a glint of moonlight glistening in the mirror. He grabbed his saddle-rimmed John Bull top hat and, with all the determination he could muster, held it securely on his head. The glass began to flicker. He started to become entranced. He called out for his beloved Eva. At first, there was not reply. After a few moments, he started to become dizzy, and his ears began to ring. Then suddenly, he saw a dark, blurred image silhouetted in the mirror. He heard her call out to him. He began to see the image more clearly. He strained to focus in on her. Then he saw her clearly. It was indeed Eva. She was seated in a hotel room. He beckoned to her. She answered back, pleading for him to come to her. The glass on the mirror's face began to ripple as if it were being dappled by a skimming stone, just like it had done before. She beckoned for him once more, standing with her arms wide open. Without further hesitation, Danny put his hand to the mirror. It went right through it. He was mystified.

"I'm coming, my love," he answered her as he stuck his other hand through the mirror's time dimension. He felt a warm, tender feeling, as though her hand was touching his. He paused a few seconds and then stepped in farther. Within a brief moment, he was totally through. He had gone back, completely back, to the woman he passionately loved. She had been waiting for him at the Erie Hotel on Turnpike Street. She was wearing the cameo brooch that he had purchased for her. It was pinned to her frilly high-neck collar. Outside, the snowstorm was still raging. The hotel was a mere stone's throw from where he must have convinced her to get off the train. She had been waiting in the room that he had rented for her and where, apparently, he had accompanied her to that day. On the floor of her hotel room sat her open steamer trunk. Her clothes were splayed across the carved Victorian walnut bed. On the floor next to the trunk lay the wooden crate, in disrepair, with a few planks missing from it. Next to it, in the corner, for the time being, stood the mirror that she had purchased in New York for her mother. He must have assisted her in carrying the beautiful and majestic work of art across the way to the room. Within the briefest period of time, he emerged from her mother's mirror, like he somehow had always done before. This time it was into her hotel room. Remarkably, he emerged wearing his black felt top hat. He looked at Eva, doffed his fine hat, and headed straight forward into her loving, outstretched arms. Daniel had gone back into the past to her, never to return to the present again.

About forty miles to the west of the Erie depot, Gustav Lindfors sat impatiently and nervously inside of the Ashtabula railroad station. He was fidgeting, his black felt John Bull top hat in his hand, tapping his knee with it, as he sat cross-legged in his chair. The snow was pounding. It was blinding. The wind howled ferociously. He once again looked at his pocket watch. It was about 7:15 p.m. He was worried, waiting for his precious daughter Eva to arrive on the Pacific Express train, which was now well over two hours late. He continued to thump his knee with his saddle-brimmed hat.

"Telegram for Gustav Lindfors1" came the strained shout from the stations telegraph office.

Gustav strode up to the telegraph office at an alarmed pace. He set his hat on the counter and introduced himself as the intended recipient of the wire. He gave the man the proper money and received the message.

"Sorry I'm a little behind in my time in giving it to you, sir," the telegraph clerk humbly confessed. Gustav ambled back and sat in the chair that he had been fidgeting in since a little after 5:00, inadvertently leaving his hat on the counter.

He read the wire. It had been time stamped at around 6:40 PM:

> DEAR FATHER, I AM TERRIBLY SORRY FOR THE DELAY (STOP)
> THE WEATHER IS DREADFUL, AND DANIEL, THE WONDERFUL
> YOUNG FELLOW WHOM I MET ON THE TRAIN THIS MORNING,

HAS CONVINCED ME TO GET OFF IN ERIE TO WAIT IT OUT (STOP)
I HOPE YOU UNDERSTAND (STOP) I AM SORRY FOR THE INCONVENIENCE
(STOP) HE WILL ACCOMPANY ME AS HE CONVEYS ME TO YOUR SIDE
TOMORROW MORNING (STOP) I HOPE YOU FIND HIM TO BE A VERY
UPSTANDING AND FINE GENTLEMAN (STOP) WE'LL SEE YOU TOMORROW
LOVE, EVA (STOP)

Gustav read and then reread the message. He frustratedly folded it up and tucked it into his vest pocket. He had waited so long at the station for nothing. He would have to spend another night in town until meeting Eva before heading back to Chicago. Out on the main line, off in the distance, a freight train was heard rumbling beyond the town. He wondered just who in the world this Daniel was who was keeping his daughter behind. A few moments later, off in the distance, a sharp, crisp whistle blared from across the river from the city's east side, echoing through the frozen air.

The welcome whistle was signaling its impending, long overdue approach to the bridge spanning the Ashtabula River Gorge, and the ensuing, long-awaited stop at the station. Gustav again peeked at his pocket watch. It was 7:27 p.m. He arose and angrily headed for the exit door and into the harsh, bitter night, oblivious to his abandoned hat perched on the telegraph office counter. A few seconds later, the whistle sounded again. After a brief moment, Gustav, seized by the frigid outside air, realized he was missing his hat. He could hear the approaching engines slow as the train neared the expansive bridge. He stopped to turn back inside to retrieve his top hat when a loud, frightening snap was heard resonating over the river gorge.

Epilogue

October 2012

"And as the loud snap was heard thundering throughout the area surrounding the gorge, everyone inside the train station darted outside to the horrendous cacophony of train cars, one by one, as they pounded one upon another like a giant, murderous sledgehammer." Paul took a long, difficult drink from his wineglass as he finished filling in Caroline and Joe on the end of the legend. "In all the chaotic commotion that ensued, Gustav Lindfors never returned to the station to retrieve his black, saddle-brimmed, flat-crowned, John Bull top hat. When he returned later to fetch it, the hat was gone. Someone must have grabbed it accidently during the tumultuous dash outside when the bridge collapsed."

"That's a remarkable story," Joe replied with amazement. "Such a tragedy."

"Yes, very tragic. You are quite the storyteller, Paul," echoed an equally impressed Caroline as she also took a sip of her Catawba wine.

"Wait, there is one more strange twist to this story," Paul chimed, interrupting his raconteur accolades. "Gustav's classy top hat was taken by mistake by someone right after the disaster. It has been said that the gentleman who picked it up and procured it for himself years later passed it down to his son, who in turn passed it to his son sometime later, as well. Eventually it would change hands around town a few times during the ensuing years until many years later it was sold to the proprietor of the Harbor Antique Emporium." Paul winked at Tracy, who was chuckling.

"No way!" Caroline and Joe shrieked their disbelief in unison. "That's not the same one Danny bought back in 1984, is it?"

Paul just shrugged as Tracy continued to laugh. "they both couldn't possess it at the same time. As long as Gustav had it, the hat couldn't accompany Danny back in time. Once Gustav lost it, and it was eventually sold to Danny in 1984, he could bring it with him to 1876."

"I had that same reaction when he first told it to me," Tracy replied with a wry grin.

"And what about the antique mirror?" Joe asked, astonished. "Are you saying that it was the same exact mirror that Eva had bought for her mother back in 1876 in New York?"

"Apparently," Paul answered. "It never made it to Chicago. They for some reason brought it from Erie and kept it here in Ashtabula. Probably just like the top hat, it was passed around the family for a couple of generations and wound up at the antique shop in the harbor."

"Absolutely amazing," observed Caroline as Joe nodded in agreement.

The four of them shared a few more laughs as they finished their wine and cheese tray. Caroline and Joe went to their room and changed clothes. They took off and spent the rest of the day at Lake Erie, walking along the sand, enjoying the beautiful early autumn evening amid the crashing waves and cool shoreline breeze. Later in the evening, they went to a nice fancy restaurant and enjoyed a romantic dinner. Paul's amazing story was the main topic of conversation.

The next morning, after sleeping in a little, they enjoyed a nice breakfast that Tracy and Paul had prepared for them. Then they got ready to check out. They thanked their considerate hosts for their splendid hospitality and complimented Paul for his artful telling of the fantastic urban legend. They assured them that they would definitely come back and spend the night again in the future. Before they left, Paul encouraged the two of them to go out of their way on the trip back home and take a nice ride through the harbor area and then around through the west side of town to Chestnut Grove Cemetery to view the bridge disaster monument for themselves.

"It's a great piece of local history that you don't want to miss... now that you've heard about it," Paul assured them. He gave them directions and then sent them on their way.

Taking Paul's advice, Joe drove along the scenic lakeshore road and snaked his way toward the historic harbor. As they neared the harbor along East Sixth Street, they drove past an empty lot where a bar that was one known as the East Sixth Street Café had recently been demolished and cleared. During the past three decades, before its razing, it had since been bought and sold and renamed a couple of different times. They both thoroughly enjoyed the view as they carefully motored over the old lift bridge and then up Bridge Street, where Joe drove past a vacant three-story brick building that, unbeknownst to the two of them, was once the home of the Harbor Antique Emporium. All around lay a multitude of empty hopper cars on the railroad tracks. Some of them were moving and jostling toward the docks where a thriving world-class reciprocal port once flourished.

Joe reached the top of Bridge Street and turned left onto Lake Avenue. He drove along until the old vacant train station, now run down and in disrepair, came into view between West Thirty First and Thirty Second Streets. Caroline pointed to it and asked Joe if that was the same depot that had awaited the ill-fated train. Joe nodded that it probably was, as he continued driving toward downtown Ashtabula and then onto Main Avenue. They repeated to each other of what an immense tragedy it was.

"What a romantic story as well, though!" Caroline gushed as she admired the view of the river that snaked its way around the bottom of the ridge.

"Sounds like they couldn't live without each other. Like they were destined to be together," Joe observed.

"Sounds like another couple that I know," she replied with a wink as she reached and grasped his hand. "He saved her life." She beamed.

"No doubt her father gladly accepted him as his son-in-law," Joe added, "No matter what his station in life was previously."

You enjoy writing. Why don't you write a story like that?" Caroline nudged him.

Joe responded with a shrug and a wait-and-see attitude. "I don't know if I'm that creative," was his only answer.

"Come on, Joseph…" she prodded. "You could do it."

"Joseph…? Since when do you call me Joseph?"

"Since Eva always called Danny Daniel," she chuckled.

Along the way, they passed by a closed-down and shuttered former establishment that was once Garfield's Restaurant. Behind it lay the empty parking lot that once was the place of the long-since-dismantled Flying Saucer Gas Station. A few blocks behind them stood an empty red brick building that for nearly sixty years had housed the thriving Swedish Pastry Shop. The shop now sat barren since 2010, denuded of its kitschy blue-and-neon sign of the toque hat wearing pastry chef. They motored past those now defunct businesses, not even noticing them. They were totally oblivious to what they even were, not to mention their former significance. Joe drove down a block or so and then turned left to continue on Main Avenue, heading south toward Grove Drive. Joe grew anxious about the cemetery and the monument the closer they got to it.

"Man, this thing is really freaking me out," Joe declared cautiously.

"What thing?" Caroline queried.

“This Eva Lindfors thing,” he replied nervously. “Is this story true or not? Is her name on that monument, or isn’t it?”

Caroline roared with laughter. “You are so silly, honey,” she responded. “The owner of the winery, Paul, was pulling a fast one on you by having you view the monument. If the story isn’t true, her name won’t be on the monument. If it is true, her name still won’t be on the monument. Weren’t you paying attention?” she said as she continued to giggle.

Joe just looked at her and sighed. Then he turned onto Grove Drive and wound his way to the cemetery. He pulled his car into the gravel parking lot and turned off the engine. They both stared at the base of the graveyard and steadily raised their heads, following the old, uneven stone steps to the top.

“This place is eerie!” they both said simultaneously as they looked at each other.

Joe’s eyes followed the steps to the crest of the tombstone-riddled hill. He spotted a young couple traversing the grounds up at the top, holding hands as they walked.

“I wonder who they are,” Joe mused out loud.

“You wonder who *‘who’* are?” Caroline retorted with a perplexed look on her face.

“The couple up there, walking around on top of the ridge,” Joe answered as he pointed to the couple. “They’re right up there, right in front of us.”

“I don’t see anybody,” Caroline assured him.

Joe stopped and stared in frustration. "On top. Right in—"

Just then, Caroline interrupted as she giggled. "I see them," she said as she playfully punched his arm. "I scared you for a second," she said as she continued to laugh.

The two of them stared silently at the archaic cemetery and took in all the surrounding eeriness.

"I wonder if they are going to view the bridge disaster monument," Joe pondered, breaking the reverential silence.

"Hey," Caroline uttered in a soft, hushed tone, "You don't think that those are the ghosts of you-know-who? You know, even Tracy said this place is haunted."

Joe turned around and gave her a frown. "He's not wearing one of those—what did Paul call it?—John Bull hats, is he?"

"I think so," Caroline chuckled.

Joe paused and then turned the car's ignition back on and put it in reverse. "Let's get out of here and get back home."

Joe whipped out of the gravel parking lot and through the exit and headed for the hour-long drive back home. Meanwhile, up on the ridge the young couple frolicked and chased one another through the archaic burial grounds. They ambled past a set of old mausoleum edifices that entombed some of the city's earlier prominent families. They stopped and stared at one in particular that had caught their attention. This particular structure was not as old as the others around it. This one was erected maybe in the 1920s or even the 1930s. They took a moment to read the names engraved above the stone door frame above the locked gated entry and then moved on, again trying to playfully frighten one another as they went. Perchance, just maybe, the names etched upon the tomb were those of Daniel and Eva Lindfors Dubenion. Yet, then again, perhaps, most likely, they were not… Or could they have been?

The End

CPSIA information can be obtained
at www.ICGtesting.com
Printed in the USA
JSHW020857220621
16134JS00001BB/11

9 781647 196004